REFRAMING
Trust

Ren@Vations Inc. * 5

REGINA RUDD
MERRICK

Scrivenings
PRESS
Quench your thirst for story.
www.ScriveningsPress.com

Copyright © 2025 by Regina Rudd Merrick

Published by Scrivenings Press LLC
15 Lucky Lane
Morrilton, Arkansas 72110
https://ScriveningsPress.com

Printed in the United States of America

All rights reserved. No part of this publication may be reproduced, stored in a retrieval system, or transmitted in any form or by any means—for example, electronic, photocopy and recording— without the prior written permission of the publisher. The only exception is brief quotations in printed reviews.

Paperback ISBN 978-1-64917-478-9

eBook ISBN 978-1-64917-479-6

Editors: Amy R. Anguish and Linda Fulkerson

Cover design by Linda Fulkerson - www.bookmarketinggraphics.com

This is a work of fiction. Unless otherwise indicated, all names, characters, businesses, events, and incidents are either the product of the author's imagination or used in a fictitious manner. Any resemblance to actual persons, living or dead, or actual events is purely coincidental.

All Scripture quotations, unless otherwise indicated, are taken from the Holy Bible, New International Version®, NIV®. Copyright ©1973, 1978, 1984, 2011 by Biblica, Inc.™ Used by permission of Zondervan. All rights reserved worldwide. www.zondervan.comThe "NIV" and "New International Version" are trademarks registered in the United States Patent and Trademark Office by Biblica, Inc.™

NO AI TRAINING: Without in any way limiting the author's [and publisher's] exclusive rights under copyright, any use of this publication to "train" generative artificial intelligence (AI) technologies to generate text is expressly prohibited. The author reserves all rights to license uses of this work for generative AI training and development of machine learning language models.

To my aunts, Rosemary, Jill, and Dee. You've loved me, you've encouraged me, and you've all been shining examples of godly women. I love you all.

Chapter 1

June

Eli Reno bit back a laugh.

"Ugh." His sister, Samantha, closed her eyes in frustration as she shook her strawberry-blonde hair to loosen the dirt clods that had fallen from the tunnel's ceiling. "And why, oh why, did I agree to come down here?"

"Because I'm your brother, and you love me?"

"More likely because you could sell ice to an Eskimo and enticed me with a milkshake." She glared at him, her flashlight causing him to wince. "Just because a person can't stand being alone for any length of time doesn't mean they should take advantage of a girl's need for chocolate."

"Noted." He grinned, shining his light to check the top of her head, then shook his head. "It's a little dirt."

"Next time, it might be the whole ceiling."

"Not likely. Del and Nick shored it up after Nick and Lisa were trapped down here during the tornado."

"Scary."

"Funny thing, I have never heard them talk about it except in glowing terms." Eli arched his brow. "Maybe the tunnel holds a special place in their love story?"

She laughed. "I think that's a definite. I've heard Del's side of the story and part of Lisa's." Sighing, she continued. "I get the distinct impression she leaves out the good parts."

"Can we keep going?" Eli wanted to get as far into the cave as possible, preferring to emerge while it was still daylight, even if the sun didn't set until nearly eight.

"Lead on. Let's see what else drops on my head."

"Hey, maybe we'll come across some bats?"

"You, big brother, are cruisin' for a bruisin'."

"Aw, come on, Sam, this is fun."

He heard her mutter, "Like a toothache."

The tunnel system started at the old Woodward homestead and branched out, leading to several openings. One branch, probably the oldest and most naturally occurring, came to the surface along the Ohio River. Another was found in the basement of Nick and their cousin Lisa's house, and another in downtown Clementville—the Clementville Café, no less.

"And I do not have a problem being alone."

She kept trudging behind him, not saying a word.

"Seriously. I'm fine on my own."

Still nothing from his sister. He shook his head, trying to tamp down his irritation.

"I mean, you didn't have to come with me." He paused. "'Course, it's always a good idea to have a buddy when exploring. Safety in numbers."

He wouldn't give her the satisfaction of stopping and turning around. Not yet.

Traipsing through the uneven path, Eli let his mind wander, thinking about the history of the place. This was the oldest part of the tunnel system, running between the

Woodward homestead and the Ohio River. From what he'd learned, it was the section that may have been used in what was called the "Reverse Underground Railroad," where human trafficking of runaway slaves was perpetrated.

History was his jam. The construction course at the vocational school while in high school was his way of avoiding higher-level math and science courses. On the plus side, he discovered he had a knack for carpentry. So, he ditched college after a year, much to his mother's dismay.

Give him a hammer and nails or hiking boots instead of a laptop any day.

When he realized he didn't hear Sam behind him, he turned quickly, shining his light where her face should have been.

"Sam?"

"Back here," she shouted.

She'd stopped several yards and a few turns behind where he'd discovered her missing. When he reached her, she was training her flashlight beam on the ground.

Samantha's wide baby blues said it all.

Somebody had been there. Recently.

JULIA ROSSI RELEASED a sigh as soon as she arrived at her car.

The three-story structure of the Louisville, Kentucky, Field Office didn't have many places where a person could be alone, and thankfully, she got her next assignment right before quitting time.

She had to be in Clementville, in western Kentucky, at 9 a.m. tomorrow.

Go home, pack for a few days, fill the car with gas, and drive southwest for three hours.

At least it was a pretty drive.

Her last encounter with Clementville had put her in a coma after she was drugged by the thugs using the series of underground tunnels in the tiny river town. A lot had happened since then.

Leaning her forehead on the steering wheel, she sat there a minute, fortifying herself against the emotions this case prompted. Taking the assignment without complaint would look good on her record, but it wasn't easy.

The FBI was all she had, so she'd better make the best of it.

Plus, she knew the area and the people. In her short time in the FBI, she'd frequented diners all over the USA, and nothing compared to the burgers and shakes at the Clementville Café.

Finally, she sat up, set her jaw, and stared into her sun visor's mirror. Dark brown eyes stared back at her, a little luminous with the tears she let sneak through when she left the building, but overall, not bad. Her neat ponytail, almost black, true to her Italian ancestry, begged to be let loose. Maybe later.

Now, it was time for a pep talk.

You got this, girl.

When the hands-free technology in her Honda Civic displayed a call, she was tempted to let it go to voicemail.

But the number that popped belonged to Dad.

"Hey, Dad, how's it going?" She sounded relaxed, breezy even. Maybe she could convince both her dad and herself everything would be okay.

"You just getting off work?"

His volume made her smile—he was also in his vehicle. How many times had she told him he didn't have to yell into the steering wheel?

"Yes. Getting on the Watterson Expressway to head home. Then I get to pack and head west."

"New assignment?"

He sounded worried as he had since the last case took her out of town.

"'Fraid so."

"Where to?"

She grinned to herself. "Now, Dad, if I told you, I'd have to kill you."

"Hardy-har-har."

He always made her laugh.

"Is the non-disclosure Dad security clearance current?" That was their joke. He claimed being her father gave him special privileges.

"You know it is."

"Would you believe I'm going back to Clementville?"

"Kentucky?" He paused. "Isn't that where ..."

She paused, heaving a sigh. "Yes.

In her mind, she finished the thought. *Yes, Dad, it's where I got put in the hospital, and my partner got arrested on federal corruption charges.*

She kept those thoughts to herself.

He didn't say anything. "Are you going down there alone?"

"I'm a big girl, Dad."

"I know."

"They've opened a field office in Paducah, so I'll be working with an agent and analyst there, as well as the local sheriff's office."

"I won't ask any more questions. Be careful, will you?"

"Of course. Remember, I'm a highly trained agent. They don't hand out these assignments to just anybody."

"Yeah, yeah, yeah. You'll always be my little girl."

Tears pricked at her eyelids, and she shook her head

swiftly to banish them. No time for that. "Doesn't matter where I go, I'll always be your girl, Dad." She swallowed. "Love you."

"Love you, too, sweetie."

Deep breathing exercises in place, the familiar flutter of panic in her chest persisted. Why had talking to Dad triggered her? In a moment, the events of the last encounter with the tunnels in rural Crittenden County crept back in. Even after a year, the nightmares still shook her out of a good night's sleep from time to time. Now, she was going back on her own, with no partner, and not as a woman about to be married. Instead, she was an independent agent—an independent woman—who would make her way without a man, both in her professional and private lives.

Take that, Lance Billings.

ONE OF THE perks of working for his cousins and having relatives who owned the best café for miles around was getting a good breakfast before starting the day.

Usually, Eli was at the café much earlier—more like seven in the morning. Today, he arrived closer to nine. He and Sam were meeting an FBI agent from the Louisville Field Office. After they showed cousin-in-law Nick Woodward and Sheriff Clay Lacey the indicators of activity in the tunnels, Clay had lost no time calling the new Paducah Field Office, which contacted a forensics pro from Louisville.

Eli stirred the sugar in his coffee. "What time is he supposed to get here?" His mind was focused on the work piling up while he sat there sipping coffee and eating biscuits and gravy.

Not that he was complaining.

Clay pulled out his phone and double-checked his email. "They said nine this morning."

Nick grinned. "Don't worry. The boss said the work would still be there when we're done."

"Gotcha." Eli looked up at the familiar ding of the jingling on the door, figuring it was the agent they were waiting for. When he saw her, his stomach dropped, and he unconsciously muttered, "Seriously?"

When Nick raised an eyebrow at the comment, Eli shook his head, causing Nick to raise both brows before returning to the conversation.

"Oh good, it's Julia." Clay sighed.

Clay and Nick rose, greeting her as an old friend. Eli stood, finally, not offering his hand, noting her expression looked as surprised as he felt. Pale, even.

"Good morning, gentlemen." She smiled, avoiding Eli as much as possible. "Are Agent Burke and Brent meeting us here?"

"Brent texted me. They're almost here."

"Good. Maybe that will save us a re-telling." Julia scanned the room, stopping short as a squeal pulled her attention to the petite blonde hurrying toward them.

"Julia Rossi! I never thought I'd see you again." Darcy Reno set down her coffee pot and enveloped the taller woman in a hug, laughing. "Eli, believe it or not, this woman impersonated me once. She saved my life."

"Fortunately—or unfortunately for me—they were watching from outside, so a blonde wig and well-timed lighting did the trick." Julia grinned.

Darcy squeezed Julia's hand. "I'm so glad to see you here and healthy." She shook her head. "I wish it were under better circumstances." Turning over the inverted mug and filling it with fresh coffee, then topping off the others, Darcy glanced at her. "While you wait for the other guys, how about some breakfast?"

"I had something on the way." Julia's pale countenance had pinked.

Darcy shook her head in disgust. "Let me guess. You probably stopped at the convenience store at Beaver Dam and got a pre-packaged pastry or a granola bar to go with the hours-old coffee you made yesterday. Am I right?"

Julia chuckled. "Busted."

"Anything you want, it's on me."

"That's not necessary."

"Honey, if it weren't for you, my life wouldn't be what it is today—or I'd be dead." Darcy's countenance sobered. "The very least I can do is make sure you have a good breakfast before saving Clementville one more time."

Julia checked out the plates of the men around the table, ending with Eli's biscuits and gravy. When she turned her eyes toward him, she paused, a strange expression crossing her face before it shuttered closed.

So that's how she's going to play it.

She turned to smile at Darcy. "Okay, if you insist, I'll have the biscuits and gravy."

"Want some eggs with that?"

"No, a biscuit with some of your amazing gravy will be perfect."

"Coming right up." Darcy winked and wove her way through the tables and back to the kitchen.

Maybe Julia had better taste in breakfast food than she did in relationships. It still bugged him that she broke the engagement with his best friend, Lance. Out of the blue, even.

Precisely why Eli was not in a hurry to rush back into the relationship game.

Between Lance's experience and Carrie's rejection and

consequent ghosting, it wasn't worth space in his brain. He didn't care if he talked to her again, but he worried about Lance. He had to be struggling, knowing that his ex-fiancée was more interested in her career than committing to a marriage. Lance hadn't answered his calls or texts in weeks.

Eli had a fleeting thought that he needed to press the issue with Lance and find out what was going on. He'd never been good at maintaining friendships, but he was trying.

His attention was caught when Special Agent Clyde Burke and Analyst Brent Rogers joined them at the table.

Clyde sat and took a long swig of hot coffee. When he set down his cup, he took out his phone and turned on the recorder. "Eli, why don't you share what you and Samantha discovered with Agent Rossi?"

Chapter 2

Julia found it increasingly more uncomfortable to sit at the table directly across from Eli Reno.

Of all the people she had to interact with, it had to be the best friend of her rat of an ex-fiancé.

What were the odds he was a rat too?

When she discovered Lance had cheated on her, anger filled her. Then, regret. He didn't question breaking the engagement. He almost succeeded in convincing her the breakup was her fault.

She spent a lot of time at the gun range during that time. It helped.

After anger and denial, she spent some time frozen in place, wondering what she might have done differently. She took her vacation days and stayed in her apartment with the curtains drawn, ordering food and binging on her childhood favorite TV shows.

The day she woke, went directly to the shower, and got ready for work, she felt a push from somewhere. From within?

Maybe.

The case in Clementville the year before came soon after she moved to Louisville. After the traumatic injury that put her in a coma and landed her on medical leave, she kept to herself, making it difficult to make friends at work or in her neighborhood. Between that, losing a partner she'd trusted, and her broken engagement, she didn't have the energy for any kind of relationship.

The possibility of moving home was always in the back of her mind. To do that, she'd have to resign from the FBI. But she'd worked too hard to get to this position to throw in the towel because some royal jerk of a guy took advantage of her.

When the "push" came, the niggling realization that what happened to her wasn't her fault crept into her headspace. Although sometimes, when she was especially tired or emotional, it warred with the niggling fear that she simply wasn't enough and never would be.

Even though she'd only met Eli a few times, seeing him across the table, she realized she'd blocked out a lot of the conversation. Knowing his taste in friends, why should she trust what he said?

"I understand the entrance has been locked since last summer?" Clyde took charge of the interview. His eyes narrowed at Julia. When things came to a head in the tunnels beneath the Clementville Café, Clyde soon proved himself a kindred spirit. Something she'd never achieved with Special Agent Frank Stafford.

Yet another thing she could have handled better. She should have seen it coming. Shouldn't have put so much trust in her first real FBI partner.

A lovely young woman with long, slightly wavy strawberry-blonde hair approached the table.

"Here's Samantha. She's the one who found the footprints first."

Eli stood and pulled a chair from another table so she could join them. Gorgeous, no doubt, and it was obvious she and Eli were close.

Figures.

After seeing the woman Lance cheated on her with, she wasn't surprised his best friend would have a similar taste in females.

Relationship theories aside, the woman's bright smile and open expression tugged on her when she held out her hand. "I'm Sam, Eli's sister." She studied the group. "What's going on?"

Okay, so maybe they weren't close the way she thought.

"I think I know everybody except you." Her grin pulled Julia in.

"Special Agent Julia Rossi, FBI."

"Wow." Sam sighed. "That sounds so much more exciting than 'elementary school art teacher.'"

Unexpected laughter bubbled up in Julia, surprising her when her reaction came out with a chuckle. "The idea of being in charge of twenty or more kids at the same time is beyond me. Especially without a sidearm."

Sam laughed with her. "There are days when I wish I had a lasso to keep them in check."

Clyde Burke glanced from Brent to Julia and then to Nick. "Is it okay if we go out to the site?"

Nick nodded. "Certainly. After Eli and Sam reported what they'd found, I put a new padlock on the entrance. "

"It'll be interesting to see if the lock's been tampered with." Julia glanced at Clyde, who nodded.

"Might give us an idea of how often it's been accessed."

Clyde stood, leaving money with the check, stopping when Darcy approached the table.

"Your money's no good here. I consider it my civic duty to feed you." The petite blonde stood her ground, hands on her hips. Julia remembered that stance and felt her lips twitch.

"Now, Darcy ..." Clyde began.

"Don't you 'now, Darcy,' me."

Clay raised his hand. "Break it up, you two. Don't want to have to run you in for a dust-up in the Clementville Café."

SOMEHOW, for a reason that only served to prove to Eli the universe was out to get him, of all the people going to the tunnels, Julia Rossi ended up in his truck.

The saving grace of the situation? Sam was with him too.

Sam kept giving him frowny looks he knew meant, "What's your deal?" He didn't care. He'd pull a card from Trace and be as grumpy as he wanted. If she wanted to think happy-go-lucky Eli was pouting, so be it.

"So, how long were you in the hospital last summer?" Sam and Julia had been discussing Julia's last trip to Clementville.

"A couple of weeks, then when I got back to Louisville, I was in the hospital for another."

"Wow." Sam shook her head. "I'm amazed you'd want anything to do with coming down here after that. Any after-effects?"

"No, I'm okay. The worst part was losing my partner."

Samantha's eyes widened. "Lose ... as in ...?"

Julia waved her hand. "He didn't get killed."

"Whew."

"It would have been easier if he had. He's still in prison

awaiting trial on federal corruption charges." Julia shrugged. "Makes you stop and think about the people you trust."

When they reached the stop sign before turning on the lane to the Woodward homestead, Eli glanced around Sam at Julia. The slight frown on her face soon cleared.

What he wouldn't give to know what happened between her and Lance. Had she been unfaithful? Put her job ahead of being a wife? When Lance told him about their breakup, he seemed pretty upset, leaving out details. Maybe he couldn't say much because she was an FBI agent.

Julia glanced back at him as though sensing his focus on her. Her deep brown eyes widened, and then irritation crossed her face.

Maybe raising an eyebrow at her was overkill, but two could play that game. Wasn't it enough Carrie had dumped him without Lance's fiancée—now sitting in his truck—breaking their engagement within a week of Eli's heartache?

Love. It wasn't worth it.

Sure, his brother, Trace, who'd never been known to be desperately seeking companionship because he was such a loner, had come down here and promptly fallen in love with a girl who wouldn't give him the time of day.

Until she did.

Now, Trace and Hannah were on their honeymoon.

Maybe all of Eli's years of making sure he had a date every weekend was the opposite of what he should have been doing.

No, that would imply he should have been getting dating advice from Trace. He would never admit to that. The very idea made his lips tug up in a smile.

Sam's mouth gaped. "What are you smiling about?"

"Nothing." When he saw her expression, he did a double-take. "What?"

"We were just talking about Julia's experience last

summer, and I look over there, and you're smiling." Sam shook her head and turned to Julia with a huff. "I can't take him anywhere."

"For the record, I wasn't listening to your conversation."

They stopped in the drive of the Woodward homestead, waiting for the rest of the contingent.

Sam chuckled. "Well, good."

He turned and caught Julia's gaze, catching humor in her glance.

"What *were* you smiling about?" Sam wouldn't let it go.

"Not that it's any of your business, but I was thinking about Trace and Hannah."

Sam turned from Eli to Julia, waving her hands as she did. "It was the most romantic thing. Trace moved down here between Thanksgiving and Christmas—he's my other brother, Eli's twin. Anyway, he moved down here, never expecting to meet the love of his life at a job site." She chuckled. "He's an electrical engineer and was between jobs. Hannah is an electrician, and he ended up being her assistant."

"I'll bet that was fun."

"Oh, it was. Both of them were determined they were 'destined for singleness,' according to our cousin, Mandy."

"Famous last words," Eli's laugh became a snort.

"That was at Christmas, and they're on their honeymoon now?" Julia's mouth fell open.

Sam chuckled. "Mandy and Clay may have announced their engagement first ..."

"I think they were dating when I was here before."

Eli scoffed. "They got engaged in front of the whole family. Talk about witnesses."

"As I was saying, Mandy and Clay got engaged first, but Trace and Hannah wasted no time putting together a wedding. Trace said, 'When you know, you know.'" Samantha shrugged.

"And now our mom has the Clementville wedding market cornered on coordinating a wedding in two weeks." Eli shook his head. While his sister may have romantic notions about romance and "knowing" your heart, he wasn't having any of it. Call it skeptical, wary, distrustful, or gun-shy. He wasn't about to jump back into the situation he had with Carrie.

Chapter 3

When you know, you know.

The sentiment, often taken out of context, stuck with Julia the rest of the day. Being around Eli meant she couldn't get away from regret concerning her broken engagement.

Put the past in the past.

Julia shook her head, irritated at herself. Her internal thought life was filled with platitudes—and very generic ones, at that.

"I thought they'd be right behind us." Eli tapped the steering wheel, obviously annoyed.

Julia opened the door and stepped on the sideboard before jumping to the ground. Who needed a truck so tall, anyway? "May as well get started."

The scenery was beautiful. She stopped when she felt the breeze and caught a glimpse of the Ohio River through the trees. "It's nice around here."

"It is."

Julia started when Eli's voice was nearer than she thought.

He was staring at the scenery, too, his expression more relaxed than she'd ever seen him. The few times they'd hung out during her engagement to Lance, they were in large groups, and he was more likely to be the life of the party than a thoughtful guy who enjoyed a view of the countryside.

She pegged him the moment she met him. Selfish, egotistical, and not to be trusted. Why she didn't recognize those traits in Lance was cemented by two beliefs—one, she couldn't trust herself with her own life, and two, she couldn't trust anybody outside her immediate family.

"This is the site Nick's great-grandparents—the Woodward side—settled in the early eighteen-hundreds."

She almost missed the first part, seething about the past. Better get it in gear. "What about the Renos?"

Sam had caught up with them by then. "The Renos got here a little after they did, mid-eighteen-hundreds." She grinned. "No Revolutionary War land grants for us, unfortunately. I think the first Reno was a Union General from West Virginia."

"Wow." Julia glanced around with new eyes. " My family came through Ellis Island to New York, then my great-grandfather moved the family to Cleveland to build a bridge in the thirties."

Sam shrugged. "Fun fact. Jesse Reno was friends with Stonewall Jackson at West Point."

"I bet that got awkward."

"No kidding."

"It's nice having such deep roots. My parents moved to Cincinnati before I was born. It's home." Julia turned when Sheriff Clay Lacey's official vehicle roared up the drive. She was glad to get back to work. If she weren't careful, she would find herself making a friend in Samantha Reno.

The idea of any kind of connection with Eli Reno irritated her.

Agent Burke smiled as he walked down the drive to where they stood. "The sound of construction is music to my ears."

Eli chuckled. "No doubt. I'm a fan too. It means steady work and getting me in *my* house quicker."

Julia tilted her head, and Agent Burke grinned. "Eli's team is building a house for Becca and me just over the hill from here, and Eli's waiting for us to move out of the house he bought."

"That's not confusing at all." Sam laughed.

Julia tilted her head toward Clyde Burke. She had only met him a few times. His story of ten years of undercover work that landed him in the middle of organized crime and a name change was the stuff movies were made of. "So, you live around here?"

"Yes, ma'am." Burke took a deep breath. "To make it more confusing, I lived under an assumed name for ten years. Becca only knew me as 'Clyde,' and since my family is few and far between, I changed my name from 'Cameron' to 'Clyde' to make the transition simpler." He shook his head and tilted his lips in a smile. "Never thought I'd marry the girl I was hired to protect. I'm not complaining. I got the girl and get to live in paradise after so long in Chicago."

"Congratulations." Julia was happy for him—and curious. How did someone keep such a secret for so long and still have anyone trust them when the truth came out?

Something to think about.

"Thanks." He smiled. "And call me Clyde—we don't stand on ceremony in Clementville."

Julia nodded. "Noted."

Clyde rubbed his hands together in anticipation. "Now,

let's make the most of your time down here. Where are you staying?"

"I've got a room at the Hampton in Kuttawa."

Clyde nodded. "It's a drive."

"Hopefully, this won't take as long as previous events."

"Right." Clyde scanned the skies. "Gonna be a nice day. Who knows? Maybe we'll get to solve the mystery and catch the bad guys by lunchtime."

"Not counting on it, but the sentiment is appreciated."

Since it was Nick's property, he took the lead. "We'll see if the new lock has been tampered with."

When they got to the old chimney ruins and what should have been a secured entry point, Nick let out a breath. "Looks like nobody's been here since yesterday, anyway."

"Not up here, at least."

Nick nodded as he pulled out the key and unlocked the trap door, wrestling it open with a loud squeak and thud.

Julia hesitated, not wanting to be the voice of doom. She didn't want her all-too-vivid memories of the case to color her judgment.

Switching on the lights Nick and Del had installed after shoring up the tunnel, Nick gestured to Eli to precede them to the evidence.

Sam got to a specific point on the path and stopped, a confused look on her face. "Wait. Wasn't this where the footprints were?"

The overhead lights lessened the deep shadows, and Julia tried not to think about the ones reaching deeper, providing hiding places for all kinds of vermin—both human and non-human. She shone her light on the area where Sam pointed, noting what appeared to be scratch marks on the ground. "Look at this." She knelt to study the indentions further, gesturing for Brent to come closer with his light and camera.

"Somebody's covering their tracks." Brent snorted. "Literally."

"Had to." Clay stood over the spot. "Last night, I saw them, too, and got pictures."

"Good."

Clyde stood and put his flashlight in a loop on his belt and turned to Brent. "Well, Mr. FBI Analyst, time for us to do our magic."

"Aye-aye." The younger man saluted. "I'll go up and get the bigger lanterns."

Julia scoured the area adjacent to the spot in question with her flashlight. "There."

Brent climbed down the narrow stairs with the lamp and brought it to her immediately.

The brighter light illuminated the area, showing every nook and cranny that would normally slink into the shadows.

When the culprit attempted to cover their tracks, they missed a partial print.

And the stub of a cigarette that still smelled of burning tobacco. The scent was all too familiar.

THE TEAM ZEROED in on what had been left behind by the trespassers.

It wasn't up to her or any of the members of law enforcement to question what Eli and Samantha saw. They simply focused, quickly finding more evidence the longer they looked.

"It always amazes me how even the best crooks can be sloppy." Julia shook her head, handing Brent the material to make a cast of the print. "They didn't count on someone putting more light on the subject." She chuckled.

"You know what this means, don't you?" Clyde queried her.

"They got in somewhere else." She gave him a sideways glance and heaved a sigh. "No quick solution here."

"No, I'm afraid not." Clyde turned to Nick. "Where are the other entrances that have been located?"

"Lisa and I found the first one by accident in the basement of my house, then the natural opening on the riverbank, and this one. A year later Darcy discovered the entrance in the basement of the café. My house and the café entrances both have locks on them, now." The line between his brows indicated the worry he had for the safety of his family. "So far, those are the only entrances we've found, but we came across a tunnel system map back in January at the old Durbin place."

"Should we split up and check all the known entrances?" Clay deferred to Clyde.

"Yes, and I want to see the map again, if it's okay with you."

Nick nodded. "Of course. I'll stop at the house. I want to check the basement door, anyway. Pray we don't find out somebody's been in there, or Lisa will never rest until our end is blocked completely."

"Hey, new mamas are pretty particular when it comes to the safety of their babies." Clay twisted his lips in a grin.

"You don't know the half. 'Pretty particular' is putting it mildly." Nick smiled, and it warmed Julia's heart. When she was in Clementville last, Nick and Lisa were about to be married. Now they had a baby, and Nick had an almost continuous smile on his face. He was obviously tickled pink at his family status.

"Lisa's always been an all-or-nothing girl," Eli said with a little snort of laughter.

Somehow, his comment hit Julia wrong. He probably didn't mean anything by it—and maybe she was searching for something to irritate her. When he turned toward her, his smile faded quickly.

Great. What kind of expression did I have on my face?

She'd been told she was unapproachable when deep in thought, as now, when she couldn't muster up a poker face.

I need to work on that.

When his face returned to the expression he bore when he first saw her in the café, she knew one thing: He'd rather be with anyone in the world but her.

It bothered her, which irritated her more. Why did she care?

"Julia, how about you ride back to the café with Eli and Samantha and check out the entrance in the safe room in the basement of the café? Clay and I will check out the river entrance."

She nodded curtly and shot a covert glance at Eli, still plainly unhappy.

Sam's laugh tinkled, diffusing the tension somewhat. "Sounds good. I've been wanting to check out that safe room ever since Trace and Hannah got stranded in it the second time. Renos seem to have a knack for getting stuck."

"The second time?"

"Oh, yeah. The first time was accidental. The second time? Totally on purpose." Sam arched a brow. "You've heard of the 'forced proximity' trope in romance novels and romantic comedies?"

"I ... guess so." Julia's lips twitched.

"Let's just say the second time, they weren't worried about being rescued, and I don't think a day went by afterward that those two didn't see each other."

Chapter 4

"Julia seems to know her job."

Eli snorted. "I guess if the job is more important than her relationships, she oughtta."

They'd dropped Julia off at her car at the Clementville Café. Eli recognized he was being a horse's behind about Julia breaking her engagement with Lance. Samantha didn't know Lance, and from the little time he'd spent with his friend over the last few years, Eli wondered how well he knew him. Not that he'd heard from Lance lately. No contact. They'd gone years without seeing one another, and then, out of the blue, there was Lance, picking up their friendship where they'd left off as if no time had passed. Until now.

When his sister didn't say anything, he glanced across the cab. "You okay?"

Sam seemed to come to herself and took a deep breath, smiling. "Sure. I'm fine."

As he approached the stop sign, he took the opportunity to scrutinize his sister more closely. She was flushed, her eyes straight ahead.

"Care to share?"

Samantha Reno, much like her cousin, Mandy, was not known for keeping quiet when she had an opinion or had knowledge of any kind of scuttlebutt.

"No, nothing to tell." She paused, then brightened. "I have a meeting at my school next Monday, so I'm heading back to Indiana on Sunday afternoon."

"Already having meetings? It's June. School's barely out." Eli scoffed. "No rest for the weary, huh?"

She shook her head. "It's an optional professional development day, and since the topic focuses on using art in different subject areas, I thought it might be interesting."

"I can't imagine sitting inside on a summer day in June, especially after a year of dealing with elementary-aged kids."

"Sometimes it's a pain, but I prefer it to stuff falling into my hair and finding the footprints of people who were not supposed to be where they were." She grinned at him. "I'll admit, though. I am curious."

"Then my work here is done. I made you curious about something historical."

"Eli, not everyone is into history."

"Shame, isn't it?" He chuckled.

The side-eye she gave him made him laugh out loud. He'd spent a lifetime, along with Trace, picking on their little sister. When she was born, he wasn't sure what to make of the little lump of humanity everyone *oohed* and *aahed* over. It didn't take long, though, for the boys to figure out she'd smile at anything as long as her brothers were involved.

Eli proceeded through the intersection, waving as he met a farmer on a tractor coming down the road. "I've been reading up on local history. The library in town has a good collection, and the museum is interesting." He quirked a brow. "I'd be glad to take you some time."

Samantha laughed. "Just don't put me to work running microfilm and doing genealogy research. The museum, I can handle."

"It's a date, then. Saturday?"

She shook her head, amused. "Sounds like a plan."

Arriving at Grandma and Grandpa's, he had to tell her more, whether she wanted to hear it or not. "You don't have to dig far to learn that Kentucky was the 'Wild West' at one time. A lot of stuff happened back then."

"Have you learned any more about the story of Jesse Reno and how our family ended up here?"

Eli nodded, his lips turning up in a grin on one side. "That's a question for Grandpa."

"I'm sure all the other cousins know their history better than we do." She slid from her seat, landing on her feet. "Do you ever feel we missed out, not living around here?"

Did he note wistfulness in her question? Curious.

"Maybe. We know about Mom's side. I guess now is our chance to learn the Reno side."

Nodding, Sam mounted the steps to the porch, stopping before she opened the screen door. She turned to Eli, her brows gathered. "Eli, give Julia a chance."

He peered at his sister. "Why?"

She stood there, frowning. "I have a good feeling about her. Can you take my word for it?"

Eli raked his hand through his hair, balking at the very idea of accepting anything Julia Rossi had to say on any matter whatsoever.

Sam was a good judge of character. Always had been. If he wasn't sure about a situation or a girl, he'd run it by Sam, and she was usually spot-on.

Come to think of it, she'd kept pretty quiet when he told

her he was considering proposing to Carrie. Maybe he should have taken note.

JULIA SAT at the booth at the café, twirling a straw in her sweet iced tea. She wasn't sure how much sugar content the tea contained, but she was certain it was more than she ever considered adding at home. She wasn't complaining.

Darcy Reno placed a piece of apple pie a la mode in front of her and slipped into the booth across from her, effectively pulling Julia's thoughts away from footprints, cigarette butts, Eli Reno ... *Eli Reno?* Where did that come from?

Probably from the same place it had all day. Unease. She couldn't figure out his blatant animosity toward her. He plain didn't like her. She barely knew him except through Lance, so what did he have against her?

"Hey, girl. Where's the long face coming from?" Darcy tilted her head, studying Julia closely. "If I didn't know better, I'd think those sober thoughts came from somewhere besides creepy tunnels."

Julia took a bite of the warm pie, scooping up a bit of ice cream and sighing with delight at the smooth sweetness. "Whatever it was is gone in light of this amazing dessert."

Darcy laughed. "Not much that apple pie and ice cream can't solve." She narrowed her eyes. "Something's still bothering you. I'm a mom. I know these things."

"Well, *Mom*, maybe your radar is off." Julia chuckled, then took a bite of sugary, fruity goodness, glancing up with a grin, then sobering in the light of Darcy's earnest concern. "It's been a long year. That's all."

"Uh-huh. And?"

"You're not going to let it go, are you?"

"No. You saved my life, and now I am honor-bound to help you out of a jam."

Julia scoffed. "I don't think that's in the FBI agent manual."

Darcy's brows flew up. "Is there a manual?"

"Of course, there is. It's a government agency, isn't it?" Julia grinned. "There are nine, I think."

"Wow." Darcy tilted her head. "That's interesting, but stop distracting me with weird information dumps."

Pressing her lips together, Julia wondered. Since she became a Feeb, she hadn't had time to make close friends, but that was her fault. The few she'd had in high school and college drifted away as she neglected the relationships. And, she was a federal agent who distrusted nearly every person she met, at least until she knew them better.

I thought Lance was the love of my life, but I wasn't enough. I thought I knew Frank better, and look how that ended up. No judgment at all.

Darcy seemed different. Darcy wasn't a criminal, for one thing. Well, as far as one knows another person and their motives.

There I go again. Will I ever be normal and have normal friendships? These days, I know TV characters better than I know flesh-and-blood people.

Emotion welled up in her unexpectedly. Her hand shook the spoon against the dessert plate in front of her, and her vision blurred. What was happening to her?

Darcy reached across the table. "Sweetie ..."

"I'm okay." Julia took a deep breath and glanced at the ceiling, willing the tears to roll back into their ducts.

"So, it's been a long year." Darcy crossed her arms and leaned on the table. "When you left here, there was a ring on that finger." She noted Julia's left hand. "And now I see no ring, or is that an FBI thing?"

"No, I didn't wear my engagement ring on duty in case I lost it. We're allowed to wear basic jewelry—which includes wedding rings." Julia shrugged, holding up her hand. "No ring, no wedding." She snorted quietly. "Once I recovered from the coma and the drugs I'd been given, by Christmas, Lance decided he wasn't ready for a relationship. I guess I scared him off."

Darcy's expression darkened. "Sounds as if he was looking for an excuse for his lack of commitment."

Julia laughed, relieved to see someone so angry on her behalf. After the rounds she'd fought with herself over his betrayal, it was refreshing. "Honestly, I think I dodged a bullet, metaphorically speaking, that is."

"I would say so."

"A week after he broke off our engagement, I heard he was seriously dating someone else. They're probably engaged by now." She shrugged her shoulders and took a long drag of sweet tea. "As I said, I dodged a bullet. What if we'd gotten married, and *then* he decided he wasn't ready for a relationship?" She put air quotes around the word "relationship."

"Oh, girl, I'm sorry." Darcy's face mirrored the hurt she saw when she saw herself in the mirror.

"I'm okay. It is what it is."

"First Frank, and then your fiancé?" Darcy shook her head, lips clamped together. "Too much. Entirely too much." She arched a brow, and then a flash of a grin came across her face. "If Del Reno did something like that, I might just kill him." Shrugging, she continued. "Or, at the very least, make it very uncomfortable for him to go out in public."

"You are fierce." Julia had an image pop up in her mind of Darcy picking up a lasso and capturing Del, jerking on it, and then the rope wrapping around him as he twirled, like in a cartoon. She laughed.

"You bet I am." Darcy laughed. "Just call me 'Mama Bear.'"

Chapter 5

The winding road back to the nondescript federal building housing the FBI, ATF, and DEA in Paducah's Commerce Park ensured that people had to know where they were going to find it. Pushing through the glass door, Julia saw Clyde leaning over Brent's desk, probably studying the footprint comparisons of the earlier events in Clementville.

Clyde looked up with a grin. "Good morning. Have any trouble finding us?"

She chuckled. "No, but I'm glad you mentioned the nursing and rehab center. Hard to miss."

"Yeah." He sent her a half-smile. "My father-in-law is in the rehab unit over there, so it's pretty handy."

"And big," Brent said, laughing. "I know we have an aging population, but ..."

"There are worse places to end up, judging from the outside."

Clyde nodded, then gestured her over to view the computer screen. "We're comparing the shoe impressions from the different sites. One from the opening to the tunnel at Nick and

Lisa's house, one from below the café, several from the river end of the tunnel, and now this one from yesterday."

"There's a match here, but not here." Brent pointed to the print the first forensic team cast and compared it to the impressions beneath the café and the one they cast the day before. Some of the prints from the river entrance were blurred, but there was one—just one—that hit all three sites.

Julia stood, arms crossed, fist up against her chin, concentrating. "Somebody's staying under the radar."

Clyde nodded. "Pretty sure that would be Gabe Torrino."

"Any way to prove it?" She glanced over at the two men.

Brent sighed and leaned back in his chair. "We haven't been able to get eyes on him."

"We're talking about a guy who was second-in-command to the crime boss of Chicago's most influential organization."

Julia nodded. "If we had some cameras ..."

"I thought about that." Clyde leaned back on a desk, probably his, situated across from Brent's. "And then I thought again, realizing now we've found out they're active in that spot., they probably won't be long. They've relocated their base of operation every time we find them." He stood, grinning. "I guess I've hung out with criminals too long—I didn't even offer you a chair." He pulled an office chair around.

"Thanks. And don't feel bad. I'm used to being 'one of the guys.'" Julia sat, scooting forward to observe the comparisons. "You'd think he'd wear a different pair of shoes eventually. What are these? Three? Four years old?"

She glanced over at Clyde, noting the tips of his ears were pink.

Brent scoffed. "These aren't just any work boots." He gave Clyde the side-eye. "Tell us what kind of boots these are, Clyde."

Clyde sniffed loudly, avoiding eye contact with either of

them. He muttered under his breath. "They're Brunello Cucinellis."

"What was that? I couldn't quite make it out." Brent put his hand to his ear.

"Brunello Cucinellis."

Julia frowned. "Okay. What even is that?"

"Probably the most expensive hand-made work boots a guy can buy." Clyde shrugged. "I may have had a pair when I was undercover."

"Tell her how much they retail for." Brent's eyes twinkled with humor.

"Twelve hundred bucks."

Laughter burst from Brent at Julia's apparent shock.

"So, as you see—" Brent teased, "—no way those boots would be worn out after ten years, much less four."

"He's right. Best boots I ever owned. I hated to leave them behind when everything blew up."

Brent pointed to the ridges and patterns in the prints. "The sole is pretty distinctive."

Clyde shook his head. "Yeah. Brent told me I needed to put out a paper on expensive shoe prints since I'm now one of the few agents in the field with a working knowledge of men's designer footwear."

Julia laughed with Brent, and Clyde began to relax. How hard had it been to reintegrate himself into the Bureau after living as a criminal for ten years? Some agents simply didn't come out of that life. It became a habit. Part of their DNA.

It was a chance every undercover law enforcement officer took to protect and serve.

"THANKS FOR BREAKFAST, GRANDMA." Eli took a deep breath and patted his full stomach. "I'm gonna have to find a gym around here if you keep feeding me like this."

Grandma waved a hand. "*Pshaw.* You'll work it off." She grinned. "But I'll take the compliment."

"Y'all still working on Clyde and Rebecca's house?" Grandpa came in as Eli rose from the table.

"Yep. Framing's done, and trusses went up yesterday. Today, we're installing the sheathing. Then, we'll get the plumbing and electrical roughed in."

"Who's doing the electrical? Hannah will be hard to replace." Grandpa accepted the cup of coffee Grandma handed him without a word. "Thank you, ma'am."

"You're welcome."

Grandpa winked, and Grandma ... was that a blush? Somehow, Eli never thought about romance and attraction in conjunction with his grandparents.

Eli shook his head, mind blown, before answering Grandpa's question. "Nick hired a subcontractor electrician he'd used before from Eddyville. Hannah will be back in time to do the finish work."

Grandpa nodded. "Good. I didn't want my new granddaughter-in-law out of a job."

"No chance. As soon as we finish Clyde's house, we've got an addition and renovation scheduled for Brent and Ellie Rogers' house."

"A new baby is a good reason to add the square feet." Grandma chuckled. "Isn't she due any time now?"

"You're asking the wrong person," Eli scoffed. "Not my area of expertise."

"Men."

Eli glanced back to see his sister's pajama-clad self enter the kitchen. She was a grouch in the morning—one of the few times he compared her to his brother, Trace, a notorious grump. To his family, anyway. The last few months had been eye-opening, to say the least, watching as Trace fell deeper and deeper in love with his now-wife, Hannah. So much so they were married before anybody had anything to say about it.

He admired his brother for his decisiveness.

"Good morning, Mary Sunshine."

The combination smile-grimace-nose-wrinkle said all Eli needed to know about her opinion of the morning.

Grandma twisted her lips into a smile and set a large cup of coffee in front of Sam as she sat at the table. "Mornin', sweetie. Pancakes sound okay for breakfast?"

"You're an angel, Grandma."

"Oh, I have an ulterior motive in spoiling you today." Grandma winked. "Your Grandpa is planting a second sweet corn crop."

"Sure goes faster when I have a young thing to drop the seeds," Grandpa interjected, grinning.

Sam smiled weakly. "I figured there had to be an ulterior motive in inviting me to spend the night." She peered into her cup, then smiled.

Eli laughed at her. "Hey, enjoy being called a 'young thing' while you can." He sighed. "After thirty, everything starts to go downhill."

"Hardy-har-har." She stuck her tongue out at Eli and turned to Grandpa. "I will be more than happy to help in the garden, Grandpa. With you, I get fresh air and sunshine. With this guy," she pointed to Eli, "all I get are caves full of who-knows-what creepy-crawlies and criminals in there."

She paused for a second. "Creepy-crawlies and criminals. That would be a great title for a book."

"Maybe for one of those 'cozy mysteries' I check out at the library." Grandma chuckled.

Did he detect a tinge of blush going up Sam's neck and to her cheeks? "I'm glad to help. I want to learn more about living on a farm."

Eli's brows lowered. "You grew up on a farm."

"I know, but it's different now." She wasn't meeting his eyes. What was going on?

He shrugged. "Whatever ..."

"Oh!" Grandma turned to Eli. "I hear Julia Rossi is here working on the case."

Eli coughed and cleared his throat, trying to cover up the snort at the mention of her name. "She's here working with the Paducah office on the continuing saga that is the Clementville tunnels."

"Where's she staying?"

"Eddyville, I think. Not sure which hotel." Did he need to explain that Julia Rossi's accommodations were the last thing he wanted to know?

"Oh, my." Grandma frowned, then regarded Grandpa. "Julia should stay here so she doesn't have to make the trip every day."

Grandpa nodded. "I hate to think about anybody making that drive out here more than necessary. It may not be deer season, but they're still out there, watching and waiting for a car to run into."

"I'll call Clay and see if he'll bring them all to lunch today, then we can invite her." She glanced at Eli, her eyebrows raised when she saw his face. "You don't mind, do you, Eli?"

Mind? Of course, I mind. Maybe she's good at her job. Maybe she saved Darcy's life and nearly lost hers in the process. That doesn't mean she can be trusted.

Did he say that out loud? Of course not.

Instead, he tried to backpedal. "She might be more

comfortable getting out of the boonies at night. City girl, you know."

"I'll give her the option. No reason to have this big ol' house if we can't share it." Grandma picked up the phone to call Clay as Eli put on his cap and headed to the back door. "You come on in for lunch, too, Eli. I'll have plenty. I told Samantha to text Jay to join us since he's planting the south field across the road."

Had he missed something here? Sam? Jay? Maybe Jay Carrino was the reason Sam didn't balk at helping Grandpa plant corn—in the garden spot adjacent to the south field of the Carrino farm.

More importantly, could Eli possibly get out of having a meal with Agent Rossi without flat-out telling Grandma he wasn't a fan?

Taking a deep breath, he schooled his features into what he hoped was everyday pleasantness, all the while cringing inside. "Sure thing, Grandma. Thanks."

Chapter 6

The screeching of the tires on her rental car and the sudden stop on the side of the road before plowing into a nine-point buck had Julia's heart pounding. Her arms, stiff from bracing for impact, relaxed as she slowly uncurled her fingers from around the steering wheel. Sure enough, a deer was observing her while chewing a bite of grass he'd pulled. No fear there. Somehow, this buck knew it wasn't hunting season.

That was close.

She remembered the large deer population in Crittenden County, but Frank had done all the driving the last time she was here. Thinking back, she should have been aware of how he was in control at all times. He drove. He sent in the reports to their supervisor. He told her where they were going and when.

And, it was the last time she'd taken everything a man told her at face value.

She closed her eyes and took deep breaths, trying to calm

herself before she arrived at the crime scene. The last thing she wanted was for the people she worked with—all men, of course—to see her flustered.

A knock on the window made her already-pounding heart leap in her chest.

Eli Reno. Of course. The one guy she didn't want to see her sweat.

"Are you okay?"

She rolled her window down and gripped the bottom of the steering wheel, trying to keep her hands from shaking.

Nodding, she glanced up with what she hoped was a calm smile. "I'm fine. The deer have no respect for the rules of the road, do they?"

Eli chuckled and scanned the area where the deer had stood seconds before. "They do not." He checked her front bumper. "At least you missed him this time, or he missed you. Are you headed to the Woodward farm?"

"Yes, I'm meeting Clyde and Brent, and the forensics team out of Louisville is due by ten. They'll work with Brent to pick the place apart.

"Clay called earlier, asking me to come by, so we're going the same way." He grinned unexpectedly. "Want me to go in front? In case Buck wants another shot at your car?"

Until now, she'd avoided talking to him, using his sister as a buffer.

No buffer this time.

"Works for me." She paused. Awkward didn't begin to describe her feelings. "Um, thanks for stopping."

He doffed his cap and lifted his lips to one side. "My pleasure, ma'am." Tapping the roof of the car, he turned and ambled back to his truck.

Watching him in the side-view mirror, she noted his

relaxed gait. She envied his confidence. Over-confidence, more likely. Who was she to judge?

As he pulled his truck around to get back on the road, she realized her heart had calmed down, and her hands were no longer slick with sweat on the steering wheel. Lance's "life of the party" friend had a side to him that was almost ... calming.

Once upon a time, eons ago, she trusted people like Eli. Never gave them ulterior motives and thought the best of everyone around her. Even in her job, seeing the worst of the worst, she tended to give people the benefit of the doubt until they proved her wrong.

Now? Now, when profiling or interrogating a suspect, she peered further into their psyche to discover the issues that caused them to hurt people. Hurt her. She wanted to know why.

Could she trust Eli Reno? Sheriff Lacy seemed to think so. Clyde and Brent too. They'd all, same as her, seen the bad guys up close and personal.

However, they were all men. Men tended to stick together, didn't they?

Now you're being ridiculous.

There was one man, and only one man, she trusted implicitly. Dad. She needed a weekend at home in Cincinnati.

WHEN ELI HAD HAPPENED upon a highway altercation between Julia's car and a nine-point buck, he was surprised that he felt bad for her. What if she'd totaled her car and been injured? Or—and the feeling in his gut floored him—what if she'd been killed?

He pulled into the drive of the farmhouse ruins and parked next to Clay's SUV. Clay, Clyde, and Brent leaned over a makeshift table near the entrance to the old cellar. Julia pulled in next to him and stepped out, phone in her hand.

No "FBI Barbie" today, but a young woman who didn't mind getting dirty. Jeans and a T-shirt, hiking boots.

"Thanks, Dad. Love you too." She paused to end the call, slipped her phone in her back jeans pocket, and saw Eli waiting for her. "Oh. Hi." Her smile was involuntary.

"Did you say your folks live in Cincinnati?"

"They do. I grew up there within spitting distance of Kentucky." She surveyed the rural countryside and the partial view of the Ohio River beyond.

"Careful, you'll pick up the local brogue."

"Thanks for the warning. I'm not quite ready to give up my Yankee card."

Falling into step with her, her humor was refreshing after the cold shoulder she'd given him since arriving in Clementville.

Seriously? And what about the cold shoulder you've been offering?

It wasn't all on her. He had to take at least half the responsibility.

The more he was around her, the more he wondered what happened between her and Lance.

And even more confusing, why hadn't Lance answered his calls or texts?

The thought of coming right out and asking her popped into his thoughts, but he squashed the notion immediately. He wasn't sure what can of worms he'd be opening.

"What's the scoop, gentlemen?"

"I oughtta write you up for breaking dress code." Clyde narrowed his eyes at her attire.

"I ..." Julia sputtered, her eyes wide.

"I'm kidding. Kinda hard to crawl around tunnels and

caves in a black suit." Clyde laughed, then held out his hand to shake Eli's. "Morning."

Nick drove up in his truck, joining them next to the crumbling chimney—the only evidence of a once-fine home. "Did I miss anything?"

Brent gestured to the map before them. "We were going over the map of the tunnel system. We had a copy made so we could mark it up. There are more entrances and tunnels out there."

Clay nodded. "Clyde wants to send some folks down in the tunnels to check out some of the areas not found on the map."

"Would there be a way of updating it?" Nick glanced from Clay to Clyde.

Clyde furrowed his brows, thinking. "It would take time, but using GPS, we can update it and make it more accurate. It won't be a professional map-making job, but ..."

Julia glanced up from the map with an arched brow. "Looks like we get to go spelunking."

"I was hoping you'd say that." Clyde smiled. "I've been called to DC on Monday, and I've already requested you be assigned agent-in-charge to explore the tunnels."

"There are some naturally occurring caves within the system, aren't there?" Julia's eyes fairly glittered with excitement.

Eli nodded. "I've explored the big cavern near Nick's house."

"I was bummed I didn't get to explore the caves further last time I was here." She shrugged. "What can I say? I always liked Earth science." Twisting her lips, she frowned. "I have some equipment at my apartment in Louisville that would come in handy."

"No need to stay over the weekend if you need to go back for a few days. I'll be back a week from Monday. Becca's going with me, making a mini-vacation out of it since her dad's being cared for at the rehab center." Clyde's smile widened. "We don't get out of town much anymore."

"I get that." Julia pressed her lips together, thinking, then checked her watch. "If I leave for home, say, after lunch today and come back Sunday night, I'll be here early Monday to start investigating the tunnels." She turned to Brent. "How about it, Brent? You and me Monday morning?"

Brent shook his head. "Sorry. No can do. Ellie has a doctor's appointment that's been on the books for a month." He grinned. "Ultrasound day."

"I thought Eli could go along if Nick didn't mind being short a carpenter." Clyde scrutinized them in turn. "You've been down there exploring the tunnels."

Eli was in a quandary. The idea of exploring the tunnels and maybe finding more evidence of shenanigans in their community was enticing. But the thought of spending days alone with Julia?

Not so much.

According to the expression on Julia's face, she wasn't sold on the idea, either.

"ARE YOU SURE?"

Julia winced inwardly at the tone of Eli's question—and the panic on his face.

Not that she reacted any better. She wanted to ask the same question, so she was glad somebody voiced it.

Nick weighed in. "I mean, we're on the home stretch on Clyde and Becca's house, and I can pick up the slack. If I know my wife, I know she'd have a fit if I committed to spending the week out of phone range and her at home with Amelia." Nick shrugged.

"She would." Eli paused, took a deep breath, and expelled it with a huge sigh. "That's fine. I've studied the map and wanted to check out some of what appear to be dead-ends."

In other words, he figured they could make it work whether they liked each other or not.

Julia bent over the map, orienting herself to their current location. She tapped on the paper. "Is this where the first evidence was found?"

Nick nodded. "Yes." He pointed to a red X on the map underneath a square. "Here's my house and where Lisa and I found the first body." Indicating another mark, he frowned. "And here's where they found the skeletal remains of my grandfather and the remnants of a still."

"I remember going in the entrance there." Pointing to the marking closer to the river, she asked, "Is this the café?"

Clay answered. "It is." He trailed his finger along the dotted line that indicated a tunnel connected to the river entrance, Nick's house, and the location at the Woodward homestead, and then he tapped on the paper. "See this area, here?" He indicated a large blank area.

"You think there are more tunnels down there, don't you?" Julia studied the map closely. "We'll be pretty far from an exit, so tell me you're not claustrophobic."

Eli laughed, surprising her. "No, not me. That would be my brother Trace's downfall."

"Good. I didn't want to have to carry you if you passed out on me." She surprised herself with a tilt of her lips.

"I don't think it'll come to that."

Wait. What?

She definitely wasn't flirting with a guy she had no reason to trust.

Was she?

"How about showing me around down there since I'm dressed to explore?"

BEFORE HIM WAS A MORE ANIMATED Julia than he'd seen with Lance, even before the break-up. Not long before. It might explain why she'd been pretty closed off when he met with them about being in the wedding. Was this the real Julia, or did she use her more approachable persona to finagle her way into his trust? He didn't buy it.

Her clothing choice for today was meant for comfort. The well-worn jeans and T-shirt made him have highly inappropriate thoughts for someone to have about a person in law enforcement.

She was hot. No other way to put it. Put her in the right party situation, and she'd fit right in.

Eli raked his hand through his dark hair, trying to read the room. All he got back was expectations of his cooperation. "Okay, then, let's get on with the orientation."

"Good. We don't have to go too far. It would help to see for myself what kind of equipment we need." Julia smiled. "I don't want to get too dirty." She paused. "I'm looking forward to lunch at Mrs. Reno's."

A real, honest-to-goodness, natural smile.

He nodded. "She mentioned it this morning." No way he would tell her about Grandma's idea of inviting her to stay at the house for the duration of the case. She was going back home tonight, and maybe, just maybe, it would only take them a day or so to map out what they suspected was another part of the tunnel system.

"It's settled, then." Clyde tapped on his watch. "Becca went to Paducah to check on her dad, and I don't plan to miss Ms. Sylvia's meal, either. Reconvene at the Renos' house in about an hour?"

Nick chuckled. "You won't be disappointed. You may want a nap afterward. No one goes away hungry from Grandma's house."

"You and Lisa coming?" Eli hoped they were. It would take some of the pressure off of him.

"I am," Nick said, "Lisa's meeting Melanie, Ellie, and Darcy at the café for lunch."

"Mom's day out?" Julia smiled.

Nick laughed. "Sort of, if taking the baby with her counts. Lisa said she was losing her ability to socialize outside the family, so she wanted to make sure she didn't stagnate."

It wasn't in Eli's nature to try to get out of socializing. Had the break with Carrie done more to him than he thought? He hadn't noticed feeling different in crowds of people, at church, or around any number of groups. His position as "life of the party" wasn't contrived. It came naturally. It simply didn't feel as important these days.

If he asked his sister—which he would not—she'd say he was living in "emotional limbo," whatever that meant. He was stalled, going nowhere. Dead still. No movement. If he moved, something bad might happen, so he'd stay safe there in the eye of the storm, not venturing out.

Something tugged at him to take a chance.

"Ready?"

Julia's voice stirred his attention. Was she reading his mind?

"What was that?"

"I asked if you were ready to go down to the entrance." She frowned. "I mean, we can wait until Monday if that would be better."

"No. No, I'm fine, I have a lot on my mind, is all." He forced his countenance back into its usual relaxed, ready-for-anything expression.

She paused, not smiling, not frowning, capturing him with her gaze. He couldn't turn away. He tried. Her eyes narrowed, and the line appearing between her brows smoothed. One side of her lips tipped in a slow smile, and she nodded. "Okay, then. Let's see what we can get into, shall we?"

He didn't plan to smile back and kicked himself internally when he found himself momentarily grinning like a fool. He pulled his line of sight from her to the path going down to the river. One more glance at her had him questioning if he'd caught a glimpse of humor. Her lips were twitching.

He knew one thing—he had to talk Grandma out of inviting Julia Rossi to stay at the house for the duration of the case, lest he forget completely that Julia was bad news. When she hurt his friend, she hurt him too.

LET'S *see what we can get into?*

She may as well have said, "Hey there, sailor."

Trekking through the dark tunnels gave Julia time to think, but thinking while in a position where she had to trust him to lead her in the right direction was a little scary. And irritating. And ... she shook her head furiously.

Time to face facts. Eli seemed like a nice guy, but she had thought Lance was too. Maybe if she'd not met Lance first, she wouldn't distrust most males she encountered. Was her relationship with Lance a case of loneliness and a lack of dating experience?

She was tired of receiving wedding invitations. It felt like the right time to do the next grown-up thing—start a relationship, get engaged, married, house, kids. Wasn't that the order of things? The prescription for happiness?

No, and she'd been kicking herself ever since she and Lance broke up. She stopped when she realized Eli was talking to her.

"I'm sorry. What did you say?" She hadn't heard a word.

"There's a crook in the trail just up ahead." Eli shone his light on the area, revealing what looked like "a fork in the road."

Julia looked at her compass app. "Is that the trail that leads to the Ohio River?"

"I think so. It's probably the most-used and longest-used tunnel in the system." Eli turned and headed that way, then stopped. "We can keep going, or we can come back after lunch. Your case, your call."

If they returned after lunch, she'd have to endure another long, stretched-out period of joining forces with Eli.

The idea had merit. If she spent more time with him, the smidgin of attraction would go away, and she'd find out he was just like all the other guys, focused on what *she* could do for *him*.

Julia casually looked at her smartwatch to check the time. "I could eat."

Eli turned toward her. "That will be music to Grandma's ears. She likes nothing better than feeding people." He stood there, looking at her, a grin on his face. He had a nice smile, and she wasn't sure when during the last twenty-four hours she noticed.

When she didn't move, he tilted his head, a slight crease between his brows. "No rush, but I'm pretty sure I smelled peach cobbler before I left this morning. I'd hate for the other guys to beat us to it."

The dark tunnel hid her embarrassment at getting caught

staring at him. "Right." She turned on her heel and led the way out into the sunshine.

There was a shift inside herself from when they entered the tunnel to now, when they exited. Maybe it was the slower pace, the nice people she'd been around, the warm sunshine after being in a dark, damp tunnel.

Or maybe her feelings toward Eli had shifted, uninvited, on their own.

Chapter 7

Julia closed her eyes and savored the bite of peach cobbler she'd taken at Mrs. Reno's table. That woman could cook.

"Mmm. So good, Mrs. Reno."

"Thank you, Julia—and please stop the 'Mrs. Reno' business and call me Sylvia or Grandma."

Julia stifled a grin when she observed Eli's jerk to attention. He'd done a pretty good job of proving his dislike—maybe not dislike, but distrust—of her. It stung a little.

Sam cleared her throat. "*Ahem.*"

Mrs. Reno chuckled. "I have to give Samantha some of the credit. She made the pastry."

"It's very good." Julia took another bite of the delectable sweet. "I'd love to learn how to make a good pie crust. Mom always bought the kind they have at the grocery."

She glanced over at the young man sitting next to Sam. Jay? Was that his name? He seemed to have little to say, his attention fully focused on Sam ... And now there was a constant flush on the younger woman's face that wasn't there earlier ...

"Julia, why don't you stay here in our home instead of trekking back and forth to Kuttawa?"

Mrs. Reno—Sylvia?—Grandma?—Julia couldn't decide what to call her—caught her by surprise.

"I don't mind the drive. It helps me to unwind." She tried not to soften, but she felt a spark of appreciation at her invitation.

"Nonsense. I understand you nearly got hit by a deer. There are plenty more where that came from. The closer you are, the fewer chances of assault by deer population."

"I appreciate the invitation ... I don't want to intrude, with both Sam and Eli here ..."

The expression of dismay on Eli's face was priceless.

Grandma waved her hand in dismissal. "It's no trouble at all. I think it would be nice to have another female in the house for a change. I've been outnumbered most of my adult life." Sylvia chuckled. "There's plenty of room. Eli's in the blue room, Sam's in the rose room—the room I re-did after Steve got married—and I'll put you in the green room."

"The green room?" Interesting.

"When Grandma last decorated the bedrooms upstairs, she did Dad and Uncle Ed's room in plaid wallpaper, blue and green."

"I thought about redecorating those two rooms a few years later when the last two boys flew the nest, maybe make one of them a sewing room, but the year I papered those rooms, I did too good a job hanging that wallpaper. I decided to go with the flow and work around it." Sylvia shrugged. "It's been pretty nice having three guest rooms with so many grandkids needing shelter from time to time." She winked at Eli. "Eli's the last in a string of part-time residents calling the old house 'home.'"

"I might have something to say about this arrangement."

Mr. Reno had been quiet during the entire conversation, not showing his opinion on the matter in any way. Some people didn't like to be involved in an investigation. Didn't want to be connected to something so unsavory. Did her role as an FBI agent make him uneasy about her coming into his house?

He harrumphed. "Not trying to sway you one way or another, but I kinda enjoy it when we have company. She pulls out her best recipes, and there are always cookies in the cookie jar." He quirked a brow as he regarded his bride. "We shoulda had more kids because she's happiest when the house is full."

Sylvia gestured in a *pshaw* motion. "You talk a big game, old man, but there's been a spring in your step every time one of these young people stays with us for any length of time."

He smirked. "Lots of perks to having company. Makes me appreciate the silence when they're all gone."

"Eddie Clarence Reno!" Sylvia's eyes were flashing.

"Settle down." Mr. Reno pushed away from the table, patting his stomach. "Just messin' with you." Shaking his head, he turned to Julia. "We'd be honored to have you stay with us, young lady." He smiled, then dipped his head. "It would be a pleasure to be able to repay even a little for the work you do for my family and the country."

Tears rushed to Julia's eyes. What was the matter with her? She didn't used to get sentimental. She was a seasoned special agent with the Federal Bureau of Investigation. A federal officer of the Justice Department of The United States of America.

She was also a woman, and—she was beginning to realize—a lonely one.

ELI CAUGHT a glimpse of himself in the mirror next to the front door. Calm, cool, collected. Happy, even.

Then why were his insides revving a mile a minute, and a sense of foreboding taking over as he considered the possibility of living in the same house with Julia Rossi for even a few days?

Get it together, man.

Lance had dodged a bullet. Julia's defection must have done a number on him to completely cut ties with everyone close to him.

He turned as Julia came to the door, flanked by Grandma and Grandpa, carrying a baggie of cookies. He snorted a laugh. "Travel package?"

Grandma patted his arm. "That's a long drive. No reason to travel on an empty stomach."

A sudden laugh came from Julia. It was the most animated he'd seen her.

"Right now, I don't think I could eat another bite for the rest of the day."

"Then consider it food to stay awake with, dear." Grandma hugged the younger woman. "I'm glad you'll be staying with us." She narrowed her eyes at Eli. "I'll make sure this young man minds his manners."

The twist of Julia's lips as she turned her eyes toward Eli had his lips curving up involuntarily.

"Thank you." Julia regarded the cookies in her hand and then glanced up. "I'd better hit the road."

"Be careful, now, you hear?" Grandpa stuck his hands deep in his pockets. "Lot of road construction on the Pennyrile Parkway."

"When is there not road construction?" Julia smiled broadly. "Thanks."

She slipped out the door, leaving Eli standing with Grandma and Grandpa. "So, she agreed to stay, huh?"

"Yes, she did, and I'm going upstairs to change out the linens on her bed right now before I forget." Grandma hustled up the stairs, leaving the two men behind.

"She'll be cooking and cleaning all weekend." Eli shook his head. "She shouldn't go to so much trouble."

Grandpa laid a hand on Eli's shoulder. "Leave her be, Eli. She's in her happy place, getting ready for company. Since most of the grandkids live close, she never had to get ready for them to stay an extended time. When you three came, she always pulled out all the stops. Now she's pulling in a few extra."

"As long as she doesn't overdo it."

"I'll keep an eye on her—and you can too. We'll pull our weight around here."

Eli nodded. The sparkle in Grandma's eyes confirmed how happy she was.

"You know, your grandma wanted to have at least five kids."

"Why would anybody ... ?" Eli sputtered.

Grandpa laughed. "The woman has a lot of love to give." He looked around the room, shaking his head. "This old house was big enough to fill it up with kids, but it didn't work out that way."

"She certainly has the gift of hospitality." Eli shook his head, then muttered. "I don't want her to be disappointed."

"What was that?" Grandpa narrowed his eyes. "Got something to say?"

He shook his head. "No, thinking out loud."

"Better be careful when she's around. She wouldn't be happy to think her grandson is passing judgment on someone staying under her roof." He winked. "Plus, her hearing is a lot better than mine."

WAS THIS WISE? When Sylvia invited her to stay at their house while she was working in Clementville, she'd hesitated, but it didn't take long to talk her into agreeing.

Eli was staying there too. He'd made it clear he didn't like her. What had Lance told him? Sam mentioned going back to Indiana over the weekend for a meeting on Monday, which meant she wouldn't be there to run interference for a few days.

Oh, brother.

She and Eli would be spending a lot of time together next week. In tight spots. In her search for topics of conversation they might have in common, would she stifle the temptation to share why she and Lance broke up? She'd overheard a few conversations and off-hand remarks about Eli's recent break-up.

They should be able to commiserate. Normal human beings were able to do that, but Julia? No. The secret-keeping aspect of her job came easy for her. She would let someone else have the pleasure of filling Eli in on Lance and Carrie's defections. While Julia could keep a secret, Samantha, not so much.

So Lance wasn't answering texts and phone calls? Did he have a new number?

Nope. She'd checked that out earlier today. She called the number, and it went to voicemail. Not leaving a message, a text from him popped up within minutes.

Everything okay?

A few months ago, she would have softened at his question. He cared. That was before he canceled their venue, the caterer, and the florist they'd secured for their wedding, and then, after doing all that, took her out to a nice restaurant and dumped her.

Her response to his text was simple.

> Sorry. Misdialed.

Then, nothing. She removed his contact information from her phone. She was done.

So, he didn't have a new number. His ghosting was the coward's way out of coming right out and telling his so-called best friend he had been carrying on with the woman Eli had hoped to marry way before Christmas. Before Thanksgiving, even. She'd found out later.

Carrie had enough class to break it off with Eli before he popped the question and made plans—unlike Lance.

Why did Eli blame her, Julia, for this mess, when the infidelity was blatantly on the heads of Lance and Carrie?

Drama. Her lack of participation in trivial fabrications of the truth had kept her out of the "cool kids" group in high school and college sororities. There was no need to store up useless information to hold over someone's head. It wasn't right, or even moral, and it certainly didn't make sense to her when it bled over into youth group at church.

Easing onto the ramp leading to the Pennyrile Parkway in Princeton, she settled in for the ride with cruise control, her big cup of ice water, and a bag of cookies. She wasn't hungry, but …

She flipped through the radio stations. Few options in this part of the state. Country reigned supreme, some classic rock, NPR, and the Christian radio station where they talked way too much for her taste. She'd never been a country music fan, news made her want to sleep after the heavy meal, and the classic rock station faded fast as she headed northeast.

So, Christian radio it was. She was introduced to some of

the newer worship songs, and every once in a while, a golden oldie would come on. Chris Tomlin, Steven Curtis Chapman, Phil Wickham, Mercy Me. Those were the stars of praise music back in the day. She found herself singing along, knowing more lyrics than she thought she would.

It hit her right in the gut that she was singing praise to God when she'd ignored Him for the better part of ten years. Working in law enforcement made it difficult to keep the Sabbath, and some of the things she'd experienced made her question everything she thought she believed.

Why did bad people do things to good people?

Why did children have to suffer abuse and death?

Why did terrorists negate the value of mankind in general?

If God loved people so much, why did He allow so much suffering in the world that there had to be a police officer on every corner?

She was on the side of the right, wasn't she? She enforced the law. Sometimes, the law didn't go deep enough to truly protect, and she was required to enforce those laws anyway. Every time a bad guy was caught, it was her job to prove her case to get anything through to the Assistant United States Attorney and then to trial.

It hurt when she saw her colleagues, fellow officers, those trusted with the same oath she'd taken, break that trust. She had to ask, once again, "Why?"

The words of the United States federal oath of office rattled through her head as the voices on the radio switched from music to talk:

"I, Julia Rossi, do solemnly swear that I will support and defend the Constitution of the United States against all enemies, foreign and domestic; that I will bear true faith and allegiance to the same; that I take this obligation freely, without any mental reservation or

purpose of evasion; and that I will well and faithfully discharge the duties of the office on which I am about to enter. So help me God."

"So help me God."

When was the last time she asked for His help?

Chapter 8

Eli pored over the tunnel map copy, calculating landmarks on the surface to place the possibility of unmarked tunnels. The large kitchen island at Nick and Lisa's house was the perfect place to spread it out.

Lisa set a tall glass of iced tea next to his hand, and, without taking his gaze from the spread-out paper, he put the glass to his lips and took a long drink. "Thanks, Lisa."

Nick stood beside him, holding his daughter, three-month-old Amelia, who had been named after Amelia Woodward, his and Becca's common ancestor. Her little hand grabbed at his collar, his ear—anything tiny fingers reached. The squeal she made when she was successful made Eli smile.

Pulling her tiny hands from his ear, Nick chuckled. "I might need that, sweetheart." The unadulterated love on Nick's face when he beheld his daughter made Eli long for a family of his own. He hadn't considered marriage and a family seriously until the year before when things got serious with Carrie. Now, watching Amelia pat Nick's face with the gentlest of touches, he realized what he was missing.

His road to happiness and a family might not be smooth, but then, whose was? He didn't know anybody in a stable relationship who didn't or wouldn't go through trials.

Eli had taken a sheet of clear plastic and traced the original map Hannah found, then placed it over the road map so he could experiment with dry-erase markers. "Does this look right?" He turned the map toward Nick.

"Let me have her." Lisa took Amelia and immediately started bouncing. "It's lunchtime and naptime for baby, and the last thing we need is for little fingers to get hold of that map."

"Sleep well, sweetie." Nick kissed his daughter on the head and turned back to the map, grinning. "She's something, isn't she?"

Proud papa? "She is. First baby I've been around in a while. I missed out on Chloe and Robbie. I think they were nearly a year old before I met them."

"Any time you want to hold the most beautiful baby in the world, feel free to stop by." Nick winked. Looking back at the map, he pointed at the well-defined road into Clementville and to the Cave-In-Rock ferry at the end of Highway 91.

"Does this show the area that's been explored?" Eli compared the markings between the old map and the new one.

Nick picked up a green marker and marked the areas they'd found. "There's the one from here to the river and the homeplace."

Eli ran his finger along another marked route. "And here's the café. So, one meets here, between the café and your house?"

"Approximately." Nick drew a circle with a red marker. "Here's the hidden drop-off, so that makes sense."

"Yeah, I'd hate to find that spot by accident."

Nick chuckled. "Del never told me which was worse, the

gunshot wound or the drop-off. The combination wasn't great."

Nodding slowly, Eli frowned. "This helps. There's not much out that way. Some farmland and a few houses. There may not be any more tunnels. If not, these guys are doing an amazing job staying out of the way."

A knock at the back door interrupted their work. Nick opened it to reveal Clyde and Becca on the porch.

"Come in."

"Thanks." Clyde smiled. "My lovely wife has picked out everything—and I mean everything—a person might need to finish out the house, and we were at loose ends."

"I want some Amelia time." Becca grinned, a slight flush on her cheeks.

"Lisa's feeding her and putting her down for a nap, but I'll bet she'll allow a cuddle." Nick gestured toward the opening between the kitchen and dining room. "They're up in the baby's room. I think you know the way."

"Oh." Becca paused before she left the room. "I'm glad I found you guys again."

"Us, too, Becca." Nick smiled.

"Funny how all this led to you finding more family." Clyde's lips tipped. "It's been good for her after being kept from any family except her grandparents for so many years."

Nick nodded. "I'm not exactly flush with family, either, so it's nice since Lisa's got cousins all over the place—this guy included,"—he gestured with his thumb to Eli—"that I finally have a cousin to call my own."

"I get it." Clyde studied the map. "The only positive thing about me not having any family is that I never put anyone in danger because of my job. Now?" Clyde took a deep breath. "Now, I wonder, every day, what trouble this job may bring me and my family."

Family had always been important to Eli, and listening to the conversation between two men who had suffered indescribable loss and found happiness afterward underlined the fact he wanted what they had. Trace found it with Hannah. He and Samantha were the last of the cousins not paired off.

Sam had some growing up to do before she got serious.

Well, in his opinion, anyway.

"Speaking of tunnels," Clyde began, "I talked to Tripp yesterday. His speech therapy is going well, and his voice is getting stronger. I asked him about the map of the tunnels."

Eli and Nick waited as Clyde continued.

"According to him, he made the map."

"Did you ask him if it was complete?" Eli hung on Clyde's every word.

"I did. He said there were more passageways he didn't put on the map." Clyde sighed. "Then he drifted off to sleep."

JULIA PUSHED IN THE DRAWER, annoyed. She'd decluttered a bathroom drawer that didn't need decluttering.

Saturday night in the biggest town in Kentucky, and Julia had nothing to do. At one point, she considered trekking up to Cincinnati to see her parents, but the idea of driving the extra two hours made it less desirable. She'd gone for a run along the river early in the morning, checked in with her supervisor, done her laundry, gathered the equipment she needed for the cave exploration, packed a bag, flipped through the channels on TV, and made brownies.

This is ridiculous.

She stared at herself in the mirror, studying, noting flaws, and shook her head, checking the time.

It wasn't even six o'clock.

Never a natural pleasure-seeker, since her broken engagement, she'd stayed busy working. Now? Now that she had fully recovered from the psychological trauma and medical issues she'd suffered at the hands of the criminals, she was once again investigating. Contemplating Lance's defection, she was mainly annoyed that she'd let it get so far.

She pulled the scrunchie out of her hair, ran her fingers through her dark mane, and then changed from her jogging shorts and tank into jeans and a T-shirt. She had planned to do some major shopping before the wedding to be ready for the honeymoon, but she never got around to it. Hitting the mall had never been her go-to for entertainment. Maybe she would reward herself with some frozen yogurt or a fancy coffee.

Shopping sounded better all the time, and staying in her apartment one minute longer was more than she could take.

Key in hand, Julia checked the back seat and all around, a long-time habit, before getting in the car. It didn't matter how many times she had, without incident, gone into the parking garage located under her apartment building, she'd seen enough movies to know the dangers. Her phone rang as she hit the unlock button on her key fob.

Clyde Burke. Frowning, she answered. "What's up, Agent Burke?"

"I told you, call me Clyde."

She could hear the humor in his voice. "Very well, then. What's up, Clyde?" It still didn't feel right to be so casual, but she'd follow his lead.

"Hey, sorry to call on the weekend."

"Weekend. What's that?" She chuckled into the phone.

"I hear you. I wanted to fill you in since I'll be gone a few days next week. Talked to my father-in-law ..."

"Tripp Durbin?"

She sat up straight in her bucket seat. Her interest was

piqued now. She'd read the file on Durbin and learned bits and pieces of the family saga.

"Yes. He had a good afternoon yesterday, so I asked him about the map of the caves and tunnels."

"Any new info?"

"Not much. Just that he drew the map and that it isn't complete. He fell asleep before he could tell me any more. It's a start."

"Good to know we're not dealing with lost information."

"I agree. Eli Reno is working on identifying the passageways we know about and marking possible off-shoots in the unmarked area. I'm planning to go back with Rebecca to see Tripp tomorrow afternoon. Maybe he'll be able to tell us more."

"Sounds good." She paused. "I remember Rebecca was in the tunnels when I was in the mix, before. Does she remember any side passages not on the map?"

"She studied the map with us this afternoon. She recalled a few places that didn't line up with the map, so Eli's marked those. Monday, I want you two to go down there armed with the map, lights, and a camera, getting every bit of information you can."

"Works for me. I haven't been spelunking in a while." The idea of getting into the caves energized her.

"Good deal. Hey, have a good rest of the weekend."

"Will do, and safe travels."

"Thanks, Julia."

The call ended, and she sat there for a few minutes, thinking through what she'd learned, making a few reminder notes on the notepad she kept in the console of her Nissan Sentra. Tripp Durbin created the map and then hid it in the cabin's attic before he got caught. Or maybe he'd hidden it up there much earlier. The farm had been in his family for a few generations.

Clyde Burke was an interesting guy. Undercover for ten years, and earlier, a stint in military intelligence, which explained his bearing and the tough exterior. He reminded her a little of the guy in the old *Die Hard* movies. Tough and charismatic at the same time.

Then there was Eli Reno, about as opposite of Clyde as possible. She shook her head, a sigh of humor and frustration fighting for her attention. She'd met way too many guys like him in college. Most of them had tried to lure her to frat parties that she couldn't care less about.

She started the car and shifted into reverse. A sudden knock on the window had her reaching for her gun. She narrowed her eyes at the one person in Louisville—no, make that the world—she'd rather not see again in this lifetime.

Lance.

Chapter 9

Julia pushed the button to roll down her window, frowning at the man standing next to her car, hands in his pockets.

"Lance."

"Hi, Julia." He avoided eye contact.

She sat there, staring up at him, her ire growing by the moment. "What do you want, Lance?"

He glanced at her and shrugged. The self-deprecating, false-humility-riddled affectation that once seemed sweet now irritated her. How did she think herself in love with him—enough to promise to marry him?

Hand on the roof above her open window, he leaned in closer. "When you called the other day, it made me miss you. That's all."

"How's Carrie?"

"She's fine, spending the weekend with her folks."

"So, since you're at loose ends, you figured it would be okay to bother me? As if I had nothing better to do?"

Her anger and a bit of fear grew. As an officer, she knew

how to de-escalate an altercation between people. However, all the self-defense training in the world didn't prepare a woman to mentally defend herself against a man who cheated on her only weeks before they were supposed to be married.

Not for the first time, she wished she had the authority to arrest him for being a loser.

At one point in time, his dazzling, over-whitened smile *might* have resurrected the appeal she'd experienced when they met. Now? When she'd been around actual men who loved and respected the women in their lives? Now, the greasy smile angered her. He was a child in a man's body.

"I figured it couldn't hurt to try." He sobered, his eyes focused down, ostensibly at his feet. "Listen, I know I did a stupid thing, cheating on you."

"With your best friend's girlfriend."

He nodded. "I feel bad about Eli."

About Eli? She felt nothing for this man except anger. The last thing she wanted to do was rehash what was becoming more tiresome by the minute.

"He's worried."

Lance's head whipped up. "How do you know?"

One side of her mouth lifted along with one brow. There were so many ways that would make him squirm. She decided the truth was interesting enough. "I've spent the better part of a week working down in Clementville. Going back next week." She shrugged, giving the gesture back to him. "Staying with his grandparents."

Raking his hand through his dark blond hair, he had the grace to appear flustered. "You haven't ..."

"No, Lance, I haven't said anything to him. The way he acts toward me, he probably thinks the breakup was my fault. What did you call me? A 'cold fish'? Pretty sure 'frigid' was one of the words you used to describe me."

If she stayed within close proximity of him much longer, she would get out of the car and put him on the ground with a couple of martial arts moves he wasn't aware she possessed. Her anger grew to the point she wouldn't be too concerned about inflicting concussions and broken bones.

"If you're worried about me ratting you out, don't be. If he finds out, it won't be from me. I make no claims about him learning what you've done from another source, though."

"Julie, I ..."

That did it. She got out of the car and stood, legs in a secure stance and hands on her hips, eyes on him. She could envision only two scenarios for the near future—put her hands on her hips or sock him in the face. She knew what she'd prefer, but as a peace officer, socking him in the face wouldn't look good on her record.

"Don't call me 'Julie.'"

"I know I should talk to Eli. I figured what he didn't know wouldn't hurt him."

"And now you've waited too long," Julia seethed.

He stood there, his face pale. "I'm sorry."

"Yes. Yes, you are. Me? I'm over you. This little meeting has helped tremendously. What I can't understand is why anyone would throw away a lifetime friendship for a woman who might as easily cheat on you as she did on Eli."

The flicker in his eyes proved her words hit home. Good.

"Lance, nothing in the world could induce me to stay here talking to you. What made me think there was any chance of creating a family together is totally beyond me. Oh. That's right. You never wanted kids. Not with me, anyway. You oughtta be in undercover work. You sure fooled me."

He stepped back, holding his hands up in surrender. "When you accidentally called the other night ..."

"It wasn't an accident."

One of his brows shot up.

Moron.

"I called the number to see if you'd changed it, for Eli's benefit. Not mine. And certainly not yours."

Eyes narrowed, he pulled his chin back and squinted at her, briefly indicating jealousy, as if he had any right.

"Taking care of Eli, huh? How do I know you and he weren't carrying on while we were still engaged?"

"This conversation is over." Her hands itched. She wanted so badly to hit him, but she got back in her car. "Goodbye, Lance."

She rolled up her car window and drove off without checking to see if he was out of the way, squealing her tires a little as she rushed out of the parking lot.

He would never know her hands were shaking on the steering wheel.

ELI WAS, both literally and figuratively, dragging his feet. The idea of working in close quarters with Julia put him in a bad mood. Party? Fun. Carpentry work? Fulfilling. Exploring? Interesting. The idea of being stuck in a tunnel with Julia Rossi? Mind-numbing.

When he arrived in the kitchen, Grandma bustled around, putting breakfast on the table.

"Now, you boys help yourselves while I make myself presentable for church." She started to leave, then stopped to pour them some coffee.

"I thought you were going to get ready for church?" Eli was not his usual sunny self, and he was aware of it.

"Well, good to know you're talking." Grandma put a hand

on her hip and shook her head. "That's the first thing you've said all morning."

Eli twisted his lips and muttered, "Sorry."

Grandma put down the coffee pot. "All is forgiven. Amazin' how much ill-will happens on Sunday morning, of all times." She swept out of the kitchen, leaving Eli and Grandpa to themselves.

Grandpa narrowed his eyes at Eli. "What's got your knickers in a twist?"

Eli couldn't stay mad. He laughed. "That's one I haven't heard in a long time."

"Don't usually have to use it on you," Grandpa said. "I had to pull out all sorts of old sayin's on Trace. That is until he and Hannah got their act together." He took a big bite of scrambled eggs and pointed at Eli with a crispy slice of bacon. "Better get it off your chest. Mandy homes in on a foul mood at first glance, and she won't rest until she gets to the bottom of it."

The thought of his cousin staring at him all through Bible Study was enough to make him less reticent about sharing his frustration.

"Dreading tomorrow, I reckon." Eli split a biscuit and poured sausage gravy over everything on his plate.

"Julia?"

Eli nodded.

"I thought I caught wind of some animosity there. I didn't know you were acquainted with her." Grandpa took a long swig of hot coffee.

"You remember my friend, Lance?"

"Sure. He always seemed to be around when we were up at your place." Grandpa sat back and waited.

"Julia Rossi was engaged to Lance. She broke the engagement. He didn't give me any details, but he was pretty torn up about it."

"Hmm. Sounds to me like there may be more to the story, right off hand."

"It would help if Lance would answer my calls or texts." Eli shook his head. "I'm worried about him, Grandpa."

"Somehow, I don't see Julia entering into an engagement, and certainly not a marriage, lightly."

"Hard to know about people." Eli shrugged. "Anyway, we're working together down in the tunnels, and I don't have a clue what to talk about."

Grandpa laughed. "Can't have any dead air, can we, boy?"

Grandpa was right. Silence made Eli uncomfortable. Being still made it worse.

His thoughts immediately went to the song *Be Still*, and then to the Bible verse, "*Be still and know that I am God.*"

"I don't know what did or didn't happen with Julia and Lance, but your grandma is pretty good at reading people. She wouldn't have invited her to stay under our roof if she thought there would be a problem." Grandpa eased back in his chair, arms crossed over his stomach.

Eli scoffed. "I don't think you get into the FBI without passing a pretty rigorous background check." He shook his head. "I'm sure it'll work out. Maybe she'll give me some idea about why Lance seems to have disappeared."

"Maybe she will, at that." Grandpa narrowed his eyes. "Now, think you can pass the Mandy inquisition stare?"

Mug in hand, Eli took one last swig of his coffee and rose, placing the empty plate and mug in the sink. "Maybe. I'm sure I'm making a mountain out of a molehill."

"We poor humans usually do. Sometimes, we have to be still and listen. God'll talk to you if you do." Grandpa checked his watch and then the clock on the stove. "Grandma is going to have to get it in gear if we're going to get to Sunday School in time."

"I'm curious why I get blamed for us being late when you don't even have shoes on yet." Grandma stood in the kitchen doorway, Bible and purse in one hand and the other hand fisted on her hip. She shook her head, muttering, "Get it in gear, my foot."

"THINK NOTHING OF IT. Looking forward to having you, Julia. Bye, now."

Grandma pressed the button to turn off the old cordless phone, her eyes shining. "That was Julia."

"I figured that out." Eli pulled his attention from his book to send a half-grin to his Grandma.

"Smarty." Grandma shook her head. "She said she'd be in around seven. I told her Grandpa and I had a meeting at church tonight..."

Grandpa put the paper down, surprised. "What meeting?"

"You heard the pastor say there would be a mission trip planning meeting."

"I did. I didn't know we planned on going." Grandpa frowned.

Grandma stood her ground. "I didn't say we'd committed to going. I thought it might be nice to learn a little more about it. After all, Ed and Christine are heading it up."

"When is it?" Eli was curious. Wasn't Mandy's wedding in a few weeks?

"Not until September in Eastern Kentucky." Grandma smiled, her excitement contagious.

"Yeah, about as far east as a body can go and still be in Kentucky." Grandpa harumphed.

Grandma waved him off, turning back to Eli. "There's a church camp there serving a lot of underprivileged kids and adults, and they depend on off-season help to keep the buildings maintained."

"Don't know what they'd want with a couple of senior citizens on this trip." Grandpa put the paper on the arm of the sofa and pushed himself up, grunting a little. "What kind of help would we be?"

"They're also hosting Bible classes in the evenings for the church members there. I think Ed has in mind for you to teach a men's class and me a ladies' class."

Heaving a sigh, Grandpa shook his head. "I'll listen, but I'm not committing to anything yet. That's about the time we'll get the last hay in, and if the weather's dry, I'll be into shelling corn and combining beans."

Eli raised his brows. "Isn't that what Dad's here for?"

"Exactly." Grandma smiled. "Isn't it about time you let Tom run the fall harvest?"

"I'll be around to help after work. Trace, too, if he's not still on his honeymoon." Eli rolled his eyes.

Grandpa huffed. "I'm gettin' too old to teach. I've forgotten more than I knew when I was younger."

Grandma came, slipping an arm around his waist, smiling up at him. "Your reasoning also applies to working all hours getting a crop in. I know we might retire from a job, but we never retire from serving the Lord."

Kissing her on the forehead, Grandpa sighed. "I suppose not."

"So, Julia will be here around seven?" It dawned on him that he'd be there to greet her unless he found a very good reason to be gone. "I thought I'd go to Bible study tonight ..."

"No Bible study tonight. Preacher's on vacation. They left right after morning service." Grandma had a triumphant gleam in her eye. "So, I didn't think you'd mind staying around to let Julia in."

The dread in the pit of his stomach went right along with the feeling he woke up to that morning. He took a deep breath, steeling himself. "I don't mind."

"I've put her in the green bedroom." She inspected the room, probably trying to see if she could find anything out of place before their "guest" arrived. "Oh, and offer her some supper. There's some fried chicken and potato salad in the refrigerator."

Eli held up a hand and nodded. "Will do."

"Good." Grandma's eyes crinkled in the corners as she smiled, and then she whacked Grandpa gently in the stomach. "We need to get a move on."

Grandpa picked up his Bible from the coffee table and grabbed his keys from the table next to the front door. "I'm ready."

They left without further ado, leaving Eli there pondering his upcoming greeting to Julia Rossi. She'd be there in less than an hour. Why Grandma thought she needed to stick her nose into an ongoing FBI investigation was beyond him, but he had too much respect for his grandparents to argue.

When his silenced phone vibrated in his pocket, he pulled it out to see a voicemail notification.

From Lance. Same number as before.

Opening the voicemail app, no words filled the space where there was usually an AI-generated text translation of audio. He pushed the "play" button anyway. Nothing. Glancing at his recents, he saw a missed call from Lance.

This was the first time Lance had reached out since Eli'd moved down to western Kentucky. Tapping the number on the screen, it rang once and then went straight to voicemail.

It wouldn't hurt to leave a message, would it?

"Hey, Lance, sorry I missed you. Call me back. I've been trying to reach you for months, afraid you'd changed your number or something without telling your old pal." Eli laughed with what he hoped was a lighthearted chuckle. "Anyway, hope to hear from you soon." He pulled the phone away from his ear and stuffed it in his pocket.

He'd done his part. Now, the ball was in Lance's court. As he pondered, the crunch of gravel in the driveway pulled his thoughts away from Lance.

She was here.

Chapter 10

Julia pulled into the driveway of the big white farmhouse where she'd be staying for a few days. A suburban girl born to confirmed urban residents, farms had always fascinated her. Dad thought the ten-minute drive from their subdivision to the nearest Walmart was sheer agony. The fact that there were three Walmarts, two Targets, an outlet mall, and a large shopping center with all the latest and greatest shops within a ten-mile radius of her childhood home made the ambiance of Crittenden County as deserted as Antarctica.

Opening the car door, the hot, steamy air swept in.

Not Antarctica.

Louisville and Cincinnati weren't much better. At least here, there was the aroma of growing things with a hint of cattle, whereas the city smelled like a dirty, unwashed dog.

She grabbed her bag and purse, heading to the front door, which opened about the time she stepped up on the porch.

Eli.

Great.

There was a car missing. That's right, Sunday night. Mrs. Reno mentioned that.

"How was your trip?" Eli held out his hand for her bag, and she gave it to him.

Maybe chivalry isn't dead.

"Good. No road crews today." She came in, seeing the comfortable home with new eyes. When she'd been there before, it was a random place where she ate lunch one day. Tonight, she was a guest in the house.

"This is a nice place." Julia smiled when Eli's brows rose. "I know, it's only been a few days. I wasn't a houseguest, then."

He nodded, eyes roaming the room. "I'm trying to see it through the eyes of a stranger." Then he frowned. "Not working. Still just Grandma and Grandpa's house."

She laughed. "Am I to assume your grandparents have always lived here?"

"Yep, my great-grandparents built it back in the nineteen-thirties, I think."

A tinge of jealousy made her lips twitch. How great would it be to have so much family?

"I'm an only child, and both my parents were only children. My grandparents, except for one, are gone, and Nonna doesn't live in her house anymore."

"I'm sorry."

His words brought her eyes to his. She shrugged. "It is what it is."

"I sometimes wonder about being an only child. Mom is an only too. It wasn't a problem until she had to care for both of her parents." He swallowed, a mist of emotion crossing his face. "They both died within a year of each other."

So they had a few things in common. They'd both suffered the loss of grandparents. Both of them had been victimized by people they thought loved them.

Aaand that's pretty much where the comparisons end.

Eli held up her bag. "My instructions are to show you to the 'green room,' noting that it has nothing to do with the entertainment industry and has everything to do with a very well-preserved re-decoration in the late seventies."

"Oh, I thought maybe we were in the White House—there's a Green Room there too."

"Huh." Eli stopped climbing the stairs and glanced back at her. "If Grandma finds out, she'll never give up that wallpaper."

Julia chuckled, then followed him up the comfortable carpeted stairs to the second floor.

"Grandma and Grandpa sleep in the downstairs bedroom now. They figured it might be a good idea to avoid the stairs as they aged."

Entering the hallway, Julia was impressed. "There are more bedrooms up here than I expected."

Eli smiled. "Grandpa had three brothers and two sisters, so his father built the house to fit his family."

The first bedroom on the left appeared to be occupied. They walked past a large bathroom, and on the right, was the green room.

He jerked a thumb behind him. "There's only one bathroom up here, so we'll have to share. I'll try to leave it in good shape when I'm done."

Entering the last door, she stopped. She couldn't help herself. She chuckled, and he joined her. "Its name is right. It is a *green* room." Taking note of the comfortable space, she nodded. "It's nice."

His sidelong glance was relaxed. She had his approval. For now, anyway. Finally, a pleasant experience with the guy most likely to hate her.

Eli hoisted her bag onto the blanket chest at the foot of the bed. "If you need anything, Grandma is equipped for any emergency, large or small." Eyes back to hers, he paused. "Have you had supper?"

She'd snacked all the way there. Did that count?

"I've eaten, but ..."

"I asked if you'd had supper, not if you snacked all the way here." His brow arched, and he smirked. "There's fried chicken and potato salad in the refrigerator if you're interested."

ELI SMOTHERED a smile when hers broadened.

"I'll not pass up fried chicken and potato salad." She put her purse on the bed and stuffed her phone into her jeans back pocket.

"Good. I'm getting hungry too. We usually fend for ourselves on Sunday night." He turned and led her down the stairs and into the kitchen. Pulling out the platter covered in aluminum foil and the Tupperware container full of potato salad, he held the door open, seeing what else he might find. "Sweet tea?"

At her nod, he grabbed the half-filled pitcher and set it on the counter.

"Believe it or not, there is sweet tea north of the Ohio River." She grinned. "Not as much, but it's there."

"Remember, I grew up north of the Ohio." He pulled two glasses from the cabinet and filled them with tea. "Since Dad grew up here, Mom had to learn to keep the sweet tea coming."

"Are the plates up here?" She pointed to the cabinet above the dishwasher.

"Yes, and silverware there." He pointed to the drawer to the left of the sink, noting she didn't hesitate to reach up and grab dinnerware and cutlery. It was almost comfortable, working side-by-side with her, putting a meal on the table.

He snorted a laugh. *What would Lance have to say about this cozy turn of events?*

"What's funny?" She regarded him quizzically.

"Sorry." He tried to tamp down the heat he sensed on his neck. "I thought of something else."

"I love cold fried chicken." She must have decided to ignore his outburst and went around to the other side of the table.

"Me too. Especially in the summertime." He held the plate of chicken out and let her choose first, then the potato salad.

"This looks good." She hesitated.

He glanced at her over the simple meal. "Not sure how you feel about it, but we always say Grace over our meals at Grandma and Grandpa's table."

Did he see a blush slowly making its way up her face? "I don't mind. Nonna would have a fit if we so much as took a bite before the blessing."

Reaching across the table to take her hand for the prayer was as automatic as brushing his teeth. When her startled eyes met his, he realized he held her hand. She didn't hesitate, either. Her fingers wrapped around his, hers a little cold, his warm enough to heat the chicken as he ate. It wasn't weird at all, and that made him angry. Was he that shallow? She'd hurt his friend, after all.

Get over yourself, Reno.

All he had to do was say the blessing. No pointed references to his opinion of her. A prayer that straight-out blessed the food and thanked God for His care. He'd pray the prayer he would pray if Grandma were sitting at the table with him.

"Father, thank You for bringing Julia here safely, and bless us in the work we'll do tomorrow. We give thanks for the food

You've provided. Use it to nourish our bodies and our bodies to Your service. Amen."

He heard a small "amen" from across the table as he pulled his hand away. He'd concentrate on his food. He didn't have to talk to her. While she might not be as evil as he'd built her up to be, he didn't have to be friends with her, either.

Did the blessing count if it wasn't from a sincere heart? Because right now, his heart was anything but honest. He didn't want anything bad to happen to her, but for some perverse reason, he wanted her to experience at least a fraction of the hurt she'd inflicted on Lance.

After a few quiet moments, the silence threatened to drive him crazy. It was one of the reasons he hadn't liked living by himself. He'd keep the television or music on during all meals he took at home. At least it was company.

Considering he'd be working with her this week, possibly for several days, they had to come to some kind of truce. He was aware of her observation of him, and he was tempted to ask her for her version of what happened with Lance.

No. It was none of his business. Lance would call him. Eventually. In the meantime, he would play nice. Be the bigger person.

He drew a sigh of relief at the distinctive sound of Grandma and Grandpa's car pulling up the drive. The social one in the family, nobody would believe he was tongue-tied around Julia. He needed someone else to carry the conversation so he could think.

What on earth would they talk about while they were alone in the tunnels?

Chapter 11

Eli paused at the foot of the stairs, listening to the conversation going on in the kitchen. He'd hoped Julia was what Grandma would call a "lie-abed." No such luck. As soon as he entered the shared upstairs bathroom, he discovered she wasn't. The room was as clean, if not cleaner, than before she arrived. If it hadn't been for the residual steam around the edges of the mirror, there would be no sign she'd been there.

"Mornin', Eli." Grandpa smiled up at his bride when she filled his cup, then turned back to Eli. "Thought we were gonna have to roust you out of bed."

"No. I thought I'd stay out of the way in case Julia needed more time in the bathroom. I see she's ready to start the day."

Grandma set a plate of waffles in front of him. "Since it's Julia's first day here, I thought I'd fix us all a treat."

Passing him the bottle of pancake syrup, Julia twisted her lips in a smile. "I was up early, so I thought I may as well get in and out of the way."

"Not in my way at all. I have a brother and a sister,

remember? I've only had my own bathroom for the last few years." Eli speared a sausage link and then a bite of waffle, closing his eyes in delight. "Grandma, have I ever mentioned you make the best waffles in the world?"

"Well, I've heard it a few times," she said drily, shaking her head. "Julia, the boys in this family—and there are a lot of them—inherited the gift of hyperbole from their Grandpa's side of the family."

"Must have skipped a generation." Eli winked at Grandpa, who chuckled.

"Maybe a little bit from my side too. I wish you'd known my daddy better. He could wrap my sisters and mother around his little finger with his compliments. My boys are as bad."

"So, are you the 'strong, silent type'?" Julia grinned, glancing up at Eli.

"Not Eli, but there's one of those in every generation too," Grandma said. "Grandpa, Eli's dad, Tom, and his brother, Trace."

Eli ate his waffles with little to say for a change. Julia fit in with his grandparents better than he preferred. He supposed, as an FBI agent, she was trained to insert herself in any situation. Had she used her position working undercover to manipulate her way into Lance's affections?

He didn't trust her. About the time she worked her way into his good graces, he had to stop and remind himself to hold her at arm's length, at least until he knew Lance's side of the story.

Raking the syrup on his plate with the last bite of sausage, Eli put down his fork and checked the clock on the range. Seven-thirty.

Julia was way ahead of him. She wiped her mouth with a napkin, thanked Grandma for the breakfast, and rushed upstairs to finish getting ready.

They'd probably run late if she was anything like Samantha, who spent the last five minutes before leaving changing outfits.

But no. Julia was back before he got his plate and mug in the sink.

"Are you ready?"

The smile on her face and a spark of excitement in her dark brown eyes put him in gear.

"Let me run upstairs for a minute, and then we can go." Now, he was the slacker.

"Might want to grab a jacket." She called out to him as he climbed the stairs.

"It's supposed to be in the 90s today," he replied.

"Not in those tunnels, it won't. A cozy sixty degrees is more accurate."

He didn't answer. When he went up to brush his teeth, he hesitated, then pulled his hoodie from the back of the closet.

She might be right, but she wouldn't hear it from him.

JULIA WAS IRRITATED. Her first night at the Renos' house, Eli seemed to have decided to be pleasant. Today was a different story. A moodier, more frustrating man she'd never met.

And they had spent all day together, for multiple days.

Has it only been a week?

Topics of conversations they'd had up to lunchtime included the merits of wearing the correct footwear when caving and whether to turn right or left when they met the fork in the path.

They went left. Eli's pick. Typical.

"If we go right, we'll be going over territory that's already been covered." Eli's confidence annoyed her.

She bit her tongue, unsure whether or not her disagreement with his choice was right or out of vexation.

"Lead on, then."

Earlier in the week, they'd gone through the passages on the map. The easy part. When they squeezed through the narrow spot in the tunnel Nick had described, she was pretty sure they were close to the drop-off where Del was shot.

Eli trained his flashlight on the ground and adjusted his headlamp to get general lighting. Julia did the same. He stopped when a blast of cold air hit them. "What was that?"

"We've been going downhill for the last half-hour. Cold air goes down. We happened to hit a pocket where air circulation is more active." Julia had explored her share of caves. It was one of her favorite ways to get into nature.

"Where'd you learn about caves?"

She paused, pushing a larger rock to one side. "My dad. We went to Mammoth Cave when I was little, and I was hooked. The excitement on his face at every twist and turn made me happy." She lifted a shoulder. "I've always been a 'daddy's girl.'"

Eli smiled. One of the few she'd seen today.

"After that, we try to visit at least one cave every summer." She chuckled. "We wait until it's hot as blue blazes outside. Makes us enjoy the cool air inside."

They walked a little while in silence, then she spoke again. "What about you?"

The deep breath he took reminded her that he was with her under duress, as it were. He'd prefer to be with anyone else, but it was out of her hands. How would he feel about the partnership when he learned the truth about Lance?

"A lot of history happened in caves. There's a historical tour at Mammoth Cave ..."

"I am aware—been on that one a few times."

"Not surprised. I find it interesting to see the ways people throughout history have used naturally occurring landforms." Eli stopped abruptly, causing Julia to come close to crashing into him.

"What's wrong?"

Eli crouched down, shining the flashlight beam in a slow trail from the path to what appeared to be a wall of rock. "I didn't see this last time I was down here." He pointed to drag marks in the damp tunnel floor. The marks shifted, going from straight lines to a curve.

With both their headlamps shining on the other, Julia saw Eli's wide eyes and knew hers were too. "Now what?"

A slow grin budded on Eli's lips. Was his sense of adventure kicking in? Had it ever really gone away?

"Elementary, my dear Watson. We go forth."

She felt her lips twitch, determined to keep her excitement about their undertaking to herself. "Well, Sherlock, I need to get some pictures and take some notes."

"Killjoy." His smile came full-on. "While you do, I'll see what's around this invisible corner."

Julia didn't want him to discover anything without her. Was she being petty? He wasn't a suspect, so there was no need to keep an eye on him every minute.

Focusing on the floor, Julia took pictures, noting on the image file the direction the marks headed. With her compass app, she took a screenshot of the exact coordinates. She scoured the surrounding area with the lights from her headlamp and flashlight, wishing for a lantern.

Next trip.

Going over the space in a grid pattern, she almost missed it. Kneeling closer, where the floor met the wall, a small object sparkled.

"Eli."

"Find something?"

She crouched down, shining her light on what she now could tell was a coin. Or was it a medal of some kind? "Has anyone else been down here?" Gloves in place, she secured the object in a small evidence bag, zipping the top.

"Before I brought Clay and Nick down here, Samantha and I were the last. Before that, I don't know. None of our folks have been down here since last summer." Eli scoffed. "Too busy having babies and getting married around here."

She held out the coin to let him see. Where had she seen this before?

Eli's eyes shot to hers and then back to the coin. With a curt nod, he handed it back to her. "We can see it better when we get up top."

He'd seen the coin before. It was written all over his face.

Chapter 12

Eli pulled into his parents' drive, glad to have a reprieve from Julia's prying eyes. She didn't have much to say after they found the St. Christopher's medal. She was as troubled as he about this piece of evidence.

He knew exactly where that coin had come from. He remembered the tiny square hole on one edge.

The last time he and Carrie tried to have a double date with Lance and Julia, Julia called at the last minute, unable to join them because of a case she was working on.

Even then, he'd scoffed at the excuse. Working for the FBI had its perks. Nobody would question an agent's alibi because their whereabouts might be part of a federal investigation.

Yeah, right.

He tried not to judge, but by then, his relationship with Carrie was tense, to say the least. From Lance's reaction, things weren't exactly rosy with him and Julia, either.

Wedding nerves.

The three of them had gone out for supper, and while they were waiting for their entrees, Lance entertained them with his coin tricks. He'd always had a thing for magic, especially sleight-of-hand illusions. He rolled a coin across his knuckles as smooth as silk, something Eli had never been able to do.

The coin he liked to use was an old St. Christopher's medal he must have acquired in college after Eli dropped out. Eli didn't remember Lance carrying the medal around in high school. The coin trick, yes. The actual medal? No.

Entering the new front door of his mom and dad's house, Eli peeked in, listening to the sounds of conversation back in the kitchen. He'd surprise them.

In his stealth, he found himself surprised, instead, when the topic of conversation turned to his and Carrie's breakup.

He stopped, listening.

"I can't believe Eli hasn't figured it out. I mean, Lance has ghosted him ever since he broke up with Carrie. It's no coincidence that their breakup happened soon after Lance and Julia broke off their engagement."

Okay, it was time to reveal his presence. The last thing he wanted to hear was his little sister's deep dive into his personal life.

"Hey, guys," Eli said, sliding into a stool next to his sister at the large kitchen island. "What's for supper?"

Sam had difficulty meeting his gaze, even as she succumbed to his side hug.

He made a show of sniffing the air. "Does my nose deceive me, or do I smell lasagna?"

"Ding, ding, ding, we have a winner." Mom laughed. "It's nice to have at least two of my chicks in the nest occasionally."

"Let's not make it a habit." Dad had slipped in and stood behind Eli, his hand on Eli's shoulder. The squeeze and wink when Eli turned to him belied his gruff comment. "But Mom's happy, so I guess I'll have to put up with you two."

"At least Trace isn't here."

"He counts as two now, you know." Mom's smile beamed. "I wonder how long I'll have to wait for grandchildren …" Her voice trailed off, and a dreamy expression came across her face.

"Good grief, Mom, let's not scare them out of the notion." Sam laughed.

"No worries. I won't do anything to slow the process of becoming a grandmother." Mom grinned, arching a brow. "Tonight, Samantha made the lasagna."

Dad frowned. "What's the occasion?"

"Does it have to be an 'occasion' for me to cook?" Sam twisted her lips. "Maybe I wanted to learn from the best."

"Plus, Jay is coming for dinner."

"Carrino?" Dad's frown continued. "Why?"

Eli wanted to know more about the conversation he'd interrupted. The current topic was seriously distracting him.

Samantha was cooking, and she was blushing a lot lately for no good reason. Or was there a reason?

Jay Carrino, the young farmer down the road, seemed to be spending a lot of time wherever Sam was. He remembered him from summers visiting the farm. He'd sneak out of Grandma's house, and he and Jay would see what kind of trouble they might get in.

Mom checked the clock. "It's not quite five … Eli, could you run up to the Amish store and pick up a loaf of bread?"

"Sure." Eli turned to his little sister. "Want to ride along?"

She twisted her lips, then nodded, taking a deep breath as she glanced at Mom. "I would love to. Jay won't be here until six."

"We better get going, then. Anything else you need?"

"No, I'm good. I didn't buy bread at the store the other day, thinking I'd stop in at the bakery. Of course, I didn't remember every time I went by." She sighed happily. "Thank you. I've missed having my runners on site."

Eli chuckled. Before the ink was dry on their driver's licenses, all three of them were the ones running to the store at the last minute. He was pretty sure Dad appreciated it even more than Mom did.

"Here." Dad held out a twenty-dollar bill.

"My treat, Dad."

"Force of habit."

"Be careful. Next time, I might grab it and go."

As he and Sam exited, their parents were laughing. Eli wasn't sure Sam would be in nearly as good a mood by the time he got through with her.

ELI TURNED the truck around and headed toward Highway 91. Catering to their Amish community, the real money came from the "English," as they called non-Amish people. A tourist destination in the summer, there was always plenty of bread on hand.

Sam was suspiciously quiet, and he let her stew in her own juice.

Serves her right.

"Sam—"

"Eli—"

They both spoke at the same time.

"Ladies first," Eli said, keeping his eyes on the road.

"No, you go first."

He glanced over at his sister, and his expression must have done his talking for him.

"Okay, I'll start." She swallowed audibly. "I know you heard Mom and me talking about Carrie." She paused.

What did she expect him to say?

"I did." When she didn't continue, he glanced over to see her chewing on her bottom lip. "And?"

"Sorry. Trying to get my thoughts in order."

Eli chuckled, his former anger dissipating in the face of her obvious dread. He wasn't excited about rehashing his former relationship, so he understood. "I don't know if we have that kind of time."

"Hardy-har-har." She punched him in the arm.

"Watch it, woman. I'm driving."

The long sigh coming from his sister instilled a little sympathy toward her. He knew she'd put off this conversation.

"Have you talked to Lance lately?"

"No. I've tried calling him. He hasn't answered any calls or texts. I wonder if he changed his number." He kept telling himself that was the case.

"When was the last time you were on Facebook?"

"I kinda ditched Facebook when Carrie and I split." His face warmed. "Too many happy newlyweds on social media for my taste. At least for my taste at that time. Then I came down here and got used to not checking it."

Eli pulled the truck into the parking lot of the store and turned toward her. "What are you getting at? We're going to finish this conversation before we go back to the house."

After another deep breath, she faced him. "I think we'd better get the bread before we go any further."

He nodded, checking the clock on the dash. Almost closing time. "Wait here. Be right back."

"Not planning on going anywhere." She gestured around at their remote location with an arched brow.

She knew something he wasn't privy to, and he had a feeling whatever it was wouldn't make him feel any better toward either Carrie or Lance. As much as he hadn't wanted his suspicions to be true, maybe they were. Maybe he'd been wrong about a lot of things.

Pulling open the door, the bell jangled, and the young Amish man at the checkout counter welcomed him in. "What can I help you with?"

"Hey, Joshua. Just picking up a loaf of bread." There it was, the last loaf, on the rack next to the counter. "Had a run on bread today, huh?"

The smile on the youth's face accented his age and status—no beard meant he wasn't married. Was he old enough to shave? "We did. Good thing I sent a loaf home with Jenny for supper."

"Jenny?"

Joshua scanned the store for other customers and then spoke in a low voice. "We're telling the family tonight." He grinned. "We're engaged."

And there again was a happy man in love.

"Congratulations."

"Keep it under your hat, if you don't mind." Joshua shrugged. "We don't tell anybody outside the family until right before the wedding."

"My lips are sealed."

"Thank you, Mr. Reno."

"Glad to keep your secret, and call me Eli." Eli picked up the long loaf of uncut bread and pointed it at the clock. "Better lock up behind me. Wouldn't want you to get in trouble by being late to dinner."

The young man laughed. "Yes, sir. Have a good night, Mr. R—er, Eli."

Eli chuckled under his breath, head down as he stepped off the porch. When he glanced at Sam in the passenger seat, his mood was swept back into the conversation he didn't want to have. Now was the time for things to be out in the open. As much as possible, anyway.

Handing her the loaf of bread, he buckled his seatbelt and headed out. "Now, what's so bad we had to wait to talk about it?"

Sam played with the twist-tie on the loaf of bread. "You haven't heard anything from either Lance or Carrie?"

"I told you I haven't, so you may as well stop avoiding it."

"Okay." Sam cleared her throat, her signature delay tactic. "Remember, you asked. Carrie and Lance are engaged."

Chapter 13

A jolt of anger hit Eli, and he slammed on the brakes. The truck skidded to a halt on the little-traveled road. His stomach roiled, and the blood rushed to his ears as the truth of Samantha's announcement sank in.

His former girlfriend and his former, as of now, best friend ...

This was a different kind of hurt. Part betrayal and part anger. Carrie hurt him when she broke up with him, but she wasn't the one who fueled his rage. He gripped the steering wheel until his knuckles were white.

"I'm sorry, Eli."

"How long?"

"What do you mean?"

"How long since you found out?"

Before they made it to the road where their parents lived, Eli detoured to Riverside Park and stopped the truck, turning it off and rolling down his window. He turned to his sister and saw tears in her eyes.

"I didn't want to be the one to tell you, Eli. I thought surely

Lance would reach out, make some kind of peace. I didn't expect him to stop communicating completely."

"How long, Sam?" He softened his tone and reached over, taking her hand in his. "I'm not angry at you. I'm angry with them and with the situation."

Tears rolled. "Oh, Eli, at first, I told myself it wasn't my business, and you wouldn't appreciate me telling you."

"Sam ..."

"New Year's Eve."

"That's when they started dating?" Eli was calculating in his head. Carrie had broken up with him between Thanksgiving and Christmas. "That means ..."

Samantha nodded slowly. "That means they were seeing each other while Lance was engaged to Julia, and Carrie was dating you."

"I went to Thanksgiving with her family. Who invites the person she's about to break up with to a family holiday meal?" He sat there, shaking his head, blood pressure building.

"I'm sorry."

"You have nothing to be sorry for. Lance, on the other hand ..."

"I know." He began to hear righteous indignation in her voice. "I'd like to give them both a swift kick in the you-know-what."

The image of his feisty sister taking on both Carrie and Lance almost made him smile. Almost.

"It'll be okay, Sam."

"How?" She swiped the tears from her face and shook her head. "Aren't you mad?"

"I am, but not at you." He scoffed. "You didn't do anything wrong, sis."

"I should have told you earlier. Then you could have confronted them."

"And what good would that do?" He started the truck. "Sometimes distance is the best thing. It wasn't your responsibility to keep them honest, and it isn't your job to make sure nobody hurts me."

"You'd do the same thing," she huffed.

"Probably. If I'd known then, I would have been a lot angrier than I am now. It's not as if I feel the need to fight for my rights. What are my rights, anyway? Carrie and I weren't married. We weren't even engaged."

Looking back, it struck him that every time he mentioned the future, Carrie clammed up or changed the subject. She was interested in the next fun thing.

"Anyway, getting mad and getting even aren't worth it."

"You've grown up, bro." Samantha turned her hand over to his and squeezed. "I love you, and I can't imagine a better big brother, and if you tell Trace, I'll deny it to death."

"Got it. Love you, too, sis." Rolling up the windows, he checked behind him and turned around. "Mom's going to wonder where her bread is." As they turned back onto the highway, he glanced over at his sister with raised brows. "Now, what's this about Jay Carrino?"

"He has become a good friend. Beyond that, I have no comment."

"I'm keeping an eye on you two."

He could have heard her sigh a mile away. "Eli Reno, don't you dare go all 'big-brother' on me. Dad's bad enough."

"I'll be watching. How's that?"

She put her hands over her face, then brought them down. "Ugh. Can't a girl who is twenty-five years old date a guy without her family treating her as if she's fifteen?"

"So you two are officially dating, eh?"

Silence as she twisted her lips, then she broke. "Jay is my date for Mandy's wedding. There. Satisfied?"

Eli reached over and tweaked her shoulder in the spot he knew was ticklish, making her jerk away in laughter. "I won't speak for Dad, but I'll try to be good." He raised an eyebrow. "Isn't it a little early to secure your date for a September wedding?"

"Ugh."

He shrugged, thoughts running through his mind a mile a minute, so fast he could hardly keep up. So many questions. Carrie and Lance. Sam and Jay.

And now there was the medal Julia found in the cave.

Plus, there was the very fact of Julia. He may have some words and thoughts to eat.

DARCY RENO HAD no trouble asking the hard questions. Julia had accepted an invitation to dinner at their apartment above the Clementville Café. Darcy wanted to do something to thank her for her part in saving her life and securing her happiness with Del. She wouldn't take a "just doing my job, ma'am" for acceptance.

After a dinner of the best chicken enchiladas she'd had outside of Texas, Julia was savoring the chocolate pie that threatened to put her over her sugar threshold for the week.

"Oh, my, that was amazing." She took a sip of freshly ground and brewed coffee and sat back in her chair, hand on her stomach. "Not that I haven't been having crazy-good meals all week. Del, your grandmother is a wonderful cook. I think I'll have gained ten pounds by the time I get home."

Darcy beamed. "Thank you, Julia. Glad you enjoyed it."

Del raised his hand. "I made the coffee."

"Noted. I don't know when I've had such a good cup of coffee."

"Don't give my husband the big head. I have to live with him, you know." Darcy gave her husband a twisted grin. "But it was good coffee, hun."

"Thank you, kindly."

"I'm still trying to figure out what God has in mind after all you've gone through in the last year." Darcy shook her head.

Del laughed. "Knowing you, finding Julia's ex in a dark alley and beating him up would be high on the agenda."

Julia had to laugh. Darcy was small but mighty. She'd proven it when she was taken, blindfolded, to the tunnels as leverage and distraction for the criminals searching for information they thought hidden in the café. If Julia hadn't come out of the drug-induced fog that almost killed her, the plan might have succeeded. As it was, her partner was caught, and the operation foiled. At least, that was the thought a year ago.

Now? Now, they were covering many of the same places and finding new evidence.

"I'm fine. I did have the opportunity to drive off with Lance standing right by my car last week."

"Tell me you ran over his toes." There was unmitigated glee in Darcy's voice.

Julia laughed. "No. I'll admit I kinda wish I had." Where did Darcy's love come from? They had never met before the incident last year. Back then, Julia was engaged, and Darcy was fighting an attraction to her now-husband.

The tables had turned.

Now Julia was fighting an attraction of her own.

"Don't say anything to Eli."

Darcy didn't say anything as her brow shot up.

"Anyway, I had dreaded meeting up with Lance again, hoping he'd stay on his side of the river and me on mine." Julia frowned. "It didn't make sense. Why would he show up in the parking lot of my apartment?"

Unless he's been stalking me.

Darcy narrowed her eyes. "I don't like that one bit."

"My wife doesn't tend to think the best of situations until she sees proof." Del gathered the dirty dishes and put them directly into the dishwasher.

"It comes from being a criminal justice major, I guess. And having a husband in the military." Darcy shrugged. "It taught me to be careful."

"You spent a lot of time alone."

Darcy's half-smile was sad. "Not alone. I had the added blessing of two babies."

The trials of a military wife. It was one thing—one horrible thing—to be alone and widowed, but alone with newborn twins? Hard to imagine.

"I would be the same way, I think. It's hard to avoid knee-jerk reactions, knowing danger lurks around every corner. And with two kids? I admire you, Darcy."

Del came up behind his petite wife's chair and kissed her on top of her head. "So do I."

Darcy turned her face upward and smiled. Not a sad smile this time. Del stooped to bestow a quick kiss on her lips, then straightened. "If you ladies will excuse me, I have two baths to supervise." He took a deep breath. "Prayers requested."

"You *think* he's kidding." He walked away, and Darcy's deadpan expression accompanying her statement made Julia laugh harder than she had in a long time.

It felt good.

Even so, she couldn't help acknowledging the niggling shadow of apprehension that came along with Lance's impromptu visit last weekend. He expected her to assume it was a random encounter. Her training prepared her for the worst.

And right now, the worst was Lance Billings. She didn't trust him any farther than she could throw him.

She followed Darcy into the living room past the table, pushing her hand in her pocket to pull out a tube of lip balm. The first thing her fingers touched, however, wasn't lip balm.

It was a hard, round, flat object in a plastic evidence bag.

The St. Christopher's medal. Was it the one that belonged to Lance?

Chapter 14

Her phone vibrating on the nightstand woke Julia from a deep sleep. Mrs. Reno told her the night before to sleep as long as possible. She thought it was a good plan.

Bleary-eyed, she picked up the phone and rubbed her eyes to clear her vision. The illuminated clock read 7:45, and as soon as she comprehended the word "Mom" on her caller ID, she hit the button.

"Mom? What's wrong." She never called early on a Saturday morning.

"Sweetie, calm down. We're fine. Nonna is fine."

That's what people said when things were *not* fine.

"Mom." Julia's heart was racing.

"Dad's in the hospital." Mom was concentrating on keeping her voice level. The last time she received a call at an odd time was when Nonna had a stroke.

"What happened?"

"They're calling it a Myocardial ..."

"A myocardial infarction?" A heart attack. Dad had a heart attack. "I'll be there"—Julia calculated the mileage between

Clementville and Cincinnati, then subtracted an hour for timezone change from Central to Eastern—"by noon."

"I don't want you driving like a maniac. All we need is for *you* to be in an accident. I'm not sure they provide adjoining rooms in the hospital." Mom's wry humor helped Julia's blood pressure to recede slowly.

"How bad is it?" Julia packed her suitcase while holding the phone between her ear and her shoulder

"They're running tests. When we got here last night—"

Julia straightened. "Last night?"

"It was so late. I wanted to wait until I had something to report before I called. There was no reason for both of us to sit here, waiting."

"Mom, what if something ... bad had happened? I should already be there." So much for calming down.

"The worst thing was having to sit up most of the night in the ER listening to your dad fuss that we could have waited 'til morning." Mom sighed. "Julia, I don't know if it's worth you driving all the way up here."

She closed her eyes and sat on the edge of the bed, willing the tears to stay inside. "I'll be there by lunchtime. When you hear anything, and I mean *anything*, call me. I'll get on the road in the next few minutes."

The soft sniff on the other end of the call squeezed Julia's heart. "I'll be glad to have you here, Jules, but I hate to interrupt your case."

"No need in either of us waiting for information alone. This case will still be here next week, and if I need to step back, other agents can take over."

"If you're sure." Mom's voice already sounded calmer.

"I'm sure. Kiss Daddy for me."

"Will do. Be careful, okay?" Mom always worried when she was on the road.

Julia grinned and repeated what Mom said. "Will do. Love you, Mom. Bye."

"Love you too. Talk soon."

The call ended, and she sat there in the green-plaid room, suddenly at a loss. What was she doing? Packing. She needed to pack, get dressed, and get downstairs to let the Renos know what was happening.

The bathroom door creaked as it opened, and footsteps went past her door toward the stairs. Eli was up, and she was glad. She didn't want to leave without telling him. Mr. and Mrs. Reno had probably been up for hours already.

Clothes and sundries packed up, she pulled a brush through her almost-black hair. There, on the dresser, was the St. Christopher's medal they'd found the day before. There was so much more of the tunnel system to explore.

No question about it. Dad was more important than any case. She wasn't deep undercover with no outside contact or out of the country with limited communication and transportation. Clementville was wildly civilized compared to some of the places she'd been assigned.

Should she make the bed or strip the sheets off and take them downstairs? She made the bed, deciding she'd ask Mrs. Reno her preference.

Jogging down the stairs, she set her suitcase by the front door.

"Leaving?" Eli tilted his head, eyes narrowed.

She nodded. "I just talked to my mom. Dad's in the hospital in Cincinnati. Heart attack."

"Wow."

Her grin came at the same time tears threatened once again.

"Is he okay? I mean, I know it's serious, but ..."

"They're running tests this morning, then they'll know

more. He's conscious, alert, and making life hard for Mom, so yes, I'm going to say he's okay."

The elder Renos came into the hallway, curious. "Are you leaving us?"

"I'm afraid so." Julia swallowed thickly, then shared what she'd learned from her mom.

"Oh, my. I'll get your dad's name on the prayer chain right away." Mrs. Reno was already rifling through the hall table, pulling out a worn address book.

"Thank you, Mrs. Reno. We appreciate it."

The older woman came and wrapped Julia in a hug, whispering a prayer in her ear, then stepped back. "No more of this 'Mrs. Reno' stuff, you hear? Please, Julia. Call me Grandma?"

Mrs. Reno—correction, Grandma—reminded her of her own Nonna's pre-stroke.

Julia nodded. "Yes, ma'am."

"Now, do you have time to sit down to breakfast, or can I put some biscuits and sausage together for a sandwich? Coffee?"

"Are you a grandma or a guardian angel?"

Sweeping her hand and emitting a quiet "Pshaw," Grandma chuckled. "I know it's like to want to get somewhere only to have it take forever to get started."

"I came down to ask if you want me to strip the bed and bring the sheets down?"

"Neither. We need to get you on the road. Do you think you'll be back?"

"I don't know. Maybe?" Julia's eyes cut to Eli's. She saw compassion on his face. It wasn't there when they parted yesterday afternoon. They'd gone their separate ways for supper, Grandma and Grandpa having previous plans with Steve and Roxy Reno. Eli had been by turns pleasant and prickly, so she wasn't sure what she'd get from one hour to the next. Maybe they'd worked too closely together. Maybe her leaving was for the best.

WHAT STARTED as a lazy Saturday quickly evolved into emergency status. Eli asked for her keys and carried her bag to the car, starting it up to check her gas level. She wouldn't have to stop until she made it to Elizabethtown. As she came down from the front porch, she pushed her hair behind her ear and pressed the phone to it.

"Thanks for calling me back, Clyde." Pause, then, as she approached him, she stopped. "Thanks. I hope to return next week, but I appreciate your understanding." She glanced at Eli. "I'll give Eli the piece of evidence we found yesterday." She nodded her head. "Right."

She ended the call with, apparently, Clyde Burke. He kept his eyes trained on her, trying to figure out what he hadn't seen before as far as Lance was concerned. Upon hearing her dad was in trouble, she continuously wiped tears from her eyes as if they wouldn't notice. Maybe she didn't want *him* to notice.

His experience with Carrie, and now knowing what had happened between Carrie and his so-called best friend, had dulled his sensitivity. Or maybe he spent so much time hogging the spotlight that he didn't notice the finer points of relationships. The cues. The little indications things weren't what they seemed.

Now? Now he realized how unfair he'd been. They'd both been treated abominably.

Julia opened her car door and threw her purse into the passenger seat, then carefully put the travel mug in the cupholder within reach. "I guess I'm on my way, then."

Grandma and Grandpa had joined them. Grandma once again put her arms around her, squeezing gently. "Remember, we'll be praying."

"Thank you." Julia smiled through real tears.

Grandpa cleared his throat and wiped his nose on the handkerchief he kept in his pocket. "Be careful on the road, and let us know when you get there."

Unbidden, Julia reached out and hugged Grandpa. His eyebrows rose in surprise, and then he squeezed her back.

"I will." She glanced from one to the other and then at Eli. "Thank you for your hospitality. I'll never forget this week."

The wistful expression as she turned toward Eli prompted a half-smile, and he nodded. "We'll learn all we can while you're away."

"I—" Julia stopped and swallowed, and then her eyes flew wider. "Oh!" She reached into her pocket, pulled out the evidence bag, and handed it to Eli. "I almost forgot. I told Clyde I'd leave this with you."

Eli nodded. "Thanks. I'll take good care of it."

She bit her lip. "If I don't get back ..."

"Oh, you'll be back." He flashed what he hoped was his signature megawatt smile.

Twisting her lips in humor and arching a brow, she shook her head. After a pause, her countenance crumbled. "If I do, it'll be because Dad's in great shape."

Julia slid into the driver's seat when Eli knocked on it softly, she lowered the window. Yeah?"

"How about we say 'when,' not 'if'?"

Eli suddenly wanted her to come back. Why? He wasn't ready to ponder that question. When her eyes fixed on his, her slow smile returned, and she nodded. "When, then? I want to see this through, especially ..."

He held up the evidence bag. "Especially since we both know where this medal came from?"

Her deep breath and slight nod told him they were on the same page. Not a page either planned to or wanted to be on. It would take some investigating to figure out the mystery of the St. Christopher's medal.

Chapter 15

Watching her drive away, Eli experienced competing emotions—relief and emptiness. Relief because her leaving gave him time to think seriously about what he'd learned about Lance and Carrie. No idea what Julia's take on the situation was.

Emptiness? That one gave him more trouble. He'd started ready to discount everything she did and said, hadn't trusted her, even if everyone in Clementville thought she should be up for sainthood.

That was before ...

Grandma called out to him. "Better come in and eat your breakfast before it gets cold."

Her voice jerked him back to the present. "Yes, ma'am." Going inside was on his agenda, but he stood there, rooted to the ground as the dust settled in the drive. She was gone. The one person he'd blamed for all his troubles was gone.

The left side of his lips crooked up, and a load lifted from his shoulders. Up to now, he thought he would have to work at forgiving Julia Rossi. It turned out Lance and Carrie—the two people he was closest to outside of family—were the ones he'd have to forgive.

Eli walked up the steps and into the house. The aroma of sausage and eggs drew him into the kitchen, where Grandma and Grandpa sat at the table, holding hands as Grandpa said the blessing. He slipped into his chair and took Grandma's hand. She glanced up at him and smiled, head still bowed.

" ... And Lord, watch over Julia as she travels. She's worried about her dad, and they need her there in Cincinnati. Thank You for putting her in our lives, and if You don't mind, bring her back. We like having her around. We thank You for the food You've provided and the beautiful hands that made the meal. In Jesus' name, Amen."

"Amen," Eli repeated softly.

"So, what are you up to this fine Saturday?"

Eli dipped gravy from the bone china bowl that was older than his dad. Then he dipped a little more for good measure. "Not sure. Maybe a little research, catch up on some emails." He met Grandpa's glance reluctantly. "You?"

"Well ... I've got a little fencing that needs doing. Your dad's taking Ginger to town for wedding supply stuff, so I told him I'd ask you."

Of course, he did.

"It won't take more than a half-hour. Forty-five minutes, tops." Funny how Grandpa avoided eye contact with Eli. It was the family joke that if Grandpa said something wouldn't take more than a half-hour, it was code for, "You're on duty at least until lunch." Didn't matter how early the project began.

And fencing was a never-ending project.

"One of our mama cows taught her calf to slip through the fence for the greener grass. Problem is, when one gets out, the other calves think they have permission to do the same thing. I think your mom is tired of getting the 'your father-in-law's cows are out' telephone calls."

Eli chuckled. Mom may have grown up on a farm and married a farmer, but she never gave in to being the quintessential "farmer's wife."

"Before either one of you leave, I need my clothesline tightened up." Grandma raised a brow and stared pointedly at Grandpa. "I seem to remember asking someone to do that for me earlier in the week."

"Guilty as charged," Grandpa said, sighing. "Your grandma is pretty patient during the week, but she gets a little steamed if her requests don't get done by Saturday." He dodged when Grandma swatted at him.

Eli scraped the last of the gravy off his plate with a half biscuit. "I'll fix it before we head to the fence."

"I'd be so grateful, Eli." Grandma came up behind him and hugged him the way she did when he was little, and he and Trace came for visits.

Grandpa might be a little gruff, but he was patient with them. Grandma? She was loving with everybody and even more affectionate with her family. Eli guessed that's why she didn't mind having a revolving door of houseguests.

"Glad to." Eli pushed away from the table, holding his stomach. "I may need a nap after breakfast. You spoil us, Grandma."

"That's a grandma's job."

JULIA STRODE through the double automatic doors of Saint Christopher Medical Center and headed straight to the information desk and the elderly lady in the pink smock. She was part of the army of volunteers called "Pink Ladies," although she'd seen a few gentlemen volunteers with a pink ribbon pinned to their shirts.

"Welcome to St. Christopher's. What can I do for you today?"

St. Christopher. He's everywhere I go.

"Hi, I'm looking for Marco Rossi's room. I think he may be in the cardiac unit?"

"Are you family?"

"Yes, I'm his daughter. Julia Rossi."

After a few clicks on the computer—which impressed Julia because she had to be over eighty if she was a day—the Pink Lady answered her query with a smile. "There he is, and there you are, on the list."

She gave Julia a brochure with a map, which was marked with a highlighter to the Cardiac Care Unit.

"Thank you." Julia smiled and turned to walk away when she heard her name.

"Miss Rossi?"

"Yes, ma'am?"

"We Pink Ladies have a little prayer meeting at shift change. Your family is on our list."

Touched more than she expected, tears formed in Julia's eyes. "Thank you. We appreciate it."

The lady nodded with a smile, then turned to the next person needing help.

The last time she'd been here was when her Nonna had a stroke. When that happened, the building had been under construction, so nothing seemed familiar. Julia was glad to have a map.

She breathed a sigh of relief when she arrived at the bank of elevators. Finally, something familiar.

Following the signs leading to the Cardiac Care Unit, she paused, then pressed the button to open the door. Relieved, she saw her parents through the strategically placed glass windows. No privacy was the price you paid for excellent care and constant vigilance.

"You must be Julia." A middle-aged nurse with short, graying hair approached her with a smile.

"I am."

"I'm Kathy, your dad's nurse. He said you were on your way."

"Is there anything I need to know before I go in there?" She wanted the scoop from a medical professional, not a garbled set of facts that may or may not be correct from her parents' memories. They weren't old, exactly, but stress affected memory. She'd experienced it herself.

"Dr. Clark is his cardiologist, and he was here a few minutes ago, discussing the results of the tests. He's recommending some stents. Two arteries were close to eighty-five percent blocked, and another was fifty. Beyond that, the arteries aren't to the point he felt needed to be treated."

Julia glanced into the room and saw Mom wave, then turned back to Nurse Kathy. "Thank you. Has anything been scheduled yet?"

"Dr. Clark said he would be back this afternoon when he's able to give you all a timetable." The nurse patted Julia on the arm and smiled. "He's in good hands. My husband was brought here two years ago with ninety percent blockages and ended up needing open-heart surgery. Now he's fifty pounds lighter and more active than he's been in years."

"Scary." Julia chewed her bottom lip. "Were you working in the unit then?"

"I was in the middle of my shift when the call came in about a patient coming in, and, lo and behold, it was Ben. Needless to say, I hightailed it to the ER and was with him from then on."

Julia remembered when, before she was injured in the attempt to flush out whoever was breaking into the Clementville Café from the tunnels, Del Reno was shot. She flashed back to Darcy's face when she arrived at the hospital, having no place there because neither had admitted their attraction to the other.

Life is short.

"God is good, and we had a good outcome." The nurse winked at Julia. "I expect Mr. Rossi will have a good outcome too." A beeping signal caught her ear. "Back to it. I'll be doing rounds as soon as I see what's going on here."

"Thanks." Julia glanced back to where her parents were sitting, waiting, as with all hospital stays, for further news or instructions.

At the full-view glass door, she started to knock softly and stopped when she saw Mom beckon her to come in. Dad was sound asleep.

"How's he doing?" Julia leaned down to hug Mom, remembering how thankful she was for her strength and level head when she'd been in a coma. By the time she was on the road to recovery, she'd learned well how strong Mom was, and here she was, proving herself again.

"Better. The nitroglycerin tablets help, and he's on a low-dose blood thinner. He's worn out." Mom sighed and shook her head, her gaze fixed on her husband. "This kind of thing happens to so many people, and yet you never think it'll happen to you."

Julia saw weariness etched on her face. "What do you need?"

Mom laughed quietly. "A nap and a shower?"

"I can stay with Dad if you want to go home for a bit."

"I don't want to leave."

"I know. The nurse I spoke to said the cardiologist would

come later today to see about scheduling his stents." Would she be able to get Mom to rest? The indecision on her face was heartbreaking. This was the woman with all the answers to Julia's mind.

"They won't let both of us stay in here very long, and I want to be with him at night." Mom twisted her lips, thinking. "How about this? After the doctor has been in, I'll run home and take a shower and change clothes while you stay with him, then I'll come back and stay overnight."

"I didn't hear anything about a nap in there."

"I can nap when I'm ..." Mom caught herself, tears overflowing her lashes.

Chapter 16

Eli arrived at the homestead entrance as Clyde was getting out of his car. He was curious about the FBI special agent's past. Ten years in deep undercover with organized crime? And now married to the woman he had been paid to protect? It had all the markings of an action-adventure novel.

"Good morning." Clyde smiled, holding his hand out. "Hate to think about being underground on a beautiful day, don't you?"

"Amen to that." Eli chuckled. "Any word from Julia?"

Now, why was Julia the first thing he chose to talk about? If Julia wanted him to know how things were going, she had his number. Would she call?

"He's stable. The surgery to place stents in his arteries is scheduled for tomorrow morning, and he may go home in a couple of days."

Is she coming back?

Eli wanted to know. Would he have a chance to undo some

of the damage he'd done in ignorance of what happened with Lance and with Carrie?

Clyde glanced at Eli as he stuffed a bottle of water and an extra flashlight in his backpack. "She said she'd be back Wednesday if nothing goes wrong." The quirk of Clyde's brow invited the heat to invade Eli's face. "I told her to take the week. We can deal with this."

"Who knows? Maybe we'll solve the case, and she won't have to come back." There. Maybe that would quash any ideas Clyde had about him and Julia.

The network of caves and tunnels connecting them became less of a mystery as they mapped them. Using GPS and a copy of the original map, Eli and Julia had found six more tributaries, and Eli expected he and Clyde would discover more today.

"How do you like living in the sticks? Must be pretty slow compared to living in Chicago."

Clyde's guffaw rang through the tunnel, echoing in the larger chamber they were entering. "I think Rebecca's having a harder time getting acclimated than I am, and she's from here." He turned to Eli. "She says the thing she misses most of all—and she says it's the truth—is shopping at Target."

Eli joined the laughter. "I suppose she's found the one in Evansville?"

"Oh, yeah, and the one in Clarksville, Tennessee." Clyde scoffed. "When we walk in, you'd think she could hear angels sing."

They walked on a little farther than Eli and Samantha had, both of them shining their lights around the stone and timber structure. In this case, instead of the stone holding up the timber, the timber supported the massive stone. Eli didn't want to think about how far under the surface they'd descended. He sensed when they were heading downhill.

Occasionally, the trek went uphill, but mostly down, into the part with features of natural caves. Judging by the fossils on the walls, he was pretty sure he was right.

Clyde was great, but Julia was a caver.

"Have you been to the Bible study Nick is starting?" Clyde's question caught Eli off guard.

"No. You?" Grandma had asked him the same question. At this point, he wasn't sure how much he trusted God. The deal with Carrie had rattled him, and now that he'd learned the rest of the story about her infidelity, he thought maybe his time would be better spent pondering life in the here and now.

"I missed last week, but I plan to go tonight." Clyde kept going forward. "If you want a ride, I'll go right by the Renos' house."

"Thanks. I'm not sure I'll go."

"Any particular reason?"

Eli took a deep breath and released it slowly. It wasn't any of Clyde's business. "Not sure about church in general right now."

Clyde knelt when his flashlight beam caught something out of place. He picked it up, holding it in the light for Eli to see. "What do we have here?"

A strap. Never been used. The little piece of paper used to hold packets of currency when delivered to a bank.

He put it in an evidence bag. "At least now we know the counterfeiting never stopped." He held the bag up. "And that Gabe Torrino is still active here."

ELI MISSED JULIA. He wanted to get things straight between them, force her to admit that the fault for their heartache was all Lance and Carrie. But she wasn't back yet. Her dad was recovering, and she decided to stay the week and planned to return next Monday.

After a few days underground with Clyde, Eli considered him a friend. Clyde was much more open and transparent than Eli expected an FBI agent would be.

On Wednesday, Eli and Clyde sat on the abandoned steps of the Woodward homestead ruins, eating the lunch Grandma packed and guzzling water. After being in the cooler tunnels, the heat and humidity took them down as soon as they emerged. While they'd found a few more minor pieces of evidence, nothing came forth that would lead them directly to Torrino and his ties to the criminal organization.

"Are you a believer?" Clyde turned to Eli. "I've seen you at church on Sundays, but you don't seem too excited about it."

Am I a believer?

Eli stretched his legs out in front of him, buying time. He was relieved when Clyde kept the conversation going.

"I haven't been for long—Nick explained how it works. I figured there was a lot of rigamarole involved in being a Christian. I was glad to hear that unless I'm missing something, accepting God's gift of grace is all I had to do." He shrugged. "Anyway, none of my business. I'm trying to figure out a whole new lifestyle."

That pinched. He'd been so caught up in his pity party that he'd pushed God to the side.

"Jesus and I haven't been speaking regularly." Would Clyde let it go now?

Clyde rubbed his hands across his nearly-shaved head. "I get it. I suppose you've been a Christian for a long time?"

Pressure was building up in Eli's chest. He hadn't had to talk about religion or God in a while. With family, it was taken for granted. They had the same history. Go to church. Sing the songs. Bow your head during prayers.

And all the time, he'd been pushing back, wondering what he'd done to deserve the heartache Carrie had inflicted on him.

Did that have anything to do with what Jesus Christ had done for him?

"I got saved at Hurricane Camp when I was about thirteen." Eli paused. "I guess after that, I took for granted my 'fire insurance' was paid up, so I didn't have to worry about it anymore."

Clyde nodded slowly. "I lost my parents when I was a sophomore in college, never knew my grandparents, so I figured if God existed, He'd left me high and dry. When I joined the FBI, I took any undercover assignment I could get. The rougher, the better. When I landed the Vic Pennington gig, I didn't have too far down to go." He grinned. "Until I got to know Rebecca."

"She had a tough time, didn't she?" Eli wanted to get the spotlight off of himself, and he was curious about Clyde and Rebecca. Especially since ...

"Wait. Didn't she date Del?" The first time he met her, Eli recognized her but wasn't sure why.

"She did." Clyde shook his head. "If Vic hadn't made her go to Chicago after her mom was killed, she'd have married him."

That would have changed the Reno family landscape.

"Is it awkward? Being around Del, I mean?"

Clyde paused. "At first it was, and when Nick roped me into his Bible study group, I wasn't ready to go that deep with other people—especially a guy who had been more important to my wife than I cared to think about."

"I get that." Eli tossed a grin to Clyde.

"It became clear neither Becca nor Del held a torch for one another." The twisted grin on Clyde's face was telling. "I'll admit, I watched quietly for a while. I'd been burned before."

Burned.

There, hidden deep inside, covered over by a veneer of bravado and nervous energy Eli had spent his lifetime perfecting, was his weak spot. His goal was to avoid getting burned. His ready smile and ability to pinpoint what the people around him wanted might have taken him to several positions of influence—teacher, preacher, or politician. Eli decided early on he wanted to work with his hands as a vocation and spend his free time absorbing information about history and making people smile. Beyond that, his main goal was finding the next good time.

Why, then, did Eli find himself in the rural community of Clementville, staring across the river, not smiling, not seeing the countryside around him?

When Clyde drove off around five o'clock, Eli decided to do some surface exploring on his own, which led him to a bluff overlooking the Ohio River. He loved watching the river flow, barges and boats traveling up and down. What went through the minds of the men and women who were the first to come down the river from the East? It was a rough life, and where he stood, all he could see was the river and trees. In his mind's eye, this was what those early settlers saw.

His mind turned to his own past. Was he going to let Carrie change his whole outlook on life, or was he being challenged on a much deeper level?

As if he'd made the request himself, God left him alone, and Eli stayed as far removed from religion as possible. It was hard to party on Saturday and then get up and go to church on Sunday, so he slid in late or skipped altogether. After a while, his parents stopped asking, and he got used to the disappointment in his mom's expression.

He thought maybe he had Grandma and Grandpa fooled.

The preacher spoke on the "narrow gate" in church Sunday. To him, that was a restriction, not a piece of sound advice. If Christians were supposed to "bring them in," wouldn't it be easier to get them through the "wide gate?"

A thought struck him: *The narrow gate depends on Jesus. The wide gate gives me the credit.*

The voice in his head sounded like Eli, but it wasn't something he would think of on his own.

I'm starting to get it, Lord.

Ever since Carrie broke up with him, he'd been confused. Wasn't it a slam to his ability to make her or any woman happy? Did he love her so much he couldn't live without her?

His gut was telling him, "No." He'd convinced himself it was time for a serious relationship, time to do the adult thing, and he would be the first to admit the physical attraction far outweighed the emotional.

And the spiritual? It didn't take a lot of thought to realize she was a distraction. The relationship with Carrie had dimmed his desire for anything concerning his relationship with Jesus.

In the last six months since she broke up with him, he'd come to realize Carrie hadn't hurt anything but his pride.

And we all know what comes after pride ...

Last night, he summoned the courage to open up his social media accounts. Sure enough, it was all there for anybody to see.

He reluctantly clicked on Lance Billings' relationship status.

When the page opened, he felt a jolt of surprise, which was idiotic.

There it was, in black and white: *Relationship status: Engaged to Carrie Miller.* Below were photos of Lance and Carrie together dating back to soon after Christmas.

His mind immediately turned to Julia. She knew all along and knew his distrust of her was evident. He'd watched the hurt expression cross her face, but she never said a word against Lance. He could be angry with her for lying to him about what she knew about Carrie, but had she?

No, she avoided talking to him about it, but she hadn't lied.

He'd been so wrong about her, and deep down, he wondered if he would be able to accept humility on his part.

Chapter 17

The doctor told Julia and her parents the procedure to insert three stents in the arteries surrounding Dad's heart might take anywhere from thirty minutes to two hours, and then he would be in recovery for a few hours.

It made for a long day when sitting in a waiting room doing nothing. Mom kept busy talking to her "sisterhood," as she liked to call her group of girlfriends who had been through so much together. One lost a husband, another divorced. Their kids were all close to the same age, and they were in an ongoing prayer group. Such a blessing that her mom had a support system. Would Julia ever be so fortunate? Her independence was a curse.

Julia took her laptop out and logged into the hospital's guest WIFI. The least she could do was get in a little research and check her email. Working away from the office had become second nature.

No news from her team leader in Louisville or anything else of a professional nature until she got down to the email from Clyde Burke.

Julia,

Did some more exploring with Eli Reno today, found a brand-new cash strap on the floor of the tunnel. Looks like our guy is still in business.

Praying for your dad. Hope the surgery is going well.

Burke

While it wasn't standard operating procedure for federal employees to offer prayers, she'd observed that Clyde Burke was anything but standard. The counterfeit operation was still in business. Gabe Torrino was once more slipping through their fingers, and with the recent evidence on top of the St. Christopher's medal find, she had to get back down to Clementville.

Clyde,

Dad's in surgery now. If everything goes well, he'll go home on Wednesday, and I'll head back. He told me he had enough women hovering over him.

Thanks for keeping me in the loop,

Julia

When the door to the surgery waiting room opened, every head turned to see if it was their surgeon. This time, it was Dad's heart surgeon.

He sat next to Mom, shaking Julia's hand as she joined them. "Mr. Rossi did great. We had to give him a little more anesthetic when we had trouble with the third stent, but other than a little more time in recovery, everything went well. He should be back in the cardiac unit by five. If all goes as planned, he should be ready to go home on Wednesday. We like to keep an eye on patients for a couple of nights."

Julia cleared her throat. "How ... what are his restrictions when he goes home?"

The surgeon smiled. "Not as many as you'd think. The usual not lifting more than a half-gallon of milk, eating healthy, taking your medicine, walking every day. The nurse will go over everything before you're released."

She nodded. This was so different from anything she or her mom had experienced. Dad was tough, and he'd raised her to be tough. She had to step up. Her parents weren't getting any younger.

"Thank you."

Mom squeezed her hand. "When can we see him?"

The doctor checked his watch. "It'll be a few more hours. The nurse in recovery will call with an update every hour."

The lines between Mom's brows eased somewhat. "That's good. One of us will be here."

Julia squeezed her hand back. "*We* will be here."

"Good. I'll check on him tomorrow, and the cardiac nurses will keep me apprised of any changes. I don't anticipate any."

"Thank you, Doctor."

She always marveled at her mother's response to a difficult situation. When her grandparents were sick, Mom was their rock. Dad was tough as nails, but Mom? When Nonna moved into Assisted Living, Mom made sure Nonna settled in. When Lance broke their engagement, Julia went straight into the arms of the woman who could take an emergency in stride and make it all better. Mom.

The thought occurred to Julia that someday, she would lose *her*, and that wasn't okay.

ON THURSDAY, Clyde had a meeting at the regional FBI headquarters in Louisville, so Eli was back on the job, finishing up Clyde and Rebecca's house. His incredulous snort at the sight before him made him dump his gear so he could inspect the progress. And there was a lot of progress.

The drywall was finished, light fixtures and plumbing fixtures were being installed, newly finished floors were covered with paper to protect them from damage, and the Amish-made kitchen cabinets were in place.

A couple of weeks would see this project done. Then, they'd start on the next one.

As he sat down to eat his lunch, his phone lit up with a text from Clyde.

> Got the forensics back on the medal.
> They were able to get partial prints.

Was it Lance? Just because the last time he saw an identical medal was in Lance's hand didn't mean it belonged to him. It was a popular one. The St. Christopher medal symbolized protection and defense.

Still, that irregularity ...

> Anybody I know?

> Maybe. On my way home, I'll get back in
> time for Bible study. Talk after?

Was that Clyde's sneaky way of getting him to Nick's group? He could wait until tomorrow to find out. Couldn't he? His brows drew in. No way he would wait a day to find out. Clyde wouldn't have brought it up if it wasn't significant.

> I'll be there.

The thumbs-up emoji was Clyde's answer.

Great.

Nick ambled onto the porch, where the crew was eating lunch. "Y'all are doing good, guys. Care if I join you?"

"If you don't mind seeing the lunch Grandma packed for me. I get dirty looks from the other guys." Eli grinned at the workers leaning up against the house.

Chuck Travis, one of the younger carpenters, chuckled. He was a big guy with an even bigger sense of humor. "Watch it, Reno. We could take you down and get to those brownies in a heartbeat."

Eli dug into his bag and held out a container. "And that's why I had Grandma put in extra. I told her if she didn't want me getting beat up on the playground, I would need more brownies."

"Smart man." Chuck lifted his brownie in salute.

"I'm glad to see you know how this works." Nick crossed his feet in front of him as he leaned on the porch post.

The rest of the crew got up, gathered the trash, and started back to work. Nick stopped Eli.

"Any thoughts about the group tonight?

Eli's lips tilted. "I'll be there. Where and when?"

"Awesome. My house, seven o'clock. Lisa's making snacks."

Eli's brow shot up. "Is that meant to entice me or warn me?"

Nick laughed. "She's improved significantly since she has Amelia and me to feed."

"That's a relief. When we were kids, she'd use Trace and me as guinea pigs when Grandma was teaching her how to cook." Eli shook his head. "It wasn't pretty."

"Then I guess it's a good thing *she's* pretty." Nick stretched as he rose. "Glad you're going to be there tonight. I haven't heard from Clyde."

"I got a text from him. He said he'd be home in time for the meeting."

"Good deal. It's a great group of guys. I'm learning as much or more from them as they are from anything I might say." He shrugged. "I hope you get something out of it."

Eli scrubbed his hand over his face and released a ragged sigh. "Let's just say this has been a long time coming."

Nick put his hand on Eli's shoulder and squeezed it gently. "From the first meeting, the group made a pact that what is said in the group stays in the group. Share or not. No pressure. We're all broken people trying our best in a broken world."

The lump in Eli's throat grew. Eli might be a blood Reno, but, after living here for six months, he felt as much an outsider as he was sure Nick did in the beginning. Now Nick was a full-fledged part of the Reno family and someone Eli had confidence in.

Chapter 18

"If you're going to drive all that way, you need to get there before dark." It didn't matter that Julia could spend another half-day with her parents if she waited until afternoon. Mom wasn't going to take *no* for an answer. She tried to explain to her mother she would gain an hour and she was heading into the sunset, so she'd arrive in Clementville before dark. Mom didn't buy it. What Julia didn't do was complain about the sun being in her eyes all the way across Kentucky.

Dad tried to reason with her, but even he had no sway this time.

Therefore, Julia would arrive at the Renos' house around five in the afternoon. She called yesterday and talked to Mrs. Reno to see if her invitation still stood.

"Pshaw. Don't even think about staying anywhere else. Oh, and you'll get here in time for our Fall Revival at church tomorrow night. I hope you'll be able to join us."

Julia gave an entirely non-committal answer. When she was involved in an investigation, she had to put that first.

Dad came home from the hospital on Thursday, and by Saturday, he was as grumpy as she'd ever seen him. "Stop hovering" was his go-to phrase. She and Mom agreed maybe it would be good for her to get back to work.

"Call me if anything—and I mean anything—happens. Promise me."

"I promise. I think Dad needs to get a few things back to normal, and if we're both on eggshells, he will be too."

During the last week, she'd had plenty of time to ponder many areas of her life. More than once, she wished she hadn't had quite so much downtime. She had too much time to think about too many things, most of which would involve her letting go of some independence or, at the very least, letting people into her world. She'd trusted once, and hopefully, someday, she could trust again.

As soon as the thought entered her mind, Eli's image came to mind.

Her first impressions of him were of the quintessential party guy, always on a quest for the next good time. Never getting completely out of bounds but leaning on the edge quite often. People-pleaser.

Had he changed? Did people really change?

On the surface, she had no reason not to think about Eli. He seemed to be a nice man. A good man. His family was great. She could trust him, couldn't she? He had many excellent qualities, not the least of which was his ready smile and clean-cut good looks.

But was he, deep down, still the frat guy who would try to entice her to party the weekend away? Was his being good only an act to keep from disappointing his family?

To be honest with herself, she was beginning to trust Eli. Was it because she hadn't taken the time to make real friends since she thought her former partner would naturally fill that role? Now, Eli filled the role of partner in exploring the caves, so it was only natural for her to treat him more as a friend.

She stretched her arms out on the steering wheel and sighed. Their last encounter had been cordial, but she hadn't heard from him since she left. Her communications had been through Clyde.

Unease coursed through her. Maybe Eli didn't want to talk to her. Had he ever talked to Lance? If so, what had Lance told him?

She'd halfway expected him to at least text her when he found out about the medal.

Would she lose a chance to have, at the very least, a friendship with Eli?

The Beaver Dam Rest Stop sign came up sooner than she expected. It was a joke in that at the rural Western Kentucky stop, much like the Spanish Steps in Rome, a person would eventually see everyone they'd ever met.

She pulled next to the gas pump and sat there a minute before pumping her gas, head on the steering wheel. Did she want more than a friendship with him, or was she so shallow she would jump at the chance to get into a relationship with the next guy who came along?

Julia had never been *that* girl, and she had no reason to think of herself in that way now.

She'd lost faith in her judgment. Part of her blamed herself for her broken engagement, although there was no way she could have known the duplicity of Lance and Carrie.

She should have known, should have seen the signs. If not, the last time she saw Lance should have tipped her off that he was no good. *Should, should, should...*

She had to get out, stretch, and get herself together before she arrived in Clementville.

ELI DID a double-take when his phone lit up with a call, interrupting his quiet Sunday afternoon.

Lance.

Interesting he would finally get in touch now, the day Julia was returning and after he'd talked to Clyde about the partial prints on the medal.

"Hello."

There was a pause on the other end of the line. "Hey, Eli. How you been?"

Eli drew in a long breath. How to answer such an inane question? He wasn't in the dark anymore. There were things he'd found out that Lance wouldn't want him to know.

"Good. You?" Keep it simple.

"Uh, yeah."

Eli heard noises in the background. Was he driving?

"I guess you heard —"

"About you and Carrie?"

"Look, it wasn't—"

"Going on while we were dating?" Eli wanted to be angry. Furious. A part of him was, the part about being duped by two people he should have been able to trust.

Back up ... he *was* furious, but not because of how it affected himself.

Wait ... What?

After months of feeding his distrust and dislike of Julia, he found himself angry on her behalf, not his. She'd done nothing to deserve being manipulated the way Lance had done.

Putting his brain back in gear, he pulled his attention back as Lance continued speaking.

"...it just happened."

He had to cut him off now. "This kind of thing doesn't 'just happen.' You made a choice."

Silence for a few seconds. "I'm sorry I hurt you, man."

"I'm sorry you hurt Julia."

More silence. "I wish I could explain ..."

"No. You made a commitment to Julia that should have lasted a lifetime. At least Carrie had the decency to break up with me before we got engaged. It became clear nothing was going to happen between us, but I had no way of knowing you were in the picture."

Eli heard a faint *beep-beep-beep*.

"I have another call coming through, Eli. Can I call you back?"

"Is there more we need to say?" Eli's teeth ground together.

After a pause, Lance spoke. "I guess not. See you around."

The call dropped before Eli had a chance to say goodbye.

What happened to change his attitude about life? The medal they found in the tunnel—the one with a partial thumbprint. Was it the same medal that belonged to Lance? The one he'd used to entertain them, distract him from Julia's absence?

Grandma's voice carried from the other room. She said Julia's name, solving that mystery. Grandma invited Julia to the revival meeting tonight.

He took a deep breath and blew it out in frustration.

Why is Grandma so pushy about church?

As a teen, it embarrassed him how easily his grandparents talked about church and spiritual matters. It wasn't a topic that came about naturally in their house. Mom came from a small family and grew up in a small country church, and Dad, the anomaly in the Reno family, went because she did.

Dad never had much to say. Samantha fully embraced her spiritual life. She was enthusiastic about everything, so when she started attending a larger church with a thriving youth ministry, their parents decided they would all go. He grew as a Christian, but at sixteen, he'd become used to being the class clown, the prankster, and the one who didn't take life seriously. Outwardly.

As time grew toward graduation, he had questions. So many questions, but he kept them to himself. For instance, did God really have a plan for everyone? How did that jive with free will? There was no way he would ask out loud. For him, it was all about keeping a wall up and being comic relief. For Trace? Nobody expected conversation from Trace.

The mix of men, a few of them Renos, at the Bible study in Nick and Lisa's home had him thinking.

"Julia should be here in about an hour." Grandma raised her eyebrows when he turned his attention to her. "I invited her to church tonight."

"I heard."

"Your hearing is better than your grandpa's. I'm used to translating for him." She chuckled. "Plus, he's nosey."

Eli grinned. "Can I do anything before she gets here?"

"Sit and talk to me, if you don't mind." She made her way to the sofa. To her spot, where her tote of yarn, needles, and scissors lived between the sofa and the end table. She automatically picked up her knitting.

"I would love to." He sat next to her, putting an arm around her shoulders and nodding toward the hands. "What are you making?

She held up the tiny garment. "A sweater for little Amelia." Grandma shook her head and smiled. "I'm so happy I get to experience my great-grands. They're pretty special."

Holding his free hand to his chest, Eli brought his head back. "I am appalled. I remember being told there was nothing more special than grandchildren."

She raised a brow. "I said that before I met our next generation. Grandchildren are grand, for sure. Great-grandchildren? They are *great*." She shook her head, smiling into the work in her lap.

"I guess I can stand competition from a little girl less than a year old." Eli squeezed her shoulders. "I'll admit, she's pretty cute."

"I agree. I expect to be starting a few more blankets and sweaters before much longer."

"There has been an epidemic of weddings in this family."

"We're down to you and Samantha."

Eli scoffed. "You know how close I am to holy matrimony. Sam too." The pleased expression on Grandma's face told him he needed to pay more attention to his little sister.

Grandma continued. "She's been in Clementville all summer." Her eyes flitted to his. "There may be a certain young farmer she's got her eye on."

Chapter 19

As she would have with her biological grandparents, Julia dropped her bags and was ready to leave for church the moment she arrived at the Renos' house. She had too much respect for them to say a word otherwise.

Grandma Reno chattered all the way from the house to the church parking lot. Eli hadn't said much beyond "hello." Sitting in the back with him was awkward because the small sedan had seats that tended to dump all the passengers toward the middle. Julia sat straight and stiff, battling the gravity that made it a struggle to stay on her side.

Solid as a rock, Eli kept his eyes straight ahead, moving as little as possible. Saying as little as possible.

Not having anything to say was out of character for him, a fact she ascertained soon after their meeting. According to Samantha, he was quieter than usual since moving down to Kentucky. He probably had a lot on his mind. She understood. It was difficult to keep Lance and Carrie out of her thoughts when there were so many connections to people down here.

Seeing Lance a few weeks before severed all ties that remained. Any feelings he might have hoped to resurrect had been decimated. Something nagged at her about his demeanor that evening. Something dark. Had he hidden part of himself too long, to the point it would come out one way or another? She didn't want to encounter him again, but she needed to see if there was a connection between him and the medal.

When Eli spoke, she was startled, missing part of what he said. "Oh! Did you say something?"

He chuckled. "I asked if you had a good drive down."

Her face warmed. "Sorry. I did. Mom made me promise to get here before dark, and with the guff Dad's giving her, I didn't want to add to her stress."

Eli nodded. "How's he doing?"

"Remarkably well. So well, he was ready for me to get out of his hair."

"You know how guys are." He shrugged, keeping his eyes straight ahead.

"I haven't had much luck in that department." She said it quietly, and Lance flew to her mind again.

He snorted. "I've dated a lot of women, but this deal with Carrie pointed out all the things I don't know about love, for sure."

He could have gone all night without pointing out his dating frequency. She lifted one side of her mouth in a slight smile. "I'm sorry." There she went again, apologizing for something she hadn't done

Eli shook his head and pressed his lips together. "You have absolutely nothing to be sorry for."

She pulled back slightly.

He turned toward her. There was hurt there, in his eyes. "I didn't mean to be harsh. I'm mad at Lance, not you."

"Because of Carrie." She nodded. "I get it."

"Not because of Carrie."

She turned, and their eyes met. He didn't break his stare, and her heart pounded, the air around them crackling with confused emotion.

"You kids going to stay in the car or go into the church house?" Grandpa Reno leaned in his open car door to speak. "Makes me no never mind, but I hear Lisa's singing a solo tonight, and I don't want to miss it."

Julia hadn't realized the car had stopped. Grandma Reno had already exited the vehicle. Her attention was fully on the man sitting next to her. Glancing over, he appeared as sheepish as she felt.

"Sorry, Grandpa, we'll be right in."

Grandpa Reno closed the car door and tapped on the car roof before heading to the front door of the church, cane in hand, occasionally allowing it to touch the ground. As soon as he was out of earshot, they glanced at one another and burst out laughing.

YOUR AVERAGE COUNTRY church revival included a schedule of meetings featuring a guest preacher and song leader. This wasn't an average revival meeting, but a series of meetings designed for the church family.

The service had the same musicians as usual, Lisa on the piano with a microphone in front of her, and men from the church were the speakers. Lisa raised her head to see over the instrument and wiggled her fingers in a wave when she caught Eli's eye. Sam, with Jay Carrino very close behind, slipped in the back door and into a pew about a quarter of the way up the aisle. Acknowledging Lisa's wave, he sat down on the pew with Grandma and Grandpa next to Julia.

At the men's Bible study the other night, Nick asked for prayer as he was first up to speak on Sunday night.

Eli never heard of Nick Woodward before he and Lisa began dating. It surprised Eli when he discovered besides being good friends with his cousin, Del, Nick also had deep ties to the area, even if some of those ties were on the wrong side of the law.

Give him words, God. Help me to see You in them.

Julia poked him in the side when the congregation rose to participate in worship. He was no singer, but the songs were fresh and catchy. More than anything, they spoke to his heart.

The last, "Trust In God," featured Lisa taking the lead on the verses, steeping the congregation in her mellow alto, and leading them into an attitude of prayer.

Wow.

When did he start attributing such to music?

Since he'd become closer to the church—God's people in Clementville—that his dad grew up in. Even Dad was known to shed a tear from time to time.

He will never fail.

Trust. That's what he'd been missing. He had run through life half-cocked, daring God to tell him "no." He'd been waiting for Eli to get together with His plan.

The sniffle coming from Julia surprised him. It endeared her to him and made him want to fix whatever was wrong in her world. It would have to be difficult to trust even God in her line of work. Law enforcement was a life of proving or disproving lies, sometimes lies on top of lies.

And then, with Lance, she'd been faced with lies on a personal level.

Eli closed his eyes briefly. He'd said a silent prayer for Nick, but now it was about Julia.

If there is anything I can do for Julia, tell me. If there's anything You need to do, get me out of the way, get my anger at Lance out of the way. I trust You.

As the song ended, Nick came forward, hugging Lisa as they passed on the platform.

Nick started with the scripture that inspired the song. "I sought the Lord, and He answered me and delivered me from all my fears." He paused, contemplating the congregation before him. "Let's pray."

As Nick offered his message, more testimony than sermon, Eli listened closely. For once, his attention wasn't pulled away. Maybe a little. Julia sat next to him—a hint of temptation to let his mind wander.

Focus ...

He knew about the tragedy of Nick's first wife and unborn child dying in a car accident, but that wasn't the whole story. Nick gave up on God and turned his back on the idea of loving again. His long-time friendship with Del brought him to the area, and when he met Lisa, this time as a woman instead of his best friend's little sister, he fought the attraction. Finally, Nick realized God had something special for him. For them.

"The Lord is near to the brokenhearted and saves the crushed in spirit."

Psalm 34 was full of hope and assurance. God watches over us—His children—even when everything goes in the opposite direction we think it should.

There was that nagging thought again: Where was God when Lance decided to dump Julia and get involved with Carrie?

I'm there. Blessed are those who see and believe, but more blessed are those who don't see and believe.

Eli closed his eyes again, trying to shut out everything except the inaudible, yet very present, voice talking to him.

When the piano music began, Eli hoped he hadn't missed anything at the end of the message.

But then, if I'd been listening to Nick, I wouldn't have heard from God.

Chapter 20

"You're about to go to sleep on your feet."

Grandpa's laugh pulled a smile from Julia. The long drive and the interesting church service had taken its toll.

After a slice of Lemon Icebox Pie and a cup of decaf, they were all ready to head to their respective places. Eli was quieter than usual. He gave her dibs on the bathroom, and when she'd finished and closed her bedroom door behind her, he quietly, except for that one spot in the floor that creaked, padded down the hallway to brush his teeth.

Had the message troubled him? There was a point, as they were leaving for church last night, that she thought he almost said something but held back.

He probably figures he'll get enough Julia time in the tunnels.

She didn't fall asleep until after she heard him return and close the door to his room.

THE LORD IS *near to the brokenhearted and saves the crushed in spirit.*

Julia woke on Monday with the words from Psalm 34 in her head. The part about the brokenhearted and seeking the Lord rattled around in her thoughts.

There was a time when Julia would have scoffed at the very idea of the Lord caring if she was "brokenhearted" or "crushed in spirit." She'd had her ups and downs, though lately, it had been more down than up.

Ready to face the new day, the new week, she felt her lips tug into a smile when she entered the hallway.

"Mornin'." Eli met her at the top of the steps.

"Good morning. Sleep well?" Julia cringed inwardly. What an inane question.

His grin relieved her. Maybe it wasn't such a stupid comment. "I did. I dreamt of sailing across a plaid ocean to Scotland."

Julia laughed out loud, his joke unexpected after the serious tone of last night. "I guess I'll be dreaming of green plaid forests, then?" She wished that was the worst of her dreams. The recurring nightmare of being trapped in a smoke-filled room still woke her from time to time.

"We'll have to compare notes." Eli gestured for her to precede her down the steps and to the kitchen, following her nose to the aroma of ... waffles?

"Grandma, you read my mind. How did you know I wanted waffles for breakfast?" Eli kissed his grandmother on the cheek before pouring himself a cup of coffee. He held up the pot to Julia, and she nodded assent as she held up her mug.

Grandpa put down the paper he'd been scanning. "Maybe because it's been mentioned several times in the last few weeks how much you love waffles?" He winked at Eli and whispered, "I'll slip you a twenty later."

Grandma laughed. "I see what's going on. Eddie Clarence Reno, you've been bribing the grandchildren to do your begging."

"Guilty as charged. It's your own fault."

"How's that?" Grandma sent a wary eye his way.

"If your waffles weren't so good, I wouldn't hanker after them so much."

Julia sat, sipping her coffee and enjoying the repartee. It wouldn't be hard to fall in love with such a family.

As the thought entered her mind, her coffee decided to go down the wrong way. She sputtered.

"Are you okay?" Eli's brows lowered in concern, which only served to make her more uncomfortable.

"I'm good. Went down the wrong way." She wiped her mouth on the napkin she'd placed in her lap, then took another sip to soothe her throat.

She had to get her mind under control before she forgot she didn't live here.

ELI WAS IN A GOOD MOOD. Usually outwardly friendly and happy, most people wouldn't notice if he weren't. This time, it wasn't a masquerade. While he received no satisfaction, personally, from talking to Lance, he was glad he had the opportunity to tell him what he thought about the way he'd treated Julia when Lance cheated on her with Carrie.

The church service had helped to open up and reveal things in Eli's soul he hadn't been aware of for a long time. Coming so soon after talking to Lance gave him perspective. When Carrie bounced right from him to Lance, he was hurt, but wasn't he more affected?

Julia had soldiered on for weeks, not telling him this thing that would hurt him. She didn't talk about what had hurt her. Deeply. Having spent more time with her, thinking back, he recognized her devastation. Last week, when she arrived in Clementville on Sunday night, she was frustrated. Maybe even angry.

Something had happened over the weekend. It was a different frustration than he'd observed in the past few weeks. He wanted to know why, and he wanted to know how she felt about Lance. Was her heart broken? Did she still love him?

If the answer to either of those questions were "yes," would he be willing to settle for being *friend-zoned*?

Eli grabbed his gear from the back of the truck. Julia had been on the phone with Clyde on the short drive over to the Woodward homestead, giving Eli plenty of time to think. Unfortunately, the more thinking time he had, the more he found himself attracted to her—and not her skills in law enforcement.

She jumped off the running board and grabbed her pack from the bed of the truck. "Clyde said he'd come down after lunch. He had to go into Paducah to finish some paperwork."

"Has he said anything about the partial print they got from the medal?"

Julia twisted her lips. "He did. He said it might be a match for Lance. But, since it's a partial, he can't confirm."

She didn't say anything else and didn't seem to want to meet his eyes.

He watched her fight the uncomfortable position Lance put her in. It was inexcusable.

"Julia, I—"

Her phone chose that moment to ring. She held up her finger and answered. "Rossi."

There was a lot of "Yes," "No," "I understand," and "Uh-huh" on her end of the conversation.

Pushing her phone into her back pocket, she took a deep breath and raised her eyes to Eli, her head tilted. "We've got three more days to find some evidence, then I'm going to be recalled back to Louisville. There's chatter about a bank robbery going down this weekend."

"Wow." Eli shook his head.

"Yeah, that's not a lot of time." Julia frowned. "This case is personal. I want to see it closed."

"I only meant, wow, you use the FBI lingo 'chatter' and 'going down.'" When he twitched his brow and tried to hide his smile, she laughed.

"Touché," she said, trying to get herself under control. "I've heard 'scumbag' and 'chucklehead' used a few times too."

"Oh, 'chucklehead' is well-used around here. The woods are full of 'em." Her laughter made him smile. He'd seen a lighter side of her since yesterday.

He wanted to tell her about talking to Lance. He'd get to it. Not now. Now was the time to get in that tunnel and ferret out some more information.

"Shall we?"

Julia pulled on her FBI windbreaker and cap. "I'm ready if you are."

Chapter 21

Nothing.

For the last two days, Julia and Eli had scoured the tunnels on the map and the ones they'd added since Eli and Sam found evidence of activity. When they got the go-ahead to spend three more days investigating, she was convinced they were about to get a break in the case.

No such luck.

Either the crooks they were close to had abandoned the site, or they were moving one step ahead of the law.

When they emerged from the tunnel, Julia threw her cap on the ground and plopped down, hard, on the ruined steps of the house that once stood there. Clutching her head with her hands, she almost growled.

"Why haven't we found anything?"

Eli walked over and sat next to her, saying nothing. After a few moments of silence, she glared at him, her eyes flashing. "Well?"

"Well, what?" Eli stared at her.

"Aren't you going to tell me we'll find something when we least expect it? That tomorrow will be another day?"

The way he mashed his lips between his teeth, she had no doubt he was trying hard not to laugh. It would make her more angry and frustrated, and he discerned her mood. The random thought occurred to her that it was a good trait to have in a partner. Rubbing her eyes to "reset" her emotions, she took a deep breath.

"Sorry." She sighed from deep within herself. "Maybe it's a little more personal than other cases."

"No maybe about it. If Lance is involved, it's very personal. More for you than for me. Yeah, it's personal."

He downplayed his pain, deflecting, making the people around him comfortable at his expense. How could she have been so wrong about him? Carrie had hurt him almost as much as Lance had hurt her.

"I saw Lance a few weeks ago."

He sat there, silent. When she hazarded a glance at him, he was calm, saying nothing. She should have told him earlier.

"How did it go?"

"Not well." She picked at a thread in her jeans pocket. "I tried to call his cell phone when you said he hadn't been answering calls or texts. Simply to see if the number was still in service."

Eli nodded, shutters closing on his expression. "So it is, right? Still in service, I mean."

"Yes."

"Are he and Carrie …"

"Still engaged? Apparently. He said she was out of town. When he saw I'd called, he thought maybe I'd forgiven him." She sputtered a laugh. "I told him he'd burned any bridges he'd ever had with me."

The small smile on Eli's face warmed her, but the way his eyes shifted from hers gave her pause.

"Where did you see him?"

She swallowed. "In the parking garage of my apartment building."

That brought him to his feet. "So he was stalking you?" He stilled, staring at her full-on, fear written all over his face. "That medal ..." After scrubbing down his face with both hands, Eli paced back and forth in front of her as if he couldn't be still if he wanted to.

"I know. And it freaked me out a little too." She rubbed her arms as a chill ran through her, even in a Kentucky summer. "I told him I only called to see if his number still worked since he ghosted you. Then he accused *me* of cheating on *him*, with *you*. I guess if that had happened, it would make them cheating on us acceptable. I don't know. It was nuts. I wanted to get away from him as soon as possible."

"He is an egotistical, self-centered, selfish—"

"I get the picture." Why did it hurt to hear Eli describe him in ways she had certainly thought of him since their breakup? If she were honest, she'd had those thoughts from time to time during their relationship. "I'm sorry to have to reveal these things about your friend."

The harsh, loud "Ha" that burst out of Eli made her smile.

"Friend?" He turned toward her, his expression more intense than she expected. He'd been intensely perturbed at her when they first met, but his current reaction confused her. This was a different animal.

"Well, you were."

The frown on his face and the way he dipped his head told her he was thinking. Deeply. Trying to sort out his emotions surrounding Lance. "I thought we were." He brought his head up. "I didn't find out he was the reason Carrie broke up with me until Sam let it slip a few weeks ago."

"I'm sorry."

"Stop saying that. Up until then, I placed the blame on you for breaking Lance's heart." He came back and sat on the stone step. "I was wrong. You had it a lot worse than me. I don't know when things changed for him. I mean, did I even know him?"

They sat there for a few more minutes. Julia didn't know what to say. Lance had never put her welfare above his own. He'd used her. He made her so sure she needed him when, in reality, she was much better off without him. For a time, she was so enamored with the idea of being in love and getting married that she sloughed off the twinges of discomfort when he made off-hand comments disregarding her feelings or opinions.

She pulled her knees up and folded her arms on them, then turned her head toward Eli. "Thank you."

"For what?"

"For being one of the good ones."

... FOR BEING *one of the good ones.*

The phrase rang in Eli's ears for the rest of the night. He didn't deserve the compliment after what he'd assumed about Julia. She hadn't revealed how it went down. Something told him Lance's infidelity had been uncovered.

In light of the St. Christopher medal found in the tunnel, they had to consider him a suspect in the criminal activity law enforcement had been fighting in this small community for the last few years.

Eli hadn't been straight with Julia. He could have told her

that he talked to him. It still rankled that his last conversation with Lance hadn't given Eli any more confidence in his former friend. Now, after learning of the recent encounter between Lance and Julia, Lance was accumulating more sins for which to answer.

And she was leaving tomorrow. Clyde and Brent would keep the case open through the Paducah Field Office, and Julia would head back to her real life in Louisville. Life would get back to normal for both of them.

Whatever *normal* was.

Eli wasn't one to sit idle. He figured he'd pick up where he left off before he and Sam found traces of something going on in the tunnels. It kept niggling at him, keeping him tossing and turning.

Two a.m.

At least it's Saturday.

Wait. He'd promised Nick and Del he'd go along with them to a new job site in Princeton. He was meeting them at nine. So much for sleeping in.

He finally threw the cover back and pulled on his sweatpants. Maybe if he went down for a snack. A drink of water, at least. Anything was better than this misery.

Padding down the stairs, he was confident he could get to the ground floor without the familiar loud creak that usually told on the younger generation—whichever generation it was—keeping them honest. He'd learned the right combination of steps to avoid getting caught when he was about fifteen. When the floor creaked in a new spot, he figured it stood to reason that in fifteen years, there might be more sounds in an old house. It couldn't be because he misremembered.

The light in the kitchen, peeking under the swinging door, drew his attention. Another sleepless soul? Pushing the door gently, he saw the table first, last night's cake and a plate next to it, and a glass of milk to top it off.

"Hey." Julia peeked around the door. "You, too, huh?"

"Yeah. Shouldn't you be in bed? You've got a long drive tomorrow."

Noting the clock on the stove, she scoffed. "Let's make that today."

"Sorry." He gestured to the cake and reached to pull down another plate. "Is there enough there for me, or are you hoarding half a cake?"

Chuckling, she cut them both a piece, then put the cake back in the refrigerator. "If I don't get it out of my sight, I'll keep eating until I do eat the rest of it." She turned back to him. "Milk?"

"Please." He sat, letting her wait on him. When she joined him at the table, he smiled. "Much obliged."

"We'd better thank your grandma." She took a bite and closed her eyes in ecstasy. "Mmm. This is so good."

"Grandma's baking has won a few county fair contests."

"I can't imagine anything else coming close." Taking a sip of milk, she grinned. "I may have a little issue with chocolate."

"You have a weak spot?"

Smirking, she took another bite. "I have a sweet tooth, yes, but chocolate is my Waterloo."

"Julia Rossi has a vice."

"You know that in law enforcement, 'vice' has a whole different meaning?"

Was she flirting with him? This fun side of Julia fascinated him.

"I am aware." He paused with the bite of cake, letting the frosting melt on his tongue. "If loving this cake is a vice, then arrest me now."

Her laughter and hand slapping over her mouth when she

realized it was the middle of the night made him laugh even harder. What was it about the wee hours of the morning that made anything funnier?

"Do I need to read your Miranda Rights?"

"Maybe."

She licked every bit of decadent homemade fudge icing off her fork, distracting him for a minute. Wow.

"Okay, how about this, 'You have the right to eat chocolate cake. Any cake you eat can and will be used against you on your waistline. You have the right to a glass of milk. If you cannot afford milk, sweet tea will be provided for you. Do you understand the rights I have just read to you?'"

"Yes, ma'am." He leaned forward.

"With these rights in mind, do you wish to continue eating cake?"

"More than anything in the world."

Chapter 22

The week was confusing, at best. The 2 a.m. chocolate cake had kept Julia up another hour after she went to bed.

Was it the cake? She didn't think so.

Julia was glad to head back to Louisville for the weekend. The dead-end of the one clue they found pulled at her. The mystery dug in and kept her mind off of anything else. Even her growing awareness of Eli.

Until last night, he'd been distant but friendly since she returned from Cincinnati. After the church service, she caught him watching her a few times. She hoped he hadn't caught her watching him.

After the conversation on the ruins steps at the crime scene, there was no mention of Lance except about the medal they'd found.

Still, something didn't sit right with her. When she left the Renos' house, bag in hand, she wasn't sure she'd be back next week. She kept telling herself Clyde and Brent had everything under control. It killed her to think about not being a part of taking down Gabe Torrino.

When she had breakfast with Mr. And Mrs. Reno and Eli, she mentioned stopping by the crime scene for another look-see. Eli objected, which annoyed her. He tried to convince her to let him call Nick and cancel the site visit so he could go with her. By the time he had to leave, she let him think she'd talked herself out of going so he would keep his appointment. Telling him she was going out there would only lead to more frustration.

He didn't need to know.

At the end of the driveway, she paused, checking both ways for oncoming traffic.

Turn left, head to Marion, then home. Turn right, the river and the Woodward homestead.

No vehicles were coming from either direction, which was the norm, so she had time to think. The clock on the dashboard said 10:45 a.m. The morning had frittered away, talking to Mr. and Mrs. Reno. She'd lose an hour switching from Central to Eastern Time zones.

Going out there might lead to more frustration. Not going didn't help, either.

They were missing something. She'd been in and out of the tunnel multiple times, as had Clyde, Brent, and Eli. Two clues weren't enough to keep an investigation open. The case was growing colder as the days progressed.

She made a quick decision—turn right. She'd stop and poke around a little bit, if only to get her mind settled. Then, she'd spend the whole leisurely drive back to Louisville pondering the situation.

Pulling into the drive of the deserted homestead ruins, the chimney stood out as the only structure left. Nothing there resembled a crime scene. That was below, through the trap door behind the chimney.

She checked her smartwatch, noting the storm watch taking effect in about an hour. She didn't need to spend more than a half-hour before getting on the road. Maybe she would get ahead of the weather system. Stuffing her keys in her jeans pocket, she picked up her flashlight, locked the car, and strode to the now-familiar spot where she unlocked the password-protected padlock and went down the stairs to the tunnels.

Scouring the area with her eyes, she tried to imagine she'd never been here before. What might she see? Had it become so familiar to her that she was blind to something that would turn the case around? It had never happened to her before, but a lot of things happening to her were beyond her experience. Maybe her emotional state, coming back here, where she'd almost died, kept her from focusing.

The counselor assigned to her—the one who had the power to clear her as fit for duty after her injuries—told Julia she had to acknowledge what happened and how she felt about it. Watch for signs of PTSD. She hadn't experienced any flashbacks in a long time. The dreams were the worst. The hardest piece of advice to follow was to avoid isolating herself.

She'd done well with that one until Lance broke off her engagement. After that, she wallowed for a while, letting her anger push her into her work harder than ever. She'd gone through two potential partners who requested transfers after three weeks of working with her.

Then came the opportunity to come back to Clementville. Her first instinct was no, but then she realized it might be good to get some closure.

She could not have anticipated Eli's presence and involvement in the investigation—two worlds colliding.

The mag light she brought from her car illuminated the tunnels better than the installed lighting, and she instinctively turned down the passage toward the café and the spot where Del had been shot.

The quiet was palpable without Eli talking. So quiet. Almost an eerie silence except for her footsteps and breathing. Was that her heartbeat?

She remembered coming out of the drug-induced coma the year before, hearing sounds sifting through one at a time and then rushing into her brain all at once, making her want to cover her ears.

She knelt where they found the St. Christopher's medal. Scanning the area slowly, in a grid, with her flashlight, Julia paused. She'd taken photographs of every inch of this section, and the mound of disturbed earth wasn't there that day.

The blood rushed to her ears, her heart pounding when a distinct thud echoed out from deeper in the tunnel. Animal? She'd heard about Lisa and Nick encountering a cat and her kittens—along with a dead body—when they found the first tunnels in the network. Maybe another animal had made their way from the opening on the river? No, this wasn't the scurrying action associated with small creatures that may or may not be friendly. Something had fallen or been dropped either accidentally or out of confidence that whoever did it was alone in the passage.

Nobody knew where she was. Eli would have been with her if she'd said the word. Merely a short side trip.

What could happen?

She put her hand to her side. Nothing. She had a lot on her mind when she got out of the car. Her phone and sidearm were there, in the passenger seat instead of with her. She had her smartwatch, but down here, there was no signal.

She needed backup.

STANDING STOCK-STILL AND LISTENING, she turned slowly, silently retracing her steps to the opening. She would call Clyde as soon as she got to her phone. In the meantime, she would get back to her vehicle as quickly and quietly as possible. Should she have marked the place where things seemed different?

No, she remembered. Someone had been down there since yesterday.

When she reached the surface, the rumble of thunder tracked the storm coming closer. She'd been underground longer than she planned. Dodging raindrops, she ran to her car and locked the doors before pulling out her phone. With lightning flashing, the series of loud *pops* didn't register until her back glass shattered, and another bullet went through the windshield. She had to get away. Now.

She punched in the contact for Clyde and immediately put her car in gear so she could get out of there. If the shooter was behind her, she had to go forward. No choice. The hilly, curvy drive wasn't meant for speed.

When she gained the first curve in the drive, her tires skidded and slid. As she worked to get control of the vehicle, the roar of a motor rushed her way, and when she turned toward the sound, a truck was barreling straight for her.

Almost in slow motion, the grill of a truck, much larger than her little Civic, advanced like a cat over a mouse. When the crash inevitably came, her airbags deployed, knocking her to the side and then back against her seat.

After hitting her square in the driver's side door, the truck kept going until it pushed her car into a tree across the drive.

Was that...? No, couldn't be. He's in Louisville. But the medal...

She tried to concentrate on identifying the driver. Things were unclear, and the light dimmed, black spots appearing in her field of vision. As her eyes drooped, her door was wrenched open, pulling her back to the present. Someone thrust a cloth bag over her head before she was cut out of her seatbelt and dragged from the car. Broken glass and bent metal scraped and cut at her skin. Her captor was ready with duct tape for her wrists and ankles. When her body hit a surface with a loud metallic thud, she lay still in what must be the back of a truck or van. Her fingers brushed the threadbare carpet under her fingers.

Van.

Have to stay conscious. Listen. Calculate movements. Press the button ...

She struggled to initiate the tracking device in her watch, straining to shift her hands enough to press the tiny switch.

One of her captors grabbed her by the neck and pressed something against her nose and mouth. Was he suffocating her? The all-too-familiar, sickly sweet smell wafted up her nostrils as her body involuntarily relaxed, and she was out.

Chapter 23

Finishing drywall wasn't Eli's favorite job, but it gave him plenty of time to think. After meeting with Del and Nick at the new worksite, they headed back to the Burke house and went to work.

How far had Julia made it toward Louisville? She planned to start the trek right after he left to meet Nick and Del, so she should be nearly halfway home. The skies were darker now than they were thirty minutes ago, and the wind howled outside the new house.

A clap of thunder and the lights flickering got his attention. Then came the blare of the storm sirens from the Clementville firehouse.

At least the new structure is weather-tight.

Nick stuck his head around the doorway of the upstairs master bedroom. "We're calling it a day. Storm warnings are all over the place. I'd rather know everyone is at home before it hits."

Eli nodded and started cleaning his tools to be ready on Monday. "It sounds rough already."

Nick tapped the door facing and went on to the master bath to tell the plumbers to head home.

What about Julia? Was she far enough ahead of the storm?

When the meteorologist on the local news mentioned they were under a watch at lunchtime, he didn't think much about it. A watch was a watch. Not a warning.

Julia wasn't happy about leaving. After their *tête-à-tête* the night before over a chocolate cake and milk, he wasn't happy about her leaving, either.

Maybe there was unfinished business between the two of them. He hoped he had the chance to find out.

He grabbed his lunchbox and empty water bottle and stepped out the front door. He had to catch the charming but useless old-fashioned screen door quickly when the wind caught it and threatened to tear it off its hinges. A storm door had that name for a reason.

He checked his phone the minute he made the pickup. No messages. As soon as he got down the drive, a message came through. He stopped, hoping Clyde and Rebecca had something in mind for cell service up here because it was spotty. And that was being generous.

Julia.

> Heading home. I'll let you know if I learn anything while I'm in L'ville. Have a good weekend.

He was correct—she'd left about two hours ago.

Unable to drive and text, he let his phone sync with the hands-free device in his truck, then asked the phone to call Julia. Sometimes it worked, sometimes it didn't.

This time, it did.

"You've reached the voicemail of Special Agent Julia Rossi. Please leave a message at the tone."

He ended the call and tried again. Maybe she wasn't quick enough to catch it.

Ring, ring, ring, ring.

Four rings. It went to voicemail again.

She wouldn't ... would she? Oh, yeah. She would.

Eli shifted into reverse and turned the truck around. He wasn't going over there alone. Julia may be reckless enough to do that, but he had no confidence in his ability to confront bad guys.

Back at the house, Nick and Del were talking on the front porch, their attention turning when Eli's truck roared up the drive.

"Hey, come with me."

Without hesitation, they got into the truck with Eli.

"What's up?" Del scrunched his brows together.

"Julia's not answering her phone."

The brows that had been bunched up flew up toward his forehead. He chuckled. "Maybe she doesn't want to talk to you, doofus."

Eli turned to him briefly, unable to say anything.

"You're serious." Nick studied him carefully. Eli kept his eyes on the road.

"She mentioned going by the homestead site before leaving. I thought she'd talked herself out of it. Now ..."

"There are lots of dead cell spots between here and Louisville. Maybe she—"

While Nick was talking, Eli raced up the drive to the homestead adjacent to the property where the new house was located. About halfway to the house, he came to a screeching halt, throwing gravel as the rain began to fall.

ELI JUMPED from the truck and ran to Julia's car, noting the open door and the extreme damage to the vehicle. He turned back to Nick and Del, following him.

"She's not here."

"Maybe she called for help."

They were trying to make the best of the situation. The twist of his gut told him he didn't have time to gloss this over.

"See the back glass and the windshield?" He pointed out the hole in the front. "That's no thrown piece of gravel."

Nick had walked around to the other side of the car, where the crumpled passenger-side door rested against the tree. "Eli."

Eli's head shot up. His eyes had been drawn to the cut seatbelt and the smudge of blood on the frame of the car door. She was injured. Dead?

If she were dead, her body would still be here. He had to keep that in mind.

"Her purse, phone, and gun are on the floorboard. Probably thrown when she got hit ... or whatever happened." Nick's face hardened into a mask of granite, and Del's very similar. Both of these men had dealt with this situation for the last few years, each time thinking the nightmare was over.

"I'm calling Clay." Del didn't stop to take consensus.

Eli pulled out his phone and called Clyde, who answered on the first ring. He put him on speaker.

"Burke. What's going on?"

The FBI already knew there was a problem.

"Have you heard from Julia?"

"No, but the tracking device on her watch was activated, the signal going directly to the Louisville office. They called me after waiting three hours." Eli could hear Clyde gritting his teeth. It wouldn't have happened on Clyde's watch, but he was restricted to what Julia's supervisor wanted to do about the situation. "They gave me the coordinates of the signal and clearance to start a search."

Eli closed his eyes tightly, his throat too thick to speak. He willed his voice back. "Clay and Ben are on their way."

There was muffled talking in the background, and he heard Clyde say to someone else, "You and your dad stay here, close the curtains, and lock up. Becca, you can't ..."

"I'll be there in five minutes." The *beep-beep-beep* indicated he'd hung up without saying goodbye. No time for niceties.

Chapter 24

"The rain is wiping out any evidence that might have been here." Brent shook his head.

The weather continued to worsen, and with no way to keep the equipment dry, Eli and the other men went to the closest location—the garage at Nick and Lisa's house. Dark came early, and the storm socked in.

Brent continued his report. "I got some partials on the car door. Maybe that will give us something."

Clyde nodded abruptly, his mouth a grim line and his eyes never leaving the hand-held satellite device used to pick up the signal. When Clyde raked his hand over his face and took a deep breath, Eli had no choice. He had to pray. He might be stubborn, but he wasn't stupid.

"Becca begged me to let her come with me. Said she felt responsible." Clyde shook his head.

Del put a hand on Clyde's shoulder. "We'll get her back. Wasn't Tripp released from rehab?"

Clyde nodded. "Brought him home today. When we moved here, I led them both into the viper's nest. I thought this was done. We got a tip that Torrino was dead or, at the very least, out of the country."

"Bad tip."

"No joke."

The storm knocked out power in some areas and wrecked electronic signals, making it difficult, if not impossible, to triangulate the signal Julia had sent. Suddenly, after an interminable amount of time, a beep.

"There it is." Clyde's eyes widened. "She's at the old Durbin place."

Eli stopped breathing for a second. "Trace and Hannah's house?"

This couldn't be good.

"Not the house." Clyde studied it further, enlarging the image on the screen. "The barn, on the outskirts of the property."

Brent gathered his gear and tossed it in the back seat of his sedan. "Saddle up."

Clyde stopped them. "We've got to go in quiet."

Eli nodded. "Tell us what you want us to do."

Clyde glanced over at Nick, then at Del, whose eyes flicked to Eli before he nodded at Clyde. "Brent, you're on communications. Clay, you take Nick and Del. Eli, you and Ben are with me."

"Do I need a weapon?" Both Del and Nick had guns. All he had was his flashlight. Granted, it would make a dandy club if needed.

"No, stick close to Ben, and you'll be okay."

Decreasing their vehicle count from six to three, they drove down the road and onto a country lane. They drove past Hannah and Trace's driveway, going toward the other side of the property to the lane used for farm equipment, which explained every rut and hole. Clay went in first. When he got to a certain point, he pumped his brake. End of the line. Any closer, and they could tip off Torrino's men.

At least they assumed it was Torrino. Eli's thoughts flashed back to the St. Christopher's medal he and Julia found.

How long had Lance been working for Torrino? Or was he running his own operation?

When had everything changed? They'd been friends since eighth grade. Played ball together. Started college together. After Eli quit, they ran in different circles. When Lance and Julia got engaged, they reconnected. Would he have noticed if Lance were different?

What happened to Lance between the ages of twenty and twenty-nine?

Concentrate on Julia. She needs you. She's waiting for you. I'm taking care of her.

The sporadic prayers he'd been whispering were being answered. There's no way Eli would have thought some of the notions going through his mind.

Only God ...

JULIA WOKE ALONE IN A ROOM, taped to the chair, with no concept of her location or how much time had passed since she activated the signal on her watch.

She tried to sling her head around to loosen the cloth bag over her head. While she was out, they'd taped her mouth shut so she couldn't use her teeth or lips to try to pull it off. She couldn't make a sound.

The place smelled musty, comparable to a room that hadn't been used in a long time. Some kind of organic material. A barn, maybe? It was damp, and she could hear the rain pinging on a metal roof.

The door creaked a warning. She hung her head, hoping they would think her still unconscious. Someone pulled her hands up behind her, hurting her shoulders. An involuntary cry worked through her closed lips, ruining the façade.

"So, little Mary Sunshine is conscious, eh?" The gravelly voice sounded familiar, and it held a distinct Chicago accent. Gabe Torrino. "And what do we have here? A smartwatch? Maybe with a tracker?"

He tore the woven band from her already sore wrist.

Would this be the end for her or Torrino? By now, surely the signal had gone from her watch to her supervisor in Louisville. By the sounds of the storm, she wondered if anyone received it. Did they get in touch with people here who might help her?

Her mind immediately flashed to Eli and his relieved expression when he thought he had talked her out of going to the homestead on her own before heading home. When she reminded him she was a big girl, he smirked, his eyes tender. He assumed she'd go straight home.

It was one thing for a mother to be concerned, but Eli? *Who would have thought?*

Looking back, going straight home would have been a better plan.

She shook her head, the woozy sensation returning. She had to concentrate. Thinking about Eli was a distraction. This was her job. She'd been trained in what to do if becoming a hostage.

When the bag tightened around her neck, she struggled. Fight or flight. She couldn't flee. Her bindings kept her from fighting. What were they doing? Was this it? Were they going to kill her and leave her for someone to find, then go on their merry way continuing their activities, maybe hurting other people in the area—people she'd grown to love?

Strange. Fingers reached up under the cover, wove into her hair, and jerked her head back. Through her head cover, she caught a whiff of something she'd hoped never to smell again. Ether.

Could she fool them? She had to try. She'd almost died the last time they'd used it on her. With the slightest change in dosage, the subject would be killed, and quickly, by the narcotic's attack on the nervous system. Maybe that was their intention.

She held her breath, glad she'd trained her lungs while on the swim team. The random skill aided her during her training at Quantico.

Making herself relax, she still held her breath. She froze, sensing another person in the room.

"Are you trying to kill her or put her out?"

That voice, she knew.

Intimately.

She'd promised to marry that voice once upon a time.

I have been so stupid.

"None of your business, kid." Torrino again. He pulled his hands away, and Julia stayed as still as possible. "You've done your part of the job. Now it's my turn to finish it. She's given them our location."

His part of the job? Julia's mind whirled, and the pressure in her chest that preceded tears ached. Her counselor had pointed out some things Julia didn't feel applied to her case, such as her reaction to her broken engagement. How she felt when she found out Lance cheated on her.

How he built himself up by tearing her down. When the engagement was broken, she hadn't done anything wrong, and yet she assumed fault that he sought comfort elsewhere.

Deep down, she knew better. Growing up, she'd had no reason to distrust the people around her. When she met Lance, it was a low point in her career. Out of money, on the treadmill of being a low-level FBI analyst. And lonely. When a work friend invited her to join them at a neighborhood bar for happy hour, she thought, "Why not?"

She'd met him that night.

"Leave her be. We'll come back for her when we have Durbin and his daughter. We'll use this one to get the information we need from them."

The low scoff placed Lance right in front of her. "Where'll we take them?"

The men walked away from her, their voices becoming too faint to make out what they were saying. A wave of dizziness that might be a concussion or possibly sickness from being bested wracked through her body.

They were going after Rebecca and Tripp Durbin, and she was as good as dead.

Chapter 25

The air changed in the room. Blindfolded, she couldn't see movement—but she sensed it. She stayed as limp as possible.

Someone pulled her wrist up to check her pulse, and it took all her strength to stay quiet as the pain radiated through her body. They ripped away the tape holding her onto the chair. It was as if they pulled her flesh off with the adhesive, but she didn't cry out. Someone—Lance?—picked her up and carried her like a baby. Rain on her skin made her feel alive for a few moments before being dumped unceremoniously into a vehicle. From the familiar smell, it must have been the same van used earlier.

This time, she wasn't alone. When she was tossed in, she slammed into another body. Rebecca? Becca's dad, Tripp Durbin? More than likely, they were either unconscious or tied up as she was.

There had to be a way out. It wasn't only her, now. There were civilians involved. She had faith in her fellow officers, but had they been able to get the signal with the storm? Now, she didn't have her watch. She was utterly cut off from any communication.

She felt every bump in the trip from where they were and where they were going. If only she could see something. Anything. Anything that would give her a clue as to their whereabouts.

The van stopped, and she heard the same voices again. The window rolled down, and Gabe Torrino spoke. "Did you get inside?"

"Yeah. Nice little hideout as long as the owners don't come back anytime soon."

"We're gonna search the house and the cabin until we find the map of the tunnels Tripp put together." Gabe Torrino again.

When Tripp's name was mentioned, she felt a slight jerk next to her. It had to be Tripp or Rebecca. She closed her eyes and prayed for him to stay still.

Please, Lord. Help them. Help me.

"Set up three chairs and get them secured. I want them to see what they're up against."

Would she possibly be able to see? As good as that seemed, the menacing words also meant they didn't care if she saw them or not. She may as well be dead.

Strange hands grabbed her roughly by the ankles, dragging, then lifting and carrying her fireman-style into another structure, where they slammed her into a hard, straight-backed chair. When she tried to call out, her captor inflicted a stinging slap in the face, her head whipping back painfully, having had no way to steel herself. Once again, she was secured with duct tape, and she heard movement next to her. The other hostages were being treated as she was. Without sight or voice, she felt useless.

"Keep 'em blind?" It was the strange voice from outside the car earlier.

"For now. If she gives us any trouble, we'll dose her again." Torrino paced back and forth in front of her. The smell of his cigar on top of the aroma of ether she'd caught a whiff of earlier made her stomach roil.

He stopped directly in front of her. She felt his hands on her and heard his voice close to her face as he knelt in front of her. She sensed his stare and smelled his breath, and the churning in her stomach worsened. When his hand slid up her thigh, she tensed. A million scenarios ran through her mind, none of them good. Would this thug, formerly a mere foot soldier in Vic's army of mobsters and now the "capo," assault her, then kill her?

"Hey."

The hand on her leg clutched painfully, then pulled away when Lance spoke. He'd come in silently.

"What?" Torrino's voice turned from anger to a jeer. "You had your chance."

"Yeah, well, one of the things we disagreed on was her level of commitment to our relationship."

"Relationship." Torrino snorted. "Right."

Lance said nothing, his footsteps giving away his location as he walked away.

Torrino spoke ostensibly to the men in the room, but it was directed at her. He wanted her to hear what he had planned for her.

"I figure this woman has made my life miserable one time too many. It's time for her to pay up."

Julia was thankful for the cloth barrier of the hood that kept her from seeing. It lightened the cigar-laden stench of his breath. His hands were on both her legs, pulling her toward him until her knees touched him, then getting into her face.

The barrier was useless when he was so close. All she could do was hold her breath to keep from gagging.

ELI HAD PULLED SOME PRETTY reckless stunts in the name of fun and adventure, but this was different. Whoever took Julia would use whatever means necessary to stop her. To stop the investigation.

On the one hand, maybe they were running scared, trying to cover their tracks. On the other, maybe they were using Julia as bait to take out Clyde and anyone else involved.

The storm had passed, but the dense cloud cover obliterated any light from the sunset. The trees in the woods were dripping, and the dead leaves left over from last winter were wet under their feet. Eli was a country boy, and this was dark as he'd seldom seen. No power. Therefore, no help from the security lights. When he'd explored the farm with Hannah and Trace, he'd seen the barn and the other outbuildings. Hannah's fear of the dark inspired her to install as many dusk-to-dawn security lights as her electrical service could handle.

Clyde followed the blip on the satellite phone, the only working communication device in their arsenal of equipment. To see their way through the dripping forest, they held their flashlights as low as possible so as not to broadcast their movements. They had to have light. Had to be able to follow Clyde in the right direction. The only thing visible was the reflective FBI letters on the back of his jacket. Eli hoped whoever they were tracking was hindered by the dark, as well.

When Clyde halted abruptly, they all stopped. A little way ahead was a solid dark blob. The barn. While the occasional sliver of light made the wet trees and leaves shimmer, no light illuminated the structure. Clyde gave hand signals, motioning

Clay to go around to the other side of the building and his group to follow him.

They made their way quietly, Eli between Clyde and Ben.

The place was deserted. As they surrounded the structure, it didn't take long to figure out it had been abandoned. Eli followed Clyde in, still following the signal from Julia's watch. In a small room built into the corner of the barn, probably formerly a tack room, there was a cot. There, in the middle of the bed, laid out neatly, was Julia's watch, the strap cut where they'd removed it from her.

Clyde swore under his breath as he studied the device in his hand, tracking the signals. "This operation has changed—they have Becca and Tripp. Got a second blip on the SAT phone."

His clipped speech held back emotion but also revealed his take on the situation.

When they started, they were set to catch Torrino and his men and rescue Julia. It wasn't so simple now.

Keeping flashlight beams to a minimum, they followed Clyde further toward where the house and cabin stood. In daylight, the place didn't seem so remote. In the dark, on foot, it may as well have been Sherwood Forest.

Within sight of the cabin, Clyde held his fist up and signaled for them to gather around him. "Lights out. We can't go in guns blazing. Tripp isn't able to move fast. If I read Torrino right, that's what he's hoping for. An easy way to get rid of Tripp ... and Becca." He paused. "And me, probably."

Ben checked the ammo in his gun with a small flashlight, then turned it off. "I understand. I'm locked and loaded. I'll cover you when you go in."

"Roger that."

With those words, Clyde stepped away without making a sound, making his way around the corner and to the front of the house. What kind of training must he have gone through to be this accurate? Calm? If Eli were married to Julia ...

That came out of nowhere.

He shook his head fiercely, hoping Ben couldn't hear his head rattle. His brain had come loose from its moorings. Caring about her safety was one thing, but marriage?

Ben tapped him on the arm, getting his attention. "Stay behind me. I figure there's at least three of them, and when things break loose, at least one of them will head for this door." Ben peered into the window within sight of both the front door, where Clyde would enter, and the door leading to the cellar, where Clay, Nick, and Del were waiting for the signal to come in. He turned back to Eli. "You okay? Not crazy about a civilian being part of this operation."

Am I okay? God, You've got this, right?

"I'm good."

The small glimpse he made out in the sliver of the window over Ben's shoulder revealed three men in the room, as Ben said. The two men standing had their backs to the window. Beyond them, he saw three chairs occupied by their captives, heads covered in cloth bags, drawstrings pulled tight against their necks. He wasn't sure who was who, except for Tripp.

The older man, Torrino, he guessed, leaned into the face of one of the women, his hands on her.

Bile rose in his throat, and his hands clenched. His heart raced. He'd seen those boots before. Julia.

Chapter 26

Julia trembled on the inside, thankful she had trained to stay outwardly calm in volatile situations.

Her mind kept darting around. Torrino's hands on her legs made her want to gag. He wanted her to know he had control. The voice of the man she'd planned to marry hurt her in places she didn't realize were still sore. Knowing there were civilians involved—civilians under federal protection—tugged at her sense of duty.

And the storm. Had anyone received the signal before Torrino tore the watch off her wrist?

She tried to ignore the pain in her shoulder. It wasn't dislocated, so it wasn't useless. She could lift her arm, so if there were tears to the rotator cuff, they weren't complete.

Compartmentalize, Julia. One thing at a time. Deep breaths.

The room wasn't big, so the men holding them had to be within earshot of one another, which meant they were within earshot of her. Two of the voices she recognized. One, she did not. Probably a new guy in the game.

A sudden thought occurred to her. Could he possibly be

aware of the terror and crime he was involved in? Did he think if he were tough enough, nothing would happen to him?

Pray for him. Pray for Torrino, Lance. Forgive those who trespass against you.

Did anyone else hear a voice? Was she losing it? Maybe the whiff of Ether was more effective than she thought. Was she imagining Torrino right in front of her, manhandling her to submission?

No., not her imagination. Her legs tightened.

Okay, God, here goes. Lord, forgive these men. Keep us safe from what they want to do to us ... and give me strength to get us out of here.

"Decided to fight back a little?" Torrino laughed, turning his head to speak to someone else in the room. "See? She just needed somebody to tell her who's boss. You're not man enough for this one."

All she saw were shadows when a person walked between her and the light source or when they stood right in front of her. She might not be able to see, but her ears never worked so well.

The click of a doorknob, to her, may as well have been a knock at the door. Torrino was busy taunting Lance, who gave back to him until finally Torrino's hands on her squeezed painfully and then left her legs. He stood and turned toward the younger man.

"I want you gone."

Torrino's voice held anger and hatred toward the man tasked with keeping her out of the way. In his eyes, Lance had failed.

She expected to hear a gunshot at any moment. At least he had taken his hands off her. Underneath the expletives and insults flying back and forth, she whispered, "Rebecca?"

"I'm okay."

"Tripp?"

"Okay."

Relief flooded her. They were alive, for now. Tripp was weak, and Rebecca was scared. If backup didn't come soon, she wasn't convinced they'd survive. Her call hadn't gone through to Clyde because she didn't have time to push Send. Her watch? Who knew? Torrino had as much as said he wanted to see them all dead. Even if backup was on its way, they might be dead within minutes.

She started praying for Clyde, for whoever else waited in the shadows to storm in the door. *God, please let it be help.*

WHEN TORRINO GOT up from Julia and faced one of the other men, Eli kept his eyes focused on Julia. As the argument grew in heat and volume, Julia's head went down, and the other woman—who must be Rebecca—raised her head abruptly and turned toward her. Tripp did the same, but slowly, still in recovery from a stroke.

Eli glanced at the front door where Clyde waited to enter. Eli would bust down the cabin door if he had to.

Maybe Clyde's a little more subtle? Better trained? Yeah ...

The front door opened quietly, and right after, the door leading to the cellar opened, smacking the third man and knocking him down. Torrino rubbernecked from one door to the other, trapped.

A shot rang out, and the man closest to the side door where Ben and Eli were stationed rushed through. Eli slowed him down as he came out, then Ben pushed him to the ground and slapped handcuffs on him.

When the deputy sheriff pulled him up, the unknown man, whose identity was unmistakable, faced Eli.

Lance Billings.

Eli stared into the face of his erstwhile best friend, anger billowing inside of him. There were no words.

When he saw the flicker of recognition, instinct and rage kicked in. Eli drew back his fist and punched him once and then again. He stopped when the cartilage of Lance's nose shifted under his fist. There had to be a way to make him suffer as much as the people around him had, but he stopped there. Payback for Carrie and his betrayal of their friendship? A little. Payback for Julia?

A lot.

As Ben stuffed Lance into the official SUV, Eli shook out his throbbing hand and turned to enter the cabin. It would be something if he broke his hand and all Lance got was a broken nose.

After the distraction of catching Lance, the blast of a gunshot screamed back into his memory. Rushing into the room, the first thing he saw was Julia, head still covered, struggling to get out of her bindings.

Immediately after removing the covering from her head, her first words were, "Get my hands and feet free!" She was frantic.

He stopped short when he noticed blood. She'd been nicked by the bullet.

Eli pulled his pocket knife and cut the duct tape she'd been secured with. "You're hurt."

"I'll be okay."

As he worked on the tape around her ankles, he contemplated her from the same position Torrino had been. Emotion rushed him when she gazed at him, tears streaming down her face. "You're not okay."

She scrubbed her face with her hands, wiping away evidence of tears, and shook her head violently. "We've got to get Torrino. No time to give in to a nick."

The tape resisted coming off her ankles but eventually gave way. That sticky residue wouldn't give up easily. What a random thing to enter his thoughts. As soon as she was free, she rose quickly, only to sway, her eyes almost rolling up in her head. He caught her before she hit the floor.

Clyde put handcuffs on the other thug. No sign of Torrino.

Pulling Julia closer, he carried her to the sofa across the room in the cabin, then went to take the bindings off Becca and Tripp Durbin.

"Are you okay?"

"I'm more worried about Dad. He hasn't said anything since he spoke to Julia." Hands free, Becca pulled the bonds holding her father to the chair while Eli finished cutting through the tape on her legs.

As Becca slung away Tripp's bonds and pulled away from hers, she tore frantically at the cloth over Tripp's head, heaving a sigh of relief when her dad peered up at her, nodding. "Did they catch him?"

Becca threw her arms around him, sobbing, and Tripp hugged her back. "It'll be okay, Becca. It'll be okay."

Duty done, Clyde came over to his little family and checked them out thoroughly. He put both arms around them, and Eli may have been mistaken, but he thought he saw a tear roll down the tough FBI agent's cheek. "We'll get him."

Eli looked over to the sofa where Julia had regained her equilibrium.

First, a horrified, then defeated expression crossed her face. The blood on her shoulder darkened as it dried. At least she wasn't still bleeding. "We still didn't get Torrino."

The loud, long-pitched sound of the ambulance drowned out anything Eli could have said.

It wouldn't have helped, anyway.

Chapter 27

One of the paramedics, a middle-aged dark-haired beauty everyone except Julia and Eli seemed to know, checked out Julia's wound. She soothed as she worked.

"I can't believe I get to say this, but it's 'just a flesh wound.'" Michele, the paramedic, released a throaty laugh. "This will be a great addition to the book."

"The book?" Julia tried to focus. She had such a feeling of heaviness as if drowning in thick, unforgiving liquid, but her mind kept jerking back to Torrino. To her not being successful in apprehending a known criminal. Again.

She pushed away the terror of being kidnapped and roughed up, but her mind kept replaying scenario after scenario about what might have happened to her when Torrino put his hands on her, bound and blindfolded. The sheer terror compounded in her thoughts, and she had to get herself out of the circular internal monologue.

Michele eyed her warily. Julia saw her glance at Eli across the room, talking to Clyde and Clay. Were they talking about her? About her failure as an agent?

The paramedic laughed, getting her attention back and holding her gaze, giving Julia something to focus on. As long as she could ground herself there, with someone talking to her, she wouldn't fall.

"Everybody keeps telling me I need to write a book about weird and funny things we encounter on the job." Michele cut off the gauze and secured it with self-adhesive bandages. "Such as an FBI agent having 'just a flesh wound,' or a girl getting stuck when her foot went through the ceiling," she laughed and scanned the area, pointing up. "Right here, as a matter of fact." She put her materials back in her pack. "Hannah Reno. Boy, was she embarrassed. Worked out pretty well, though."

Julia smiled weakly, her breathing beginning to calm. "I've heard. Smitten at New Year's, engaged on Valentine's, married by Easter, I believe?"

"You got that right." Michele peered up at her from her position in front of her. She watched Julia's movements carefully. "Any other aches and pains? You've been through the wringer."

"A little neck pain. Nothing I can't handle."

The woman probed the tissue around her neck and skull until Julia yelled, "Ow!"

"Uh-huh. Bend your neck side-to-side and back and forth."

Julia complied, grimacing when she turned her head to the left.

"I understand you were in a crash earlier."

"Yes."

"It'd be smart to get an X-ray, especially since you passed out. Concussion is nothing to fool with."

"I'll be fine."

"Just sayin'. We've got an ambulance here, and"—she glanced over where her partner finished checking out Becca and Tripp—"looks like we're going back without a load if you want to get a second opinion."

Eli walked over, concern written all over his face. How had she arrived at the sofa? She couldn't remember ... unless maybe it was the dream she had where she was floating. Maybe she did have a concussion. Eli had been nice to her, but she wasn't sure he trusted her yet. She didn't think he would go as far as to lift her into his arms and carry her over to the sofa ...

She put her hands to her cheeks, heat rolling off them. The thoughts following surprised her as much as Lance had when he broke their engagement. Had she developed more than friendly feelings for Eli Reno?

No, no, no, no, no.

But why not? He wants to take care of you.

Because I don't need him to take care of me, and I don't want ...

Her eyes drooped as the pain shot through her head. Nothing made sense. Why would she put herself through that again? And wouldn't it be too creepy to fall for a guy who was best friends with her ex, who—

Then, it all came back to her. Eli ... chocolate cake ... the caves ... the medal ...

Rushing back, the good thoughts, the ones that made her feel warm and happy, were being overridden by the horror that Lance was a part of the criminal organization she'd been tasked with stopping. They said it right in front of her. Seducing her was part of the bigger plan. He'd been involved from the beginning.

Michele patted her on the knee. A much kinder touch than Torrino's. She looked up at Eli. "Somebody needs to keep an eye on her tonight."

"Doesn't she need to go to the ER?" The concern on his face, in his voice, was comforting, but she didn't need his interference.

"I'll be fine. I think I can still drive ..."

"There's no way you can drive back to Louisville this late and injured."

And there Eli was, putting his foot down. Anger tore through her.

"I think I'm the better judge ..."

He knelt in front of her.

"Julia. Your car is totaled."

Any gumption she had demonstrated wilted in the face of facts. "Oh ..."

The back glass breaking, the car being shoved from the side into a tree, being thrust back to the seat by the airbags when they deployed, the seatbelt jerking her neck. She had been hurt before they even took her.

"Pretty bad, huh?" She would have to eat some crow. Tears very near the surface, she glanced up at him. "I don't want to impose on your grandparents. Maybe I should ..."

Eli sighed. "Julia, let's go home, okay?"

THE CLOCK on the dashboard of Eli's truck read after midnight. It had been a long day, and Eli regretted Julia having to climb into his over-tall pickup truck. She uttered no complaints.

She said little as they made their way back to the Reno farm. She was exhausted but had refused to leave the crime scene until she gave her statement to Clyde, who was, himself, distracted by what had happened to his family.

Would Clyde and Becca decide against living in Clementville? Was it safe for any of them?

"How did he get away?" Her soft voice pierced him as if he'd failed her somehow.

"When the gunfire started, Torrino saw his chance and slipped through the cellar and into the tunnels. The other two were a distraction. Expendable. Clay and Ben went after him, but Torrino knows his way around better than they do."

"And we know it better than any of them." Her voice was strained.

When she sniffed quietly, he jerked his head around. Tears ran down Julia's face as her eyes lifted to his. "I'm sorry."

What?

Understanding this woman would take a lifetime. Was he up to the task?

"What on earth do you have to be sorry for?"

"If I'd listened to you, I wouldn't have been alone. If I'd taken my phone and gun with me into the tunnel, I would have been prepared. If I'd ..."

Pulling into the drive at the Reno farm, he turned off the engine and rolled down his window to get a breeze. Then he turned to her. "Julia Rossi, you have nothing to be sorry for. Sure, if I'd been there, you might have had backup, but I'm no trained agent, remember? Your gun and phone might have given you a little edge, but after seeing your car—" Eli looked away briefly, swallowing thickly. "After seeing the car, I don't think anything would have stopped a big truck from smashing you into a tree or gunshots blowing out the back glass."

She studied her hands, smoothing and re-smoothing the tissue she'd had in her hand since they were in the cabin. It had outlived its usefulness and would be in pieces within minutes.

When she raised her eyes to his, tears stood in her lashes. "I'm sorry I didn't tell you about Lance. And Carrie." A hiccup led to another, and then the tears came in earnest.

He was so out of his league. The life of the party seldom had the role of comforter, and yet, here he was.

Eli pulled her into his arms, careful of her wounded shoulder and sore neck. Surprisingly, she did not pull away. Instead, she seemed to cling to him, her arms going around him as she cried.

"Shh. It's okay." He threaded his fingers through her black hair. It was so much softer, even after her ordeal, than he would have believed. Smooth as silk. They sat there. He wasn't sure how long. When she stopped sobbing, she stayed in his arms, occasionally shuddering and catching a breath, her emotions still raw.

His were too. Holding Julia in his arms was right, more right than anything had been in a very long time. He touched his lips to her hair unconsciously, reveling, after he realized what he was doing, in the smoothness of her dark tresses. Continuing to rake his hand through her hair at regular intervals, her body relaxed into him, her breathing steadier.

He was anything but relaxed.

When she pulled back and stared into his eyes, his hand tangled in her hair. If he'd thought things through, he would have pulled away and helped her out of the truck. It would have been the gentlemanly thing to do. Instead, he stared right back at her, the only light coming from the porch and the greenish glow of the dashboard. Was there a way to make time stand still? He needed time.

His brain told him he needed time to consider, to think things through. Part of him, usually hidden deep inside, resembled his brother, Trace. The other part of him wanted to experience everything life had to offer. His better-to-ask-forgiveness-than-permission self desired her lips more than anything he'd ever wanted in his life up to now.

Julia wasn't just any girl. She was injured both physically

and emotionally. He didn't know what had happened before they found her in the cabin. Had Torrino or his men hurt her in any way? His heart surged at the very idea.

She had seen so much more of life than he had. He was sorely provincial by comparison. And yet, Nick's message at church touched her as much as it had him.

NOTHING FELT SO RIGHT to Julia as being held in Eli's arms. When he ran his fingers through her hair, she stilled and then relaxed, burrowing deeper into his embrace. She hadn't felt so at peace in a long time. With Lance, she never knew what kind of mood he would be in. She thought Eli was the same with his mood swings, but she was wrong. So wrong.

Maybe it was her.

After a time—she wasn't sure how much time—she pulled back, unsure of everything, including her feelings. His hand still in her hair, they sat there, eye-to-eye, staring at one another. Where her heart rate had eased from the comfort she'd received, it ramped up once more, this time not from fear.

No. Not from fear.

When his eyes dipped to her lips, hers dipped to his. What would it be like to be kissed by Eli Reno?

Was she still suffering the aftereffects of her latest adventure? Maybe she did have a concussion, after all. Maybe she should have gone to the hospital for X-rays.

No, she felt perfectly fine except for a twinge where the bullet grazed her shoulder and her neck where it was wrenched earlier. Hardly worth noting in light of this moment.

Would he kiss her? Could she get up the nerve to kiss him first?

Eli's hand tightened on her scalp as if he were about to pull her closer, but he stopped. He pulled away quickly at the sound of a voice outside the truck. She was cold, even in the summer heat.

"Everything okay out here?"

Mr. Reno.

Eli's eyes closed. He was frustrated. Then he opened them and smiled, winking at her.

"We're good."

"Well, we heard the truck, and you've been sitting here for about twenty minutes. Your grandma is bursting to hear what happened, and it's way past bedtime for decent folks." Mr. Reno turned to go back into the house, then stopped. When he turned back around, his eyes were narrowed, one brow raised. He opened his mouth as if starting to say something, then thought better of it. "Anyway, come in when you get ready. Mosquitos will eat you alive out here." With a jaunty grin, he turned back toward the house and waved.

Eli sighed, then chuckled. "Busted."

Julia didn't know what to say. Had they lost their moment forever? What about tomorrow? Her head began to pound, and the injuries and lack of sleep were catching up with her.

"I guess we'd better go in and fill them in." Julia gathered the things they'd rescued from her wrecked car. She overheard Clay telling someone they had to open the back door with a crowbar to get her carry-on bag out of the back seat.

Eli reached over for her hand, waiting, saying nothing, until her eyes met his.

"You're hurt."

"I'll be okay, Eli." She smiled, tears near the surface again, this time because of the compassion she saw in his eyes. Attempting a grin, she wrinkled her nose. "I'm beginning to feel those mosquitos." Did he believe her?

He held her gaze for a moment more, then nodded. "Let's get you inside."

Hands shaking, she attempted to unlatch her seatbelt. When he leaned toward her to release the buckle, the pressure of emotion in her chest threatened to melt her to the spot. She reached for the door handle, surprised when Eli was there, opening the door for her and helping her out of the tall vehicle. Either he ran around the truck, or her body was moving more slowly than she thought.

When she landed on her feet in front of him, he kept her hand in his. She observed so many emotions flitting across his face. Fear, worry, tenderness. He shook his head and groaned. When he drew her close once again, she relaxed and sighed into the cottony softness of his T-shirt as his arms tightened around her.

Would it be possible for her to simply stay there, standing in his arms? Like, forever?

"Julia." His voice shook. He had the expression of being, as the British would say, gobsmacked.

When she nodded affirmation, the right side of his lips tilted up in a half-smile.

As he leaned toward her slowly, she had time to decide whether or not she was dreaming or it was really happening.

Eli's lips touched hers briefly. Then he pulled away to check. Was she agreeable?

Standing on her tiptoes, ignoring the pain in her shoulder, she wound her arms around his neck, kissing him back. They'd both instigated a kiss, so they were even. When he deepened the kiss, she knew one thing for sure.

She was agreeable.

Chapter 28

The last thing on Eli's mind was his brother, and the last thing he wanted to do was answer his phone when the family ringtone sounded and Trace's name and bearded mug popped up.

Groaning, he lifted his head, still holding Julia close. He had to smile. When he pulled away, he saw she no longer appeared fearful or distraught. Even in the darkness, lit only by the porch light and the dome light in his truck, she was more beautiful than he'd ever seen her. *If this is how she reacted after a kiss ...*

"Answer the phone."

Julia grinned up at him. Was she thinking the same thing he was thinking?

If so, he wasn't sure he'd survive when she left again.

The ringing stopped. Missed Call displayed, then it started again.

"It's Trace."

Pushing the Accept button, he had to wonder if anyone had told Trace and Hannah what was happening on their property.

"Hey."

"Uh, do you know why there's crime scene tape at the end of our driveway?

Eli's brows shot up. "I thought you weren't getting home until the weekend?"

"It's Friday, bro."

"Oh, yeah. Come over to Grandma and Grandpa's, and we'll fill you in."

Eli heard Trace relay the message to Hannah and her reply, "Let's get over there now."

"We'll be there in a minute."

Trace sounded like a husband now instead of a brother.

Eli had to chuckle. "We'll be here." The call ended abruptly.

Julia stared at him. "What's so funny?"

"I always thought it was funny when guys had to clear every movement with their significant other before making a decision." He shook his head and grinned. "Trace is an old married man already."

She twisted her lips as if trying to hide a grin, then arched a brow, saying nothing. "We'd better get in if they're coming now. Grandma and Grandpa have been up too long already."

Warmth spread through him. She called them Grandma and Grandpa for the first time.

Eli wasn't sure he should trust his feelings. That's all it was. Sure, there were physical symptoms involved, but he wasn't ready to call it *love* yet. He learned his lesson with Carrie.

But, if he'd had his druthers, he would have pulled her back in his arms and kissed her thoroughly, testing the overwhelming feeling once more. It was his duty to make sure, for both their sakes, wasn't it?

Julia tugged on his hand, still holding hers. "Let's go, cowboy."

He wasn't sure if she was flirting with him or reading his mind. Or both. There was a certain quality in her voice when she called him "cowboy." He raked his free hand across his face.

He let go of her long enough to grab her carry-on from the small backspace in the cab and then slammed the door before he led her to the porch.

Standing under the front porch, he chuckled. "I've stood on a lot of front porches, under a lot of porch lights, with a lot of pretty girls. I'd hate to buck tradition."

Reaching up, she kissed him briefly, so softly he wondered if it happened. "Now your record's intact." The amused, saucy expression would have spurred him on to a more satisfying conclusion if she hadn't let go of his hand and opened the screen door.

"You poor thing." Grandma came bustling into the entryway as Eli set down the suitcase at the foot of the stairs.

"I'm okay." Julia accepted her hug, wincing briefly. "Just a little sore."

"And nursing a gunshot wound." Eli wanted to make sure everyone was aware she'd been through a traumatic experience, even if she made light of it.

"Oh, sweetie, I'm sorry. Did I hurt you?"

Julia dismissed her apology. "I'm fine. A little headache, some soreness. I'll live."

Eli stuffed his hands in his pockets and observed her with his grandparents. When her glance met his gaze, her sparkle made his lips curve in a smile. She was hurt, but she would heal on all fronts.

He'd see to that.

TRACE AND HANNAH entered to a warm welcome from Grandma and Grandpa.

Julia stopped in her thoughts. She'd called Mr. and Mrs. Reno Grandma and Grandpa in her mind. It occurred without a second thought. Would she, in her weakened state, be able to keep it to herself? Things were different, and she knew it. Could she trust the sensation to be long-term, or was she exhibiting bad judgment again, as she had with Lance?

She remembered a flutter in her stomach when she first met Lance, and, pulling on her memory, he'd done everything possible to keep her attracted to him.

Was it all part of a plan created by Gabe Torrino?

Some of the sparkle drained from the euphoria of Eli's kiss. She couldn't trust herself.

Julia lost track of the conversation surrounding her. She found herself wrapped in a crocheted blanket on the couch, Eli sitting beside her.

"... and he got away through the tunnel in the cabin's root cellar."

Hannah shook her head. "That's such a small hole in the ground. We just found it a few weeks ago, but how did we miss an opening there? I mean, it doesn't appear anywhere on the map."

"Tripp Durbin created the map, and he left part of the network off in hopes of keeping his family safe. It didn't work." Eli's words and his expression were grim.

"So, we're homeless until they get the crime scene cleared," Trace said it as a statement, not a question.

Grandma shook her head. "You'll never be homeless as long as I have a floor to sleep on. And fortunately, I have better. You two can have the rose room."

"The girls' room?" Trace and Eli looked scandalized.

"Don't tell your Uncle Steve. It used to be his room, you know."

Eli turned to his twin and smiled. "I won't tell the other cousins."

Trace went out to get their bags, and Grandma turned to Julia. "You need a shower and bed."

"That sounds marvelous. I don't want to be in anyone's way. There will be four of us sharing one bathroom."

"Not to worry. It'll take the newlyweds a bit to get settled in, even if it's only for one night." Grandma tilted her head, a worried frown on her face. "We need to take care of you, not the other way around."

Tears simmering close to the surface filled her eyes. Mom and Dad would be happy to take care of her, but since she'd been on her own, she was used to fending for herself. Last year, when she was here in the local hospital, in a coma, she kept her condition under wraps, being in a different city.

"Thank you, Mrs. Reno." She hugged the older lady.

"You called me Grandma earlier. I'd love it if you'd continue."

Julia nodded, unable to speak.

"Eli, help this girl up the steps and carry her bag. I'll go get a heating pad to put in Julia's bed. It may be summer, but aches and pains are the same year round."

Julia unwound the blanket from her legs. She wasn't sure how she got there.

"What's wrong?" Eli stopped before leaving the sofa. "You had a frowny thing between your eyes again." He gestured to her face. "Are you in pain?"

"Of course, I'm in pain." She was testy. "And I don't remember how I got wrapped up in this blanket."

Eli's lips twitched. "As soon as we came in the door, Grandma swooped in and wrapped you up, then ensconced you onto the sofa." He leaned in and spoke quietly. "I had to fight for the spot next to you."

Warmth spread through her. Or was it spreading to her face? She didn't know what to say. She'd talked herself into and out of trusting her feelings, and now she was toying with the idea of *into*.

"I need a hot shower." She rose stiffly. "And apparently, I will need that heating pad too."

Eli put his hand on her back as she went up the stairs, following a step behind, carrying her bag. After he set her bag on the chair where it had been earlier in the day—had it only been that morning?—he reached out and took her hand, drawing her closer. He let go to cup her face in his hands.

She wanted to rub away the slight crease between Eli's brows, but her body wouldn't cooperate. "I'm not sure what's happening, but it feels right. Am I making sense?"

Julia put her hands over his, gently, nodding, drowning in his gaze. She wasn't sure what to say.

He leaned down and touched her lips sweetly with his as she'd kissed him on the front porch. Then, he left.

His kiss told her all she needed to know. For now, anyway.

Chapter 29

"Since when did you start getting up at the crack of dawn?"

Eli turned from his position on the front porch to face his twin. He'd been watching as the sun came up and the world awakened.

"Lot on my mind, I guess." Usually the talker in the family, Eli didn't keep much close to the vest. Now? Now, trying to figure out things, he wasn't ready to hear advice from anyone, especially a newlywed. Trace was so happy it was disgusting.

"I know that look."

"What look?"

"The am-I-ready-to-commit-or-will-it-pass look." Trace scoffed. "It's the only time you get quiet."

Maybe the twin-telepathy theory was real because Trace nailed it.

"How do you do that?"

"What?" Trace's ginger brow shot up.

"Know what I'm thinking."

"You're not so complex, brother."

"Thanks a lot." Eli shook his head. "I had that coming."

"It's not a bad thing. You read me pretty well too." Trace made his way to one of the rockers.

Eli sat next to him. "I'm trying to figure out if I can trust my feelings."

Trace rocked back and forth, staring at the horizon and the fence row where the sun would bring forth heat and typical Kentucky summer weather by the minute. "I said you weren't complex. I didn't mean you didn't have emotions."

The two brothers rocked in comfortable silence. Finally, Trace broke the silence. Not typical.

"Did I ever mention how glad I was I found Hannah first?" Trace turned and leaned on the arm of the chair nearest Eli. "And when she didn't seem interested in you, I couldn't believe it."

"I may be a lot of things, but I wouldn't steal a girl from my brother. I knew you had a thing for Hannah the first time I saw you two together." Eli laughed and then noticed the grim expression on Trace's face. "When did I steal your girl?"

"Where to start ... Middle School? Junior Prom? Senior Prom?" Trace raised his brows and shrugged. "When we were younger, there were a couple of girls who went out with me just to be close to you."

Eli leaned forward, hands clasped between his knees as he studied the porch floor. Closing his eyes, he thought back to all the times he'd seen the familiar shut-off expression on Trace's face when he went out with someone they both knew.

"I know a lot was my fault. I was slow on the draw and had to think it to death before I got up the nerve to ask somebody out. To me, rejection was the biggest, most horrible situation I could imagine. Pure failure. It wasn't worth it for a date."

"Is that why you didn't go out much?" Eli wanted to know. He wanted to know his brother not as a kid but as an adult.

Trace leaned back and shrugged. "I didn't want to go to the trouble of going out with someone when I knew it wasn't going anywhere."

"I think that's called wisdom, bro."

"And being an extreme introvert," Trace countered, laughing. "As it turns out, I think we were both right."

"How? I've dated quite a few women for fun, no strings attached, and the one time I think I have a shot at future happiness, this is what happens." Eli leaned back and expelled a long breath. "And now ..."

"Now here's someone you were wrong about who's different from the women you've dated in the past, and—"

"And I almost lost her yesterday."

"If you boys are done solving the world's problems, your grandma has pancakes ready to put on plates."

How had their grandfather reached the door without either one of them hearing?

Trace waited until Grandpa turned to go back to the kitchen, much louder than he'd walked up to the door. "If it weren't for Grandpa, I might not have had the chance to marry Hannah." He stared straight across the field. "He told me about when he and Grandma got together. Dated six weeks before they got married, then he went to Vietnam."

He turned to send Eli a half-smile. "Because Grandpa talks about as much as me. He waits until he has something wise or hilarious to say before he speaks."

"Sounds about right." Eli got up and stretched. "Good talk."

Trace held out a fist, and Eli bumped it. "Same. Let's get pancakes before our women come and distract us." His waggling eyebrows were the perfect end to the conversation.

The screen door slapped as Trace went in, and Eli followed him, laughing under his breath.

JULIA HAD to take another shower the next morning to be able to move without wincing in pain. The paramedic had put a waterproof bandage on her shoulder wound, so she luxuriated under the steaming stream until she worked the kinks out.

She was the last one up, and after her shower, she followed the sounds of laughter, talking, and the clink of silverware from the kitchen. She'd never met Hannah or Trace, and it made her a little nervous. Her FBI training helped when she had to meet new people in a professional capacity, but a little part of her tended to step back at the anticipation of being forced into that situation.

And this time? With the Reno family becoming more and more dear to her as the days progressed? This time was even more nerve-wracking. Trace was Eli's twin brother, after all. No closer than that.

She shook out the hair she washed the night before. It was a little damp from today's shower. In light of her sore shoulder and arm, she put in some styling mousse and scrunched it until the waves she normally straightened became more pronounced. Giving herself a smile of approval in the mirror, she touched her lips, thinking of the kisses from the night before. Eli hadn't seen her hair in its natural state. This was the *real* Julia.

Had the kisses happened? Maybe she'd been dreaming ... until she saw the bruise on her cheek turning different colors. She hadn't noticed it last night.

If the bruise happened, then the kisses had too. A slow smile bloomed at the thought. She bit her bottom lip, wondering. What would he think about the bruise on her face and probably other parts of her body? She'd seen his face when he released her from her bonds. He'd seen Torrino's hands on her.

At least she had been able to follow protocol up to a point. Triggering the tracking device on her watch had saved her. If she hadn't, she and the others would be dead, or worse. She paused at the top of the stairs, trying to stop shaking.

It was too soon. Too soon after her last encounter with Torrino. She shouldn't be here. Her psych eval may have cleared her, but she'd been careful to leave out details of the dreams—no, nightmares—plaguing her.

Before today, she would jerk out of a sound sleep after the recurring nightmare. In the months after the incident above the Clementville Café, details had gradually slipped away. Lately, it came back stronger than ever. In the dream, she stayed conscious longer. Before, she would wake from the dream when she heard glass breaking.

Enveloped in smoke, she saw no flames, but the deadly gas thickened by the moment. It was difficult—almost impossible—to breathe. More recently, running feet enticed her to follow the sound of breaking glass below. Her body screamed out to move, but she was paralyzed. Where was Frank? Her last thought before waking was an old idiom, "Where there's smoke, there's fire."

Today, the images invaded her waking hours, and the emotions these traumatic events evoked in her took over, the dream more real than the newel post under her hand. She stopped at the top of the stairs. Closing her eyes, she tried to bring back sweet memories. Mom and Dad, her cute apartment in downtown Louisville, her Nonna's gingerbread cookies, Eli's kisses …

Eli's kisses didn't instigate her tears. Memories of Nonna did. Since before she could remember, Nonna had been such a mainstay in her life. Close didn't begin to describe their relationship. She swiped away the tears, but more came.

Angry at herself, she shook her head furiously.

What would Nonna do?

Her grandmother was the strongest person Julia had ever known. She survived wars and was widowed as a young mother, raising Julia's dad, his brother, and two sisters on her own. Julia remembered asking her why she never married again, and Nonna laughed, telling her she didn't blame folks for wanting to remarry after being widowed, claiming she was so busy raising kids and making ends meet that she didn't have time for such.

Before the stroke brought on dementia, she would have told Julia to pull herself up by her bootstraps, and while Julia wasn't sure exactly what bootstraps were, the message was clear. Besides reaching down and finding inner strength, Nonna would also tell her to pray. Pray and trust God to handle whatever was bothering her. Even with dementia to the point she wasn't sure who Julia was at times, Nonna still trusted God to take care of her.

Praying, Julia could do. Trusting? Another matter entirely.

Chapter 30

Eli immediately noticed Julia had been crying. Red-rimmed eyes and obvious bruises. It killed him to see her upset.

He didn't say anything. Not now, in front of everyone, but he had to know—had those men hurt her worse than she'd revealed?

His grandparents had gone about their business, preparing for church, and Eli stayed to keep her company. Trace and Hannah were going over to their property to see when they might be able to go home.

Now, watching Julia pack away a hearty breakfast, Eli was astounded at how pretty she was. Her hair, usually perfectly straight, had a beguiling wave to it, and she left off the makeup that hid her beautiful eyes and olive complexion. She glanced up at him, catching him as he stared, chin on hand, a full second cup of coffee cooling at his fingertips.

"Take a picture, it'll last longer." The teasing tone of her voice was heartening.

"How'd you sleep?" He reached out to touch the bruise,

pulling back as she flinched, grabbing his wrist. Instead of pulling away, he turned his hand to link his fingers with hers.

"Sorry. Force of habit." She squeezed his fingers, then let go to pick up her mug. She'd decided to keep her aches and pains to herself. "Okay, I guess. I'm now an official fan of heating pads."

She was hiding something.

"Does your face hurt where you're bruised?"

"Only when I touch it. It'll be fine in a day or two. Makeup will cover it up."

"No need around here." He couldn't tear his eyes away from her.

"I know." She smiled, and Eli was relieved. "I checked the bandage on my shoulder, and it's fine. No bleeding. As Michele said, it's just a flesh wound."

"Big, tough FBI Special Agent."

"I wear the title proudly." She grinned at him. "It wasn't easy."

"I know." He took a sip of cold coffee and wanted to spit it out. "Cold."

She took the cup from him. Grandma made a second pot, so there was still plenty left. Disposing of the cold brew, she poured him a fresh cup and set it down in front of him.

"Thank you." He took a sip.

"Welcome." She put her dish on the counter and then poured herself a little more. "I need to go out to the crime scene."

Eli frowned. His first instinct was a resounding *no*, but he resisted. It wasn't his call. She at least needed to wait a day. Heal a little more.

"Eli, I won't be bundled in bubble wrap."

"How'd you ..."

"It was written all over your face." She pursed her lips with a combination of humor and irritation. "I've been hurt worse than this."

"That was before ..."

"Before I met you?" She closed her eyes and sighed, then sat across the table from him, taking both his hands in hers. "It's the job, Eli."

His agitation had to be noticeable. Did she see the way his fight response triggered at the the situation she was in last night? In his mind's eye, he couldn't squelch the images of her mangled in a wrecked car, at the mercy of thugs, getting shot more seriously than a flesh wound.

It was uncharacteristic of him to keep his thoughts to himself. If he were ever to do it, now was one of those times. He'd have to channel Trace. "Can I at least go with you?"

She sent him a small smile. "I would like that very much." Her lips twisted. "Plus, I have no vehicle."

He pulled her hands up to his lips and kissed them, his eyes never leaving hers. Did he detect a slight hitch in her breath?

"I'll tell Grandma where we're headed, then I'll be ready when you are."

Julia pulled her hands away—reluctantly, it seemed. He hoped so, anyway. She rose from her seat and gently pushed in her chair. "Sounds good. I need to put on my work boots, and I'll be ready."

"I'll be by the door, Agent Rossi."

"Thank you, Civilian Reno."

She would probably deny it, but Eli's grin broadened when an involuntary giggle burst from her lips.

What was it they said about the Grinch's heart growing two sizes? Unlike his brother, he could never be mistaken for the grouchy character, but a smile from Julia Rossi was enough to send his heart into overdrive.

AT LEAST IT'S *a sunny day.*

She had to face the site of her abduction. When they drove up, the trooper assigned to block the road waved them through.

Yellow crime-scene tape rustled in the breeze around the cabin, and she saw Trace and Hannah talking to Clyde Burke and Clay Lacey.

As she and Eli walked up the slight rise toward them, Clyde held up a hand when he saw them. "I didn't expect you here today."

"It's the job," Eli spoke before she had the chance. "At least that's what Agent Rossi told me. Julia, on the other hand ..."

"Hush." Heat rushed to her face. Would she be able to work with him nearby? "I'm fine, and now it's personal. Found anything?"

"I'd say it's personal for you and me both." Clyde shook his head. "Good to have you."

"Thanks."

Clay pulled out his notebook. "My guys followed Torrino's trail as long as they could, then it vanished."

"As in, disappeared?" Julia frowned. "How did he have time to cover his tracks?"

Clyde held out the copy of the tunnel map folded to highlight the area where they were now. "Good question. Here's what we know—the map of tunnels is not complete. There are crevasses he could've slipped into. Then he could take his time leaving the tunnel after our guys were gone."

Julia shook her head. "We need to get in there." She felt Eli stiffen next to her, and she had to head it off. Facing him, she put her hands on her hips and stared him down. "Look. You and I know these caves as well as anybody around here. Maybe

Nick and Del, but even they haven't been in there as recently as we have." Did Eli sense her urgency?

"She's right, you know." Those were the first words she'd heard from Trace.

"Thank you." At the sight of Eli's defiant glare, she said two words, "Bubble wrap."

While his defiant glare at his brother was endearing, she didn't have time for this.

"It's not as if I'm going down there alone."

Clyde nodded. "I'm coming with you. Got your sidearm?"

Julia reached underneath the flannel shirt she'd thrown over her T-shirt and pulled the gun from her waistband. Checking the cartridge, she nodded. It was full. If they ran into Torrino, she would be ready.

"Handcuffs?" Julia grinned at Clyde's low chuckle.

"Check."

"Hey," Julia stopped, touching Clyde's arm. "How are Becca and Tripp?"

If she hadn't been so busy trying to deflect Eli's overprotective streak, she would have asked earlier.

A gentle smile appeared on Clyde's face, changing his appearance from a tough, no-nonsense law enforcement officer to the roles most important to him—husband and son-in-law. "They're good. Tripp was pretty addled when we got home, but this morning, he seemed better. Becca was more worried about him than herself." He shook his head. "I don't know what I'd do if anything happened to them."

His words hit hard. As an FBI agent, loved ones were the main line of offense between the criminal element and the officer. When a criminal threatened an agent's family, the criminal not only had the agent, but they also had the upper hand. Since becoming an agent, she'd never lived in the same city as her parents, who were the closest relatives she had. She wasn't sure what she'd do if anything happened to them.

She glanced at Eli, still stone-faced with disapproval, and spoke softly. "Are you coming with us?"

He pursed his lips. She could almost see the conflict between being overprotective of her and giving her his support. He wanted to prove himself, and he would never know how much she appreciated the gesture.

"I'll grab my gear." His lips lifted in a half-grin. "At the first sign of exhaustion, we're going home. Agreed?"

"Agreed."

"You know, Eli, you'd make a good agent."

"Nah, I'd get distracted and make bad calls. I think you guys have it under control. I'm happy being the grunt."

His words hit Julia wrong. He was so much more than a "grunt." Did he, down deep, think that because he chased a good time all his life, he wasn't as smart as his brother and sister?

A humble Eli was unexpected. And, if she were to be perfectly honest with herself, rather sweet.

WHEN CLAY and his deputies followed Gabe Torrino into the caves after he escaped, they followed a blood trail until it stopped. They started their search there.

Eli had the map, Julia the GPS, Clyde and Clay both carried guns, and Brent held the light. Eli kept his eyes on Julia most of the time, watching for signs of fatigue. She'd been injured, and determination wasn't going to heal her wounds. They kept quiet, not sure if they were alone in the cave.

Where the trail stopped, a larger bloodstain soaked the ground. Clay and Clyde stopped to study it further, inspecting the area for any other spots. There were none. All signs of Gabe Torrino vanished into thin air.

"It doesn't make any sense unless there is a tunnel here we haven't found yet." Julia tilted her head back, stretched her neck, and blew out a breath. "If we don't find him, there's no way of knowing when he'll be back. The safety of our—your—family is at stake."

Eli smiled in the darkness when she said, "Our families." Was she beginning to consider herself one of the Reno clan?

He spoke up. "This is where we stopped mapping the new tunnels. We must be missing something, and with so much blood loss, he couldn't have stayed upright much longer."

"I agree." Clyde turned to Brent. "Mr. Analyst, what do you think?"

Brent Rogers' former military intelligence training made him top in his field, a crack analyst, enabling him to choose his post. He chose Paducah.

"I say we get ground-penetrating radar back out here. We haven't run it since we mapped more of the system. I want it checked both above ground and in the tunnels."

Clyde nodded. "Consider it done. I think we've done as much as we can today. Until we get the geological report, we'd be spinning our wheels to keep going."

"But—" Julia interrupted, eyes wide.

"Julia, I'm not sending you back if that's what you're worried about." Clyde smiled. "I know you're bound and determined to find Torrino. I am too. I worked with the man, and I know how shady and slippery he is." He turned to go, then stopped. "Oh, and I've already cleared it with Banks. He's sending another team to the bank robbery scene."

She nodded and glanced Eli's way, a glimmer of a smile on her face. She wanted to stay. Maybe it was to catch a criminal.

But it would also give them a little more time together to explore the shift between them.

As the others were making their way out of the tunnel, Eli saw Julia kneeling, flashlight on the pool of blood. She pulled out a bag and knife, scraped the ground, and put some of the blood-soaked earth inside. Fastening the zip-lock on the evidence bag, she noticed they were alone and shook her head. "I'm not convinced this is Torrino's blood."

"Wait. What? Shouldn't we call Clyde back?"

She shook her head again. "I'll give it to Brent and have him get it to the lab to check for DNA evidence. See if it's even human blood."

It was getting personal for all of them.

Chapter 31

"I should be doing something."

Eli had one job. Keep Julia out of the tunnels until they are done with the drone-mounted GPR in and around the Woodward homestead site. "Hey, at least we can sit out here and watch the drone do its thing."

Julia held the laptop, recording the results of the fly-over. "Not exactly the kind of investigating I prefer."

"Were you ever an analyst?" Eli turned in his lawn chair toward her. She had her hair pulled back in a ponytail, revealing her long neck and classically Italian profile.

"For a year. I couldn't stand it. An analyst is at the beck and call of the agents, and they do all the dirty work."

"You were the grunt." He laughed out loud at her expression.

"I guess I was. I decided I wanted to be the one calling the shots instead of digging the shots out of the mud." She shifted her eyes at him. "I seem to remember you calling yourself a 'grunt' the other day."

"Can't argue with facts." He relaxed back in his chair, head leaned back, following the drone with his eyes. "Typical middle child. Trace was the smart one. Sam was the talented one. And me? I'm the fun one and the one to call when manual labor is needed. Doesn't take a genius to do my job, so it worked out."

She didn't say anything. When he lazily turned his head toward her, still leaning back, he saw her lips were twisted in impatience. "What?"

"Why do you joke about not being as smart as your siblings?"

"Hey, I don't mind."

"I do." She huffed. "You are every bit as smart, and most likely smarter, than most of the agents I know. So you didn't finish college? When you talk about history, you have more insight than a lot of the history professors I've had. Underneath the 'fun guy' facade, I see a lot of common sense." She reddened. "Just sayin'."

Laughter bubbled out of him. He'd never had anyone call him on his self-deprecating humor. With Trace and Sam in the picture, the pressure was off, and he didn't mind it.

"Thanks for sticking up for me." He leaned closer to her. The smell of her shampoo teased him. Then his eyes flew open. "Do I smell vanilla?"

She swished her ponytail around and sniffed it. "I believe so."

"Nice."

"Thanks." She gave him a sidelong glance.

"You smell like cookies baking." Before she had time to answer, he leaned over and kissed her. She settled down.

"What was that for?"

"That's one of my favorite scents."

"Noted." She pulled out binoculars to focus on the drone. "Lance didn't care for it."

"Which should have been your first clue he was no good. He's an idiot." Eli settled in again, enjoying the company and the fresh air after spending so much time underground.

Eli closed his eyes, thinking about how wrong he had been about Julia and Carrie. Was Carrie in on it too? Did she even know her fiancé sat in the Crittenden County Detention Center?

Clay's Jeep roared up the drive and stopped abruptly. Barely putting it in gear, he exited his vehicle, his expression grim.

"Hey, Clay. What's going on?"

He stood, silhouetted against the sun, in front of Eli's chair. "We need to talk."

This wasn't "friend and almost family," Clay. This was Crittenden County Sheriff Clay Lacey. He was way too serious.

"What about?" Eli stood, wincing as he noted, once again, that Clay had at least six inches on him.

"Brent has had Lance Billings in interrogation, and he's making some ... allegations about you and someone you might know." Clay pulled out his notebook and flipped it open. "Carrie Miller?"

Eli's heart pounded. He knew he didn't have anything to worry about. Truth always won out, didn't it? But sometimes it didn't. What was Lance pulling? Did Lance think that implicating him would make him look better—or at least slow down the process of convicting him?

"Carrie Miller and I broke up seven months ago. She's engaged to Lance now."

"According to Lance, there was some bad blood between the two of you, and Carrie was in the middle of it."

Julia held up her hands and shook her head. "This makes no sense. Lance was engaged to me, Clay. He was cheating on me, and Carrie was cheating on Eli."

"I'm not sure what's going on here, Clay. Am I being accused of something?" Eli's brows furrowed. "If I am, I want to know what it is."

"Better come with me. Agent Burke wants to talk to you at the office."

Clay was serious.

"I'll drive myself." Eli glanced at Julia and shrugged. "I'm interested to know what Lance is saying since, before last week, I hadn't talked to him in six months."

Clay pushed the notebook and pen into his chest pocket. "I'll follow you."

"I'M COMING WITH YOU."

Julia had to be a part of the operation. If something was going on involving Eli, she had to know. Had to know if she was completely clueless when it came to falling in love with men who were trouble.

"Julia, what can you do?" Eli had his hands on his hips. "You need to rest."

"I won't rest until I know what's going on." She climbed up into the truck before he stepped up on the running board. "Besides, if you leave me here, I'll be without transportation." The cheesy grin she flashed while buckling up made him shake his head.

Looking out the windshield, he frowned. "I wonder what Lance has cooked up."

"He's going to try to implicate you somehow."

Pulling out of the smaller road and onto State Road 91, Eli didn't say anything for a couple of miles.

"You ... weren't involved, were you?" She winced when she saw his head jerk her way when the words came out, so she sat there, eyes closed, trying to block out any idea of his involvement.

"Do you think so?" His quiet voice cut her, as, she was sure, her question had cut him.

How could she be completely sure about anyone?

She thought she had a good working relationship with Frank Stafford. He turned out to be up to his neck in organized crime, working directly with Gabe Torrino. They tried to kill her.

Lance, her *knight in shining armor*, had somehow morphed into a criminal working for the same man. How did she keep getting involved with this same group of people?

His voice broke into her thoughts. "Do you trust me?"

Please, God. Not Eli. Give me someone to trust.

As soon as she prayed the words silently, she knew the answer.

Trust me.

She turned to him, unable to say anything for the emotion welling up in her, hoping all that was inside of her projected through her gaze.

He glanced her way and nodded. He was becoming quite the mind reader.

She took another deep, cleansing breath and changed the topic. After the sunshine of the morning, clouds rolled in. Just as those clouds overtook the sun, mental clouds crowded out rational thought in her mind. Her phone chirped with a weather warning. Another storm.

"Another storm coming through." She'd stick to the weather. Nothing personal or emotional.

He nodded. "The ground is saturated after the storm night before last."

"I remember it well." She caught his glance and gave him a

partial smile. When he reached across the seat to take her hand, she let him.

"It's going to be okay." Eli knew what she needed. Comfort. Stability.

"I know."

"God's got this." Emotion shook his voice.

"Eli ..."

"Yeah?"

"Is there anything you may have inadvertently seen tying you to this case?"

"Julia—"

"Hear me out." She wanted to choose her words carefully. "These aren't penny-ante gangsters. They're the real deal. They're drug dealers, counterfeiters, murderers, and kidnappers, and some of them are even federal officers on the take, like Frank Stafford. We don't know how deep it goes or how local it is. They have ways of framing innocent people with circumstantial evidence appearing out of nowhere. It happens."

He scoffed, frustration oozing out of him. "I haven't had anything to do with Lance in months. I've only talked to him once." He paused. "He called me after I left him a voicemail."

"When?" The sharpness of her tone struck home.

"The weekend after we found the medal." Eli glanced over at her. "It was a strange conversation."

She nodded. "Close to the same time he approached me in Louisville."

Giving him the benefit of the doubt, which wasn't a good idea for a federal officer, she pondered. If Eli was innocent, then Carrie had to be involved in some way.

"What about Carrie?"

"What about her?"

These were questions that must be asked, and she

wouldn't apologize for being the one to broach the subject. Better her than an agent who didn't know him.

"You mentioned going to her parent's house last Thanksgiving." She paused, finger tapping her chin. "Where do they live?"

"Indianapolis."

"Okay, driving distance to Chicago."

Eli pulled into a parking space on the street in front of the courthouse in Marion. The old building was slated for demolition and replacement within the next five years. "I guess I need to go in. Should I be happy they didn't insist on escorting me to the office in Paducah?"

"Maybe." A thought occurred to her. "What are Carrie's parents' names?"

"Charles and Melissa Miller."

She nodded. "When we get done here, let's go over to the library. I have a couple of ideas."

Chapter 32

Eli had been in some crazy shenanigans in his lifetime. He knew he'd never get away with the big-ticket items like drugs or bullying, so he stuck to mild stuff like TP-ing houses or egging select teachers' mailboxes. In retrospect, he saw it for the vandalism it was, and his daddy had taught him better. He only got caught once, and Dad made him make restitution for a destroyed mailbox. Lesson learned. In college, he tried the frat rush lifestyle and, after a semester, decided it wasn't worth it. He disliked his classes and the restraint of school in general, and it didn't take long to realize that what these guys considered fun was a good way to get in major trouble—or killed.

Oddly enough, Eli received an invitation to join the fraternity, and Lance did not. The next year, when Eli was out, Lance got in. They'd gone their separate ways until they reconnected a few years ago, both of them a little older and, Eli thought, a little wiser.

Maybe not.

Eli opened the door to the sheriff's office and ushered Julia in ahead of him. Darla, his administrative assistant, was on the phone and writing furiously on a notepad. Acknowledging them, she pushed a button, and a swinging half-door opened, letting them into the inner sanctum of the office.

In a room to the side, Clay appeared at the door. "We're set up in here."

The basic 1960s government-issue conference room sported green vinyl upholstery on the worn metal chairs, a few of them showing signs of repair with duct tape. Yes, it was time for a new courthouse.

Clay sat at one end of the table, Clyde and Brent across from them. Eli was glad he had Julia on his side of the table.

Was she on his side?

"Sorry to drag you down here, Eli." Clyde stared down at the papers in his hand, a slight furrow between his brows. "Our suspect had a lot to say when we got him to town, and there were some statements we need to verify."

"I will be glad to answer any questions you might have." Eli glanced at Julia, who sat quietly, nodding encouragement.

"And Julia, I know we didn't send for you, but since you're here, there are some points we need to clarify, as well."

The surprise on her face made Eli nervous. He didn't expect it to turn on Julia.

She cleared her throat. "I'm happy to help."

"You may not be when you hear what Lance had to say." Clyde continued studying the documents. Clay hadn't said anything.

"Do you mind if we tape this conversation?"

"It's standard operating procedure, so, no, I don't mind. Eli?" She turned toward him, nodding almost unperceptively.

"I have no problem with it."

"Good. Clay?"

So Clay's job was to man the recorder?

"For the record, please, both of you, state your names and occupations?"

"Eli Reno, Carpenter."

"Special Agent Julia Rossi, Federal Bureau of Investigation."

"Thanks. Eli, describe your relationship with Lance Billings."

Eli scoffed quietly. "We became friends in middle school, played ball together, graduated together, and started at IU together. We were friends."

"Did you observe any indication that Lance Billings was involved in gambling?"

That was unexpected.

"No. I went with him to the casino a few times. We weren't high-rollers. I think we both took a hundred bucks and stayed until we either lost it or made a little more."

"Did Lance Billings have a drinking or drug problem?"

"I'm not aware of any. From the time I left college to his engagement to Julia ..." Eli paused. " ... we didn't have much contact."

Clyde nodded, scribbling away. If this was being recorded, why was he taking notes?

When he finally glanced up, it was to pin Julia down. "I understand you were engaged to Lance Billings at one time."

"Yes, for six months."

"How long had you been seeing him before your engagement?" Eli saw past the professional veneer to the strain on Julia's face. She was still not a hundred percent after her kidnapping.

"Nearly a year. We met socially."

"Where?"

Julia reddened. "At a bar in downtown Louisville."

"Were you there alone?"

"No, I went with a friend after work."

Clyde's piercing gaze swept from one to the other, then he raked his hand across his face. He gestured to Clay to turn off the recorder.

"You see why we needed to talk to you, don't you? You both have ties to Billings. Close ties, at different times."

Julia sat up straighter in her chair. "Eli hasn't spent time with Lance in years."

"When he did, you were involved, as well." Clyde pinned her with a grave expression. Eli could see why he was successful as an agent, undercover or not.

"What is it you want to know?" What had Lance cooked up?

Clyde nodded at Clay, who restarted the machine and then concentrated on Eli. "Were you in Clementville two years ago, between Thanksgiving and Christmas?"

"Yes, I visited my grandparents and extended family Thanksgiving weekend, then again at Christmas."

"Was this before or after you reconnected with Billings?"

Eli thought for a moment. When did he meet Lance accidentally and find out he was engaged?

He looked over at Julia, then at Clay, his gaze finally landing on Clyde. "After."

JULIA'S HEART RACED. She didn't want to believe Eli was involved with Lance in any way. Had Lance drawn Eli into his web of underworld contacts? He said their gambling was harmless, but isn't that what addicts say? Eli and Carrie met in a bar ... the same way she met Lance.

She closed her eyes for a few seconds to block out her surroundings. *Think, Julia.*

"Agent Rossi, please describe your first encounter with Lance Billings." Professional. Clyde demonstrated respect and stuck to the law, and she appreciated it. She couldn't tell if he had bought what Lance had to say or if he was willing to listen to reason.

"As I said, I went with a friend—"

"And the friend's name?"

"Chrissy Edgewood. She was the administrative assistant for our unit at the field office in Louisville until she left for another job later that year." A thought flashed to her, unbidden. Chrissy quit not long after she introduced her to Lance, taking a job in Indianapolis.

"Were you close?"

"As close as work-friends go. We had fun together shopping and eating out. Regular stuff single women do."

Clyde lay a photograph on the table. "Can you identify the woman in this picture?"

It was a crime scene photograph.

Tears rushed to her eyes. "It's her."

"I'm sorry. Her real name was Crystal Torrino. Gabe Torrino's niece."

Julia couldn't stop her mouth from dropping open. She'd worked side-by-side with a real part of the crime family she'd sworn to take down. She put her elbows on the table and put her face in her hands, groaning. She fell right into their trap.

"Were the two of you drinking heavily?"

Hands trembling, she laced her fingers together and rested them on the table. "No. I only went for the social aspect of it. I played with my glass of wine and only took a couple of sips."

"What about your friend?"

Julia frowned, thinking. Amazing the things she could think of when she had time as perspective.

"She did drink more than I did. She left soon after introducing me to Lance."

If the floor could have opened up then, she would have gladly offered herself up as a willing subject to disappear in it. She'd been caught in a honey trap.

No one said anything for a moment.

"Did the introduction to Billings feel planned?"

"Chrissy told me she knew some guys she thought I might be interested in and wanted to introduce me to one of them." Julia shook her head. "Is it all right if I play Monday morning quarterback here?"

Clyde gestured to her. "You have the floor."

"I never figured out Chrissy's connection to Lance, except she was much more social than I was … am." She swallowed. "I always had a feeling I wasn't the kind of girl he usually dated, and Chrissy was."

Clyde leaned forward. "Why did you go out with him?"

Julia once again clasped her hands together, the strain on her shoulder painful as she stiffened. "He was fun. Interesting. I thought it might be good for me to date someone different from the guys I usually gravitated toward. Not that I gravitated toward many." She flashed her eyes toward Eli, begging him, silently, to understand.

He responded with a sad half-smile she couldn't interpret. How could she explain to him that she was lonely? People took one look at her and figured she had dates every weekend, and guys buzzed around her as flies to—

Bad analogy for someone caught in a honey trap.

"I get it." Clyde raised a finger to Clay, who once again cut off the recording device.

"Julia, I'm not trying to scare you." He paused as she shook her head. "According to Billings, you were feeding him information about the operation down here even before you came by being part of the Louisville Field Office."

"That's crazy. Before I came down here, I'd never *heard* of Clementville, Kentucky. Torrino, yes. Clementville? No."

She glanced at Clay and then Eli and caught the amused expressions on their faces.

"I get it." Clyde raised his eyebrows. "Who knew there was a place like this with ties to an organized crime family?"

Joking aside, this was serious. Career-ending serious. "What am I supposed to have done or allowed to happen? I never talked about cases to Lance. I always had my computer locked, although I know a lock is no guarantee of privacy." Turning to Eli, she continued, the strain becoming evident on her face. "And Eli? What is he supposed to have done?"

"So far, we don't know many details beyond the incriminating bits Billings has fed us to deflect attention. We do, however, have to take his statement seriously." Clay straightened the papers in the stack in front of him. "For now, I've been instructed to take your gun and badge—"

Her heart almost stopped. She knew the drill. Taking her gun and badge was the first step toward losing everything she'd worked for. "Am I suspended?"

"Somewhat."

Eli leaned forward. "Either she's suspended, or she's not."

"It means we're requesting neither of you leave Crittenden County until we figure out what's going on. I'm supposed to tell you to leave the investigation to the on-duty officers. I never said you couldn't do some digging. Off the record, of course." Clyde arched a brow, and Julia let out the breath she'd been holding.

"So this is a formality?"

Clyde paused. "This doesn't leave the room, understand?"

She nodded.

"Eli?"

"Scout's honor."

"I've stayed out of Lance's interrogation, and according to his statement, Billings doesn't remember me from before Vic Pennington was arrested ..." Clyde clenched his jaw. "But I remember him."

Chapter 33

The ride back to Clementville was quiet. Eli had experienced his first interrogation and wondered if it would be the last. He had to get somewhere where they wouldn't be interrupted. Forget Grandma and Grandpa's house. It was a revolving door these days.

One thought rattled through his brain: No one would convince him that Julia was involved in the illegal side of the case.

Then, going back to their earlier conversation, another thought plagued him. Did she think *he* was involved?

She'd only said a few words since they left the courthouse, skipping the plan to visit the library across the street.

Eli was better at enduring silence than he used to be, but this? This would drive him crazy.

"What happens next?"

Julia jerked her head toward him. She *had* been deep in thought.

"Sorry. Thinking." She tightened her lips in a sad smile.

"Didn't mean to interrupt. You're much better at the

thinking part than me. I have to get all the information out there, whether it's right or not." Eli snorted. "Another way I'm different from Trace or Sam."

She tilted her head and frowned at him. "You say that as if you're somehow *less than*. You're not."

Eli shrugged. "Maybe." They rode a few more miles in silence. The facts they'd learned were swirling around in his brain. It brought to mind a murder board on television, except on theirs, the pieces kept moving around.

"So, what are you thinking about?" Julia twisted her lips and raised her eyebrows in question.

"We know Lance has been involved with Torrino. And, before, with Pennington, but he doesn't remember Clyde? Does that make sense?"

"Maybe he's still trying to pull one over on the FBI." Julia had a habit of tapping her chin with her index finger when she was concentrating.

Eli paused, then said what was on his mind. "I'm not suggesting this because I have a case of sour grapes, but where does Carrie fit in? Or does she?"

"Good question. When you went to Indy to visit her parents, did you notice anything ... odd?"

"Her mom was more talkative than her dad. He seemed to hole up in his study most of the time."

Julia nodded. "Hard to get a bead on someone when they avoid contact. Were they well-off?"

Eli laughed. "I'd say so. I couldn't believe her neighborhood. Meridian Hills. Lots of gated estates, and theirs was one of them."

"Even I know about Meridian Hills. Richest part of Indianapolis. Wow." Julia grinned. "Kind of a city-mouse, country-mouse situation?"

"Definitely. When the butler answered the front door and

took our bags, I knew I was out of my league, so I wasn't surprised Carrie broke up with me." Eli pulled into a parking space at Riverside Park. "What's our next move?"

Julia's eyes widened in surprise. "Where are we?"

Eli chuckled. "Riverside Park. Thought it might be a good idea to talk where we wouldn't be interrupted." Did he detect stress in her question?

"Oh." She flashed a smile his way, but it didn't quite meet her eyes. "Right." She squeezed her eyes shut for a second, then pulled out a notepad and braced herself. "We need to get the timeline right."

He nodded. "What month did you meet Lance?"

"We met in October and started dating in November, two years ago, not long after I was assigned to the Louisville Field Office. We got engaged last spring, I had the hospitalizations, and then we planned to get married in November." She paused. "When did you and Carrie start dating?"

The timeline was crucial. His history with Carrie meshed almost seamlessly with Julia's and Lance's.

"I met Carrie through Lance, believe it or not, last summer." His laugh was hollow.

"Oh, I believe it."

"I saw him, as I said, in our hometown in Indiana, at the bar and grill. He was with Carrie and introduced her to me as someone he went to grad school with at the University of Kentucky. They invited me to join them, and I thought we hit it off." Eli shrugged. "So, basically, reconnecting with Lance and meeting Carrie was some coincidence." He shook his head wryly.

"Yeah. Like Chrissy and Lance."

Julia jumped out of the truck and walked toward the river, then stopped. She stood there facing the water, arms folded across her stomach. The clouds were churning, similar to the last storm. But the air felt different, somehow. He couldn't put his finger on it.

Eli sat a bit, then grabbed a jacket and followed her when the rain started. When he saw her shoulders shaking with sobs, he knew they were in trouble.

He didn't believe in coincidences.

RAINDROPS BEGAN to fall along with her tears, but Julia was numb. The roll of thunder did nothing to distract her from the facts swirling in her brain.

Was she running away from Eli? To a point, yes.

She needed to be alone. To wallow. To heal from the wounds she'd sustained. To think about what this latest development meant to the case and her life. Now, she was trapped here, at least temporarily.

Lance had used them both, hadn't he? Was Eli as much in the dark as she? Was she so lonely that the flash of a smile and a few compliments would sway her so completely? How did she overlook warning signs that she, as a trained agent, should have immediately recognized?

Think.

She couldn't think. When she tried, her head ached, and the overriding thoughts she pulled up were of the kisses she shared with Eli. Unexpected, but not unwelcome.

The jacket coming around her shoulders warmed her, the umbrella a relief from the pelting rain. Her only complaint was now she couldn't blame the rain for her tears. Eli's arm went around her, and she immediately, without hesitation, leaned into him.

When Eli pulled Julia closer, her cheek resting on his chest, she relaxed for a moment and then pounded him gently. "Why is this happening?" She gazed up at him. At one time, she would have wondered about her face. Was her makeup obliterated? Was she a splotchy mess? Eyes red-rimmed? Mouth in an ugly cry expression?

She didn't care. She couldn't figure out why God wasn't answering her prayers. Why bad luck seemed to follow her around.

"I'm a good person."

"I know you are. Your only vice is chocolate," Eli said, laugh rumbling as he pulled her closer, tucking her under his chin. "Sometimes bad things happen to good people."

"Old news."

"No kidding."

She felt his head lift to the skies when it thundered, tempted to burrow further into his chest. "Are we in danger of electrocution?"

"Probably. I counted the lightning five miles away."

"I guess we need to take shelter." The very thought of leaving the warmth and strength of his arms here, where the main witness was the Ohio River, scared her. What would happen to them?

"When you're ready." He didn't move.

Was it the possible concussion, the gunshot nick, or surviving a kidnapping making the sobs come harder today than they had directly after? She pulled her head away from him and nodded. "I'm ready."

He squeezed her harder and bent to take her lips gently, and then, when she was fully on board, more intensely. The emotions of the last few days were poured into their kiss.

If lightning hadn't struck a tree at the edge of the park, Julia wasn't sure how long the kiss would have lasted.

Not long enough.

"Let's run for it."

Eli picked her up with his free arm and ran to the picnic pavilion. He didn't let go of her until they reached the shelter.

"This isn't the truck." Julia shook the rain off her hands and followed his lead as he sat on the top of the picnic table.

"No, but I figured my instincts were right. We need to talk away from other people."

She nodded. "Until we make some sense out of this." When he didn't say anything else, she studied him as he stared out at the rain from the protection of the shelter. She pulled out her notebook, studying the timeline they'd put together. It wasn't long. Two years.

"In the last two years, we've both met people we thought we wanted to marry." She shook her head. "I feel so stupid."

"Join the club." He snorted.

Julia shook her head. "At least you had the brains to stop things before they went too far."

"Carrie broke up with me, remember? I was ready to go full steam ahead."

"Okay, so maybe both of us are stupid." She'd survived a torrent of tears and kisses, and now, her smile was real, as was his when their eyes met. "We're two of a kind, aren't we?"

"I guess we are." He shook his head, sobering, his eyes glittering. "But if you keep staring at me like that, I don't think we'll ever make it back home."

She had to ask. "Do you trust me?"

He met her gaze. No smile, just serious perusal as if trying to read her mind.

Chapter 34

Do you trust me?

Her words rolled over and over in Eli's mind. Two could play at this game. Had he been too trusting in his life? Carrie and Lance aside, had he taken too many people and situations at face value?

Yet, here she was, an arms-length away, close enough to pull her into an embrace at any moment, and she asked for his trust. *His* trust.

She had every right not to trust him as a long-time acquaintance of Lance Billings. At one time, he would have said friend. The sentiment was out the window.

And she goes and asks if he trusts her.

"Of course I do."

The relief on her face gave him an itch to pull her close. He couldn't. Not yet.

"I guess the next question is, do you trust *me*?"

"If I'm wrong, I'll resign from the FBI and get a job waiting tables. I love working for the FBI and would be a terrible waitress." She took both his hands in hers, making him focus on her. "Eli Reno, I *do* trust you."

"All right then, what do we do now?" He raised an eyebrow and grinned. "I have a few ideas ... but they have nothing to do with the case ... so I suggest we discuss those after we figure out why we're being framed for something we didn't do."

Red engulfed her face. Her slow smile told him she knew exactly what he meant. *Later.*

He went on. "Somebody's got something on him. Gambling?" He paused. "Lance is trying to cast blame on us. I don't think it's because we were close by."

"Agreed. When I met Lance, I didn't know Eli Reno existed."

"You were missing out." Eli winked at her.

"I was," she said, twisting her lips. "When did your parents move to Kentucky?"

"March of last year."

"Not long before he met you *accidentally* at the restaurant. Let me get this down while it's fresh in my mind." She scribbled more information in her notebook, the rain beginning to curl the corners of the pages. "Here's what I have so far:

June 2022—Julia assigned to the Louisville Field Office
October 2022—Julia meets Lance at a bar in Louisville with Chrissy
November 2022—Julia and Lance start dating
March 2023—Ginger and Ed Reno move back to Clementville
March 2023—Julia and Lance get engaged, plan fall wedding
May 2023—Eli meets Lance and Carrie in their hometown restaurant
June 2023—Eli and Carrie start dating/Julia sent to Clementville on case

August 2023—Julia released from medical leave
October 2023—Julia and Lance break their engagement
Thanksgiving 2023—Eli goes to Indy with Carrie
Christmas 2023—Eli and Carrie break up
June 2024—Eli meets Julia in Clementville

Julia stopped reading and focused on him. "Does that sound right?"

"I think so. Now we need to fill in the blanks."

"Clyde remembered Lance. We need more info. It would help the timeline." Julia wrote the question down.

"What about this? I arrive at the Louisville office, Lance is told to get a contact there, so he arranges to meet me through Chrissy, who was responsible for selecting an inside contact. Me." Julia shook her head as the image Clyde showed her crossed her mind. "This makes me sad."

Eli nodded. "If she hadn't been involved, she wouldn't have met the kind of end she did. Maybe her job was to find a likely candidate for an information leak."

"Find someone lonely enough to have their judgment compromised. That would be me." Julia clenched her lips and growled. "Ugh."

"Do you think, after what went on last year, Lance found out my parents moved back to Clementville and used me as an *in*?"

"What about Carrie? Where does she fit?" Julia stared at the list. "Eli, did you ever wonder why we never really got to know one another while we were in pre-wedding mode?"

"Lance led me to believe you let your job come before your relationship."

Anger swept across her features. "You've got to be kidding me."

"There were several excuses. Visiting parents in Cincy and

not inviting him, out of town on a case, working late with your boss—and he made it sound as if you were cheating on him."

"Wow. If you met my boss, you'd know how ludicrous that is."

"Really?" Eli grinned.

"Sixty and on his way to retirement with a wife, four kids, and six grandkids." She shook her head, gritting her teeth in frustration. "Did you ever sense he and Carrie were closer than they let on?"

He considered it. Did he? Had he focused so much on rebuilding the relationship with Lance that he overlooked some blatant red flags?

"He did seem to hug her a lot." He blew out a breath. "I may as well face it. I wasn't paying attention because I wasn't looking for it. What about you?"

She shifted, obviously uncomfortable.

"What is it?"

"During counseling, some ... things came out that I didn't realize were happening."

What had Lance done to her? He wanted to know. And yet, he didn't. He was a coward.

"Some of those times you mentioned, I didn't find out about the plans until after they had passed. When I asked him why he didn't tell me, he always said he did, and I didn't remember." She closed her eyes. "Any time I questioned it, he got angry, so I didn't press it. I figured I was under a lot of stress at work, so maybe I didn't treat our relationship as important as my job. I decided to take the blame and keep the peace." She shrugged. "I wasn't sure if I was crazy or not. Not sleeping at night will do a number on you."

"Emotional abuse." Eli gritted his teeth, wishing he'd landed more than two punches when he had the chance.

"I knew something was off. I was determined to have a

committed marriage like my parents. I figured if I kept a low profile, I could manage the tantrums without getting hurt physically."

SHE HADN'T TOLD ANYONE, not even her mother, about the abuse, but telling Eli hurt in a way she didn't expect. Lance had been on best behavior when they were with her folks, and sometimes, it made her think the same guy had to be there, somewhere, when they were alone.

"When did you break up with him?"

Julia scoffed. "Not soon enough. When I was released from the hospital, it got worse. He said I was lazy, and if I'd been smarter, I wouldn't have been hurt." She didn't say anything for a few minutes, and neither did Eli. She blessed him for giving her time.

"The final straw came when we were viewing places to live, and the realtor pointed out a small room and mentioned it would make a good nursery. She was teasing, and I laughed. He was livid. As soon as we got back in the car, he started yelling. Among other things, he said he'd never have a child with me." Tears filled her eyes. "At that point, I didn't want to have a child with him, either." She closed her eyes, trying to get the image of the horrible moment out of her head. It was hard, but Eli had to know. Had to decide for himself if she was worth the trouble. "Then he said nobody would want to get me pregnant ... that I was lucky to have him."

Eli squeezed his fists, letting them relax, only to clench them again. The muscles in his arms, already corded from his job swinging a hammer, had veins popping to the surface. She didn't know this side of him.

When she moved her head, things were distinctly off-kilter.

The last thing she wanted was for Eli to be angry. She was weak, as Lance said. Maybe she didn't have any discernment when it came to relationships. At least she was decent at her job—wasn't she? She had to realize not everyone was good at being close to someone. Maybe there was something wrong with her that stirred anger in the people she was closest to.

"Julia."

She sat there, unfocused, staring across the park. Her vision blurred, probably from crying. But things sounded odd, too, like she was in a barrel. When she tilted her head, the world went sideways, as well.

"Julia."

His voice finally came through the fog, and she turned slowly toward him.

"You're angry." She was afraid to meet his gaze.

"Julia, look at me." He touched her chin, and she flinched, so he took her hand instead. She stayed still, hoping he wouldn't hurt her. He was powerful. She heard about him hitting Lance when he was captured and saw her ex-fiancé's bloody nose.

What was wrong with her? Nothing made sense. She could hear words coming out of her mouth, but she wasn't herself enough to carry on a reasonable conversation. Things were fuzzy. Eli's face was fuzzy.

She was having a hard time concentrating. The world around her shrunk to a pinpoint.

WHEN SHE SAGGED AGAINST HIM, Eli realized she had passed out.

"Julia!"

He laid her back on the table and said her name a couple more times. Nothing. She was breathing, unconscious. Scooping her up in his arms, he left the umbrella behind.

Still clasped in his arms, she shifted a little and opened her unfocused eyes, but when he got her to the truck, she was out again. He strapped her in and headed back to town, spending half the time on the road checking on her.

When she told him about her experience with Lance, before she lost consciousness, it was all Eli could do to keep from getting in his truck and racing to Marion, where Lance Billings was temporarily housed in the county jail. If he made it there, he would undoubtedly kill him. Their friendship going back decades meant nothing in the face of his treatment of Julia. Nobody talked to a woman with such cruelty.

Especially not this woman. *His* woman.

He should have insisted she go to the ER. She'd laughed, assuring him she'd seen enough hospital interiors to last a lifetime.

Thank you, God, for keeping the deer and vehicles to a minimum. Help her, God. Help her.

As he reached US Highway 60, he turned left and then into the hospital's drive, laying on his horn and squealing his tires as he stopped at the sliding doors to the ER.

Not used to so much noise, a nurse and orderly came out immediately with a gurney.

"She passed out on me. She had a head injury a few days ago, and she has a wound on her shoulder, maybe some other injuries she didn't know about. I couldn't get her to go to the hospital."

The nurse patted his arm as the orderly pushed Julia in the doors. "Slow down. We got this. Come on in, sweetie, and we'll get her information, okay?"

Her calm demeanor soothed, and as much as he wanted to keep his head, he was still frantic. He dipped his head in assent and followed her in the door. Through the partial view into the cubicle from the registration desk, he strained to watch as nurses hooked Julia up to monitors and checked her vitals.

He'd grabbed the purse she'd thrown on the floorboard, so he handed the clerk her wallet, unsure of protocol. She was a federal officer. Was it against the law to give the hospital her ID?

Pulling his phone from his pocket, he pulled up Clyde's number, and Clyde answered on the first ring.

"Burke."

"Clyde, it's Eli. Julia is in the ER. I've given the clerk her wallet."

"Slow down. What happened?"

"She passed out, and I couldn't get her roused." Eli stretched his neck around to see what was happening.

"I'll be there in five minutes. Eli, you did the right thing."

Eli pushed the red button to end the call and turned to the desk behind the sliding glass window. "Can I go in there now?"

The young woman at the desk stood. "I'm sorry, sir. Only family is allowed."

"She doesn't have any family here." Frustration gnawed at him. "I've called one of her co-workers. Did you get an emergency number from her wallet?"

"Still checking." Her eyes widened as she studied Julia's credentials. "She's an FBI agent?"

"Yes."

"It says here a Lance Billings is her emergency contact?"

Eli closed his eyes. "Don't bother. He's in the county jail."

"Wow. That's a new one."

The sliding door swept open, and Clyde came in, phone in his ear. "Got it. Eli Reno is here." Clyde glanced up at Eli and lifted his chin in greeting, then kept talking. "I'll keep you in the loop."

"What happened?" The granite was back on Clyde's face.

"We were at Riverside Park, talking ..."

"In this rain?"

"Yeah, we wanted to talk it through, figure this thing out."

"Get your stories straight?" Clyde's eyes were narrowed.

"Yes ... I mean, no." Eli took a deep breath. This was a waste of time. "We were trying to figure out the timeline."

Clyde nodded. "Got it. I had to ask." Maybe he would let it go. He pulled out a badge and spoke to the clerk. "This man is with me. Would you please buzz us in?"

The young lady rose without question and stood back for them to enter the tiny ER.

Eli swept past both her and Clyde and stood next to the gurney. She was so pale. Was she ...? No, the heart monitor beeped regularly.

The nurse came in and patted Eli on the arm. "She's okay. The doctor on call will be here shortly. We checked her fluids, she's a little dehydrated, and her blood pressure is low. You said she was in an accident?"

"Two nights ago."

"I think a little more than a wreck took this sweet girl down." She checked the wound on her shoulder, nodding when she saw Clyde's credentials. "I thought I recognized her."

Chapter 35

Once Clyde went outside to call Becca, and the nurse responded to another call, Eli sat in the undersized chair next to the gurney where Julia lay peacefully. He couldn't take his eyes off her.

Hair splayed on the white hospital pillow curled enough to make him want to touch it. He didn't dare. The kiss they'd shared had been memorable, but he'd had memorable kisses before.

Looking at it pragmatically, he had to ask himself, was Julia on the rebound? Maybe she thought kissing Eli would be a good way to get back at Lance. On the other hand, maybe she thought the same thing about him. He leaned back and blew out a breath, closing his eyes.

After a few minutes of silence, except for the beeps, he heard a groggy "Eli?"

Her eyes swept the room, and as she glanced around, the blood pressure and heart rate monitor numbers climbed enough that the nurse returned, followed by the doctor.

Wild-eyed, Julia asked, "What happened?"

The doctor answered the questions this time. "You passed out on us."

"When?"

"At Riverside Park. Don't you remember?" Eli rose and stood next to her.

She shook her head and then winced. "Ouch. Remind me not to do that again."

The doctor chuckled. "Noted." She studied the chart on the electronic tablet. "I'm Doctor Greer. Says here you were in here about a year ago?"

Julia nodded carefully.

"You'll be okay, but we want to keep you overnight for observation. You're dehydrated, and your blood pressure dipped. We're going to run a few more tests we would have run had you come in right after the accident." Dr. Greer peered at her over her reading glasses.

"I'm supposed to be on my way to Louisville." Her eyes widened, still a little wild, as if she were being detained against her will.

Dr. Greer laid a calming hand on her hand. "I think everything is being arranged." She turned to Eli. "Are you her husband?"

"Uh ... no."

"Then I'm assuming you're either family or the FBI agent out there had something to do with you being allowed back here."

The nurse spoke up. "Since there was no family, and she was unconscious, we figured it was okay. How's the government going to get us on HIPAA if the feds are the ones requesting they be allowed in?" She checked her IV drip. "I'm Amy, by the way."

"Our services have downgraded to emergency triage, but if we find anything troubling, we'll send you to Paducah or

Evansville." The doctor turned when the X-ray technician came in.

"Hey, I'm Erin from radiology." She grinned. "I understand somebody wants their picture taken?" Holding the tablet, this time with paper on it, she gave it to the doctor for a signature.

"That was fast."

"Slow day in radiology." Erin shrugged. "Shouldn't be more than twenty minutes." She checked the list, and then her head shot up suddenly. "Any chance you're pregnant?"

Julia's face grew rosy. "No."

Eli's lips twitched. He couldn't be sorry for where his mind went. He needed to put any ideas about the future in its proper place—the future.

"Gotcha." Erin's eyes moved between Julia's rosy cheeks and Eli's twitching lips. She was probably forming her own conclusions.

"Alrighty then, CT scan of your skull, Cervical spine C-1 to C-7— Hey, you're getting the full-meal-head-injury deal, aren't you?" She chuckled. "We'll be back before you can say Magnetic Resonance Imaging." Winking, she put the sides up on the gurney and hung the IV fluids on the hook close to Julia's head. "A little radiology humor. Captive audiences love it." With a wave of her hand, she pushed Julia through the wide doorway and across the hallway.

Eli's mind and heart followed Julia to radiology as he sat in the waiting room with Julia's bag of belongings.

The television was on, turned down quite a bit, showing some DIY competition show. Beyond noticing the topic was in home building, he didn't care. Now would have been a good time to think, but someone joined him.

Clyde.

"I'm still trying to make sense of what you two were doing out there?"

And he wasn't going to let it go.

The question hit Eli wrong. Maybe it was worry about Julia or his dislike of being questioned as if he were a criminal. Whatever it was, he had to be careful not to snap. It wouldn't help the situation and might hurt it. He needed to channel his inner Trace and think before speaking.

Eli took a deep, calming breath. "Like I said, we needed a quiet place to talk. To try to figure out what could have been in Julia's and my life that coincided with the criminal activity in those tunnels for the last however many years, only two of which we know about

"ELI RENO, I'm not some China doll, nor am I going to melt if I get a little wet."

It was a stormy drive back to the Renos' house after Julia's overnight stay at Crittenden Community Hospital. When Severe Thunderstorm Warnings were forecast, she was released but restricted from driving. Dr. Greer wanted to see her again in a week.

A week.

A week of living in the same house with Eli, and with all this rain, a week with an antsy carpenter unable to work, stuck in the house with her. She glanced at him, her lips curving in a grin at the thought. *I can think of worse situations* ...

When her phone lit up with a call, she sighed. Mom. Wrinkling her nose at Eli, she said, "Well, here's another person who wants to wrap me up in bubble wrap."

Eli laughed. "Somebody's got to take care of you."

She stiffened. Had she still not proven she could take care of herself?

The glare she sent him was missed when he turned his focus back to the road ahead. She'd give him another one later.

"Hi, Mom."

"Julia, are you okay? I called the hospital, and they said you'd been released. Why didn't you call me?"

"Because there wasn't much to tell. I'm stuck here for another week until I follow up with the doctor." Mom didn't need to know that she also couldn't leave the county. That would have her down in a heartbeat.

"I spoke to Mrs. Reno, and she said they're happy to have you for another week. Do you want us to come down and get you?"

Mom's tone had a knowing quality about it. What else did she talk about with Grandma—Mrs. Reno? She had to remember to call her Mrs. Reno. There were too many hurdles to cross before she could call her Grandma ...

"Agent Burke is going to get me an FBI-issued car, and I'll come back to Louisville in a week."

"You should come stay with us."

"If they clear me to drive to Louisville, I'll be okay at home. I'll come up for a visit in a few weeks. How's Dad?" Change the subject. Maybe it would help settle the distinctive tone in Mom's voice.

"He's doing quite well. We're up to walking thirty minutes a day, per doctor's orders. I think it's making me feel better too." Julia was relieved to hear laughter instead of worry in Mom's voice.

"I'm glad."

When they turned in the drive to the Reno homestead, she expelled a sigh and glanced over at Eli. "We're getting back to the Renos' house, so I need to go, okay?"

"All right. Be careful, and call me, you hear?"

"I hear." She paused. "I love you, Mom."

"Love you, too, sweetie."

The call ended, and for some unknown reason, tears pricked. Was it the concussion?

"You okay?" Eli had put the truck in park and leaned over to get a better view of her face. "Do you need to lie down?"

"No, Mom, I do not." She shook her head in disgust. "I only need one mom."

"Good luck with that. We are about to enter a zone even more nurturing, if possible. The Grandma Zone."

Cranky as she felt, Julia's lips twitched. "Is the 'Grandma Zone' anything like the Twilight Zone, only instead of creepy, it's overly nice?"

"Maybe." He grinned, then furrowed his brow at the sight of the FBI-issue vehicle in the drive. "Looks like Clyde decided to meet us here."

And there went her attitude. *Kerplunk.* "Here we go again."

Eli reached over and squeezed her hand. "Maybe he'll have news."

There was another pickup truck in the drive as well. Jay Carrino again?

"And Sam has company, too. Full house?" It would be nice to concentrate on somebody besides herself for a while.

Eli came around to the passenger side to help her out. "You don't need to jostle yourself. Doctor's orders." He put his hands on her waist and set her on the ground in front of him.

"I don't remember those orders." His hands still rested on her waist. She couldn't quite meet his eyes.

"I read it in the handout from the nurse." He grinned. "I'll show you later."

"Uh-huh." She tried to read his face and failed. When the raindrops became larger, she hurried to the front porch before the bottom dropped out of the sky. It was a deluge. "I'm glad we got home before the storm started." There she went again. Calling the farmhouse "home." Maybe he didn't notice.

The flash of lightning and roll of thunder indicated the storm was getting closer. "Let's get inside."

As soon as Grandma—Mrs. Reno—saw them come in, she headed toward them. "There you are." She hugged Julia gently. "I'm so glad to have you home before ..."

"She said the same thing." Eli raised his eyebrows in surprise when Julia glared at him. "What?"

There it was. He finally got the full effect of her glare. Unfortunately, it didn't seem to have the effect she preferred. Not on Eli, anyway. His smile broadened instead.

"I've put clean sheets on your bed, and there's a heating pad warming it up whenever you get ready to lie down."

"Sylvia, it's July. What's the deal with the heating pad?" Grandpa—Mr. Reno—shook his head.

Why did Julia have such a hard time staying on a proper footing with these people? Yes, she'd shared with Eli the most amazing kisses she'd ever experienced. And, yes, she owed him her life. What about the feeling of her insides melting when she looked at him—and even more when *he* looked at *her*?

She was a professional federal law enforcement agent. Feelings were just that—feelings. Not something she could depend on.

Grandma continued talking ...

"It doesn't matter what time of year. When you're hurt, a little heat feels good. Am I right?"

She was.

Chapter 36

Eli gave Grandma a side hug and kissed her on the cheek. "You hit the nail on the head, Grandma."

He turned to the additional men in the room. He knew why Jay was here. It was raining, farmwork was on hold, and anyone would be hard-pressed to slide a piece of paper between him and Sam.

Clyde, on the other hand ...

"What can we do for you, Clyde?"

"I tried to catch you at the hospital, but you'd already left, so I headed this way. How are you, Julia?"

"I'll be fine. Restricted from driving for a week, which is a pain."

She downgraded the severity of her condition for Clyde. On the other hand, maybe he was biased.

Eli led Julia to the overstuffed armchair and ottoman and ignored her huff. It made him want to laugh, but now wasn't the time. He'd take care of her if it was the last thing he did.

Clyde leaned forward. "We have a lead."

Julia sat up straighter. "Anything you can share?"

"Is there a place we could talk?" Clyde turned to Grandma.

"Eddie Clarence, you, Sam, and Jay, let's vamoose to the kitchen. I need to check on my roast, anyway."

"Didn't know it took four people to open the oven door?"

"Come on, anyway. No need for Julia to get back up when she's just got settled."

"I don't know about you, Samantha, but I could use a fresh cup of coffee, and when Grandma uses my first two names, I guess I'd better hop to it." Grandpa hoisted himself out of his recliner and followed.

As they entered the kitchen, Grandma said, "Samantha, get your grandpa a cup. Jay, would you care for some too?"

Eli didn't hear the answer before the kitchen door swung closed. If the last few weeks were any indication, Jay Carrino would take whatever was offered as long as it involved Sam.

"We don't think Torrino made it very far." Clyde's eyes were shining.

Julia narrowed her eyes. "I'm listening. What did you find?"

"More blood evidence."

"So you think he was hit by the same slug that glanced off me?"

Eli shuddered inside when he considered another scenario. It could have been Torrino grazed and Julia shot.

"What's our next move?" Eli wanted this to be over. He was certain Julia felt the same.

"We haven't found evidence of anybody down there except Torrino, and he's starting to get sloppy." Clyde leaned forward, "If he's hurt, this might be the best chance we have of capturing him."

"Would getting him end this nightmare?"

Eli noted the redness around her eyes. In her weakened state, it would be understandable if she cried with relief at the very thought.

"Maybe. Between what Becca knows and if we can get his stooges to flip on him ..."

"You mean Lance?"

Clyde nodded solemnly. "Julia, you are out of commission. Eli, you've mapped those unknown areas of the cave. I need you to guide us through."

"Eli—" Julia interrupted. "Clyde, Eli isn't a trained agent."

The idea that she worried about him had merit, he'd admit.

"But I know my way around the tunnels."

"I can—"

Eli stared her down. "No, Julia, you can't." He swallowed thickly. "I don't want you in a position to get hurt again."

"What about when I go back to Louisville? You won't be there to protect me, then." She spoke quietly, holding his gaze with hers.

He didn't flinch.

Before the situation devolved into an argument, Clyde interrupted once more. "Do you think you can handle communications?" He glanced at Eli, tilting his head in question.

Eli wasn't sure. It could still be dangerous. "From where?"

"Right here?"

"I can do com work in my sleep. And I wouldn't be in the line of fire." Julia rushed her words.

Was she excited to have a part? Unreasonable though it might be, he'd be happy if she never took part in a dangerous operation again.

She sat a minute, staring at Eli, her eyes troubled. "But that puts you in harm's way." She frowned, biting her lip.

"Welcome to the club."

JULIA UNDERSTOOD she would be a hindrance to any operation requiring physical strength. She wasn't going to let Clyde and Eli know how much.

Who was she kidding? They knew.

Grandma kept watch over her and brought her painkillers from time to time. Julia refused any opioids. The head injury kept her from Aspirin and Ibuprofen, but the Extra-Strength Tylenol helped take the edge off the aches and pains. From experience, the hard-core drugs, even spacing them out ridiculously far apart, played with her senses and her judgment, and the last thing she needed was to steer the investigators in the field the wrong way.

These investigators were too important to her. One of them in particular.

She couldn't think about it. She had a job to do, and to do it right. She had to work with Brent Rogers to make sure the SAT phones and trackers were connected at all times.

"Cell service is dismal, I'm afraid. On the other hand, satellites are as good in the boonies as in the big city." Brent was, without a doubt, a techie and proud of it.

Hooking up the receiver to a computer, Julia would be able to keep an eye on them through bodycam footage streaming video to the phone.

"What about the storms? Will it mess us up?" She'd noted a slight frown between Brent's brows, and she wanted to be fully informed.

"Maybe, but it's the best we can do." He hit a few keys on the keyboard, and an image came up, but no sound. In the monitor, Julia saw Clyde talking to someone, his source of light, the LED headlight strapped around his skull.

Brent pointed to the action. "Clyde's putting the bodycam on Eli."

Julia nodded. "Can we unmute, or do they have to?"

Brent grinned. "Oh, we have the power. We can mute our mics, but theirs are consistently on. It's a safety feature." He hit the volume button, and their voices came through, loud and clear.

"Nice."

The monitor showed a split screen between Clyde's camera and Eli's. They were in the tunnel, next to the opening. When they were no longer muted, the sounds of the storm raging came through.

"It's getting late. I hope we don't lose the signal."

"If we do, it shouldn't be more than a few minutes. We're hooked up to a system of satellites."

Julia didn't say anything. A few minutes had the potential to be deadly in this kind of situation.

At a quick knock on the door. Sam was on door duty, opening it to allow Clay Lacey, covered head to toe in rain gear. He gleamed in the glow of the porch light against the backdrop of the pitch-dark night. "Come in, Clay."

"I don't want to get the floor wet."

Sam laughed, seeing the mess of boots, umbrellas, and other rain gear tossed around the entryway. "Too late for that."

Julia came to attention. "Clay? What's going on out there?"

"A monsoon, that's what." He gratefully accepted the towel Grandma handed him when she met him at the door.

She'd gathered a stack of fresh towels and placed them on the table within easy reach. "Don't worry about these floors. They've survived worse than a little rain."

"Thanks." Clay scrubbed his dark blonde hair. "It's pretty bad. Water is getting up, and in an hour or so, traveling from Clementville to Marion will be impossible. Hopefully, not for long. You know how it is this close to the river."

"Won't you be needed in town?" Julia appreciated him

being here, but did his presence with them leave the rest of Crittenden County wide open with him out of pocket?

"Ben and Darla are manning the phones in the office, and a couple of part-time deputies are on call. With Clyde and Eli going back into the tunnels, I didn't want to leave y'all without local law enforcement."

Julia nodded.

The mention of flooding hit her suddenly. If they were going to be cut off because of it, what would happen in the tunnels as the water rose?

"Clay ..." She paused, frowning. "What about water in the tunnels?"

His face was grim. More than she'd seen up to now, except when they realized Torrino had escaped capture. "Yeah, there's that too. I need to be ready to activate Search and Rescue if they get trapped down there." He kept his voice low. "No reason to worry the folks."

Chapter 37

The area around the opening of the tunnel system was sloppy with mud. It had to be worse farther into the maze, especially the areas grading downhill. Would water collect in those places?

Eli put the earpiece in his ear and hooked the antenna wire around the outside for security.

"I think we're set." Clyde reached for Eli's bodycam, flipped a tiny switch, and then did the same for his. He tapped the earpiece and spoke. "Brent, you read me?"

"Loud and clear, boss."

Clyde grinned.

"Sheriff Lacey is here, and Julia."

"Good. Give Lacey a mic too."

"Yes, sir."

Eli wished he and Clyde had the luxury of seeing the folks on the other end of communications as well as they could see himself and Clyde.

"Testing." He tapped the earpiece to see about clearing some of the static.

"Reading you, Eli." Ah, the gentle voice of Julia. "Clyde, adjust Eli's frequency. We're getting feedback."

Clyde came near and turned Eli's bodycam around to access the controls. "Test it now."

"Testing 1-2-3."

"Much better. Thanks. The concussion gives me a headache anyway. I didn't want to add to it."

"Ten-four."

THROUGH THE SPEAKERS, Julia and the crew in the house heard Clyde's voice. "Ready?"

"Ready when you are." Eli didn't sound nervous, simply anxious to get going.

On the dining room table, they laid out a copy of the revised tunnel map. One monitor had the body cam footage from both men, and the other gave them the GPS location of the two men. If the signal went out, Clyde and Eli were on their own.

"I see movement," Julia spoke into the mic attached to the headset.

"Good."

Clay shook his head and muttered, "Wish we had a tracker on Torrino."

"No kidding."

Tracking them on the map, she found they'd entered the area she and Eli had mapped last week. The two men were quiet, listening.

Tripp Durbin had purposely left this part of the network of tunnels off the map to hide access to his house, where his wife and daughter had been. He'd written down everything he knew about the organization. His goal was to get out of Vic

Pennington's organization and lead a normal life with his family.

It never happened. By the time Tripp's plan was in place, Vic was onto him, and he barely had time to hide the documents in the floorboards beside his bed before they came in and killed his wife. He'd hidden a copy of the map in the attic of the cabin where Julia, and maybe Gabe, had been shot.

During Julia's recovery last year, after Torrino and his men infiltrated the Clementville Café, she read the transcripts of the interviews with both Rebecca and Tripp Durbin. Their family had been torn apart, and Rebecca thought her father had, indeed, killed her mother. She'd wanted nothing to do with him.

The night Julia went to evening services at their church, she'd talked to Rebecca afterward. She didn't repeat her whole story—Julia had read the report, after all. One thing stuck with her. Rebecca's attitude was summed up in two words.

"But God."

An hour into the search of the caverns, Clyde spoke up. "I think we've got something."

Julia, Brent, and Lacey perked up.

Sheriff Lacey spoke up. "Keep us posted."

The thumbs-up gesture Clyde made, directed at Eli's bodycam, indicated they were going radio silent for a time.

Julia continued watching both monitors. Brent and Sheriff Lacey pulled dining room chairs up to either side of her so they could watch too.

IT GOT WETTER the farther they went into the tunnel. At first, puddles of water accumulated in low spots. Now, water ran down the walls, collecting in the path and moving to points lower.

Eli had never been afraid of water any more than the average guy. He was a strong swimmer, but the idea of getting trapped down here with no way to get out gave him pause.

They moved as quietly as possible through the inch or so of water now consistently covering the path, trying not to splash and give away their position. When Clyde declared silence, Eli focused on the sounds around him.

Dripping rocks and likely clods of clay fell from the ceiling of the tunnel. Not good. Wasn't that how cave-ins started? Not something to think about now. He had to keep his eyes and ears open. Sounds of sloshing water not from their boots. Signs of an injured party. With all this water, Eli didn't see how they could recover any blood evidence. Before now, Torrino had done a good job of covering his tracks. If the pool of blood they found was any indication, he'd lost a lot of blood. That could make him careless.

He couldn't last forever down here.

Clyde held his fist up, signaling a stop. They froze.

When Clyde pointed to the wall next to him, they were close to where he and Julia had planned to pick up and continue, about halfway between the Woodward homeplace opening and the cabin on the old Durbin place.

There had to be another access point.

Focusing both their headlamps deep into the shadows, they saw the narrow opening, similar to the one Nick had found between his house and the café. The drop-off. Same place, or was there another, similar formation? Had they come at the same trail from a different direction?

Clyde put his hand on his holster and began the process of squeezing his thick, muscular body through the opening. He pushed through—barely.

Eli wouldn't have as much trouble getting through because he was lankier than the FBI agent, but he also wasn't armed. When he got through the crevasse, he looked around. They were definitely in the same area as the drop-off where Del had been shot in an earlier altercation. He shook his head. They had to put a stop to this.

Following closely, Eli went forward, step for step, farther into the cave, where the walls were smooth, with subtle signs of erosion. Was this where water had been high at other times? The water they waded through had increased to a level of two to three inches now, making stealth a thing of the past.

When Clyde stopped abruptly and pulled his gun, Eli steeled himself at the sound of a subtle splash ahead of them. Someone? Something? They inched their way toward what appeared to be a simple opening with level ground behind it. That's where the surprise came in. Immediately through the opening, there was nothing but a five-foot drop-off.

As Clyde crept closer to the opening, his light shone inside, and they heard the feeble *click, click, click* of a gun with no ammunition.

Chapter 38

Eli peered over the edge of the drop-off as Clyde began his descent into the pit. Shining his light, he saw something he hoped Julia and the others were seeing—a side of Gabe Torrino no one had ever seen before. No more the tough, no-mercy gangster slipping through their fingers.

Now, only a weak, angry man who lacked the humility to end things well.

Clyde reached him and plucked the gun out of his hand. "This isn't doing you much good now, is it?"

The expletive coming from Torrino's mouth gave Eli even more to dislike about the man. At the last tirade, his eyes rolled back in his head, and he passed out.

Clyde called out to Eli and the folks on the other end of the communication setup. "Looks like he's got an infected gunshot wound in his leg, and he's lying in about six inches of water."

Eli spoke into the mic. "Did you get that, Julia?"

"Roger that. Good job."

"Any way we can get an ambulance out here?"

Clay came on the line. "We're cut off, Eli. Let me make

some calls and see if there's an EMT on this side of the flooded road." He paused, then asked, "Will he make it that long?"

"Hope so. I'm going down to help Clyde get him out of the water, at least, then we'll know more about what we're dealing with. No way we can get him back through the slit in the wall we came through. Maybe from the other direction?"

"I'll call Nick, then we'll go over and meet you. Same drop-off, huh?"

Eli held the bodycam in front of his face, then down to where Clyde worked with a barely-moving Torrino. "The idea of Del ending up down there, even without water, is terrifying."

"Be careful down there. Don't trust him for a minute, even if he is injured." Julia had come on the line. Did she sound ... worried?

Eli looked into the camera again and smiled. "Yes, ma'am."

He put the headlamp back on and jumped from the last ledge into the water. Clyde managed to pull Torrino up onto a higher spot even as the water rose.

"He's dead weight."

"Is he ...?"

"No, he passed out a few minutes ago. He has a weak pulse. If we don't get him out of out of this cavern, we'll have a serious problem, and not only for Torrino."

"What can I do?" Eli was ready to serve. Ready to get this done for his family's sake. More, he thought, for Julia's sake. She desperately wanted to close the case on the Vic Pennington crime organization.

"Let's try tag-teaming it to get him to the top of this hole."

Clyde's Search and Rescue training made all the difference in their success, because Eli didn't have a clue what to do next. A random thought crossed his mind about joining the volunteer fire department. An idea for another day.

They worked until they finally got Torrino's almost lifeless body to the top. With a litter, they might be able to get him back through the tunnel, going the other direction, toward Nick and Lisa's house. Someone needed to make arrangements, including forming a litter out of something. It was a process Eli had only seen on television, and those weren't how-to videos.

Laid out, Torrino didn't wasn't nearly as big as he seemed when he had a gun in his hand or when he threatened a blindfolded captive. A surge of anger swept through Eli. He wanted to kick him, to finish off what had slowly weakened him almost to the point of death, but it wasn't his place.

How long had this man had terrorized their community? First, as Vic Pennington's right-hand man, then as his replacement, stalking the café and kidnapping Darcy to find information that implicated him in the operation. He was culpable on attempted murder charges when Julia came close to succumbing to smoke inhalation and then, after recovering from that, drugging her to within an inch of her life. He still didn't kill her in the car accident, but they took her, getting her shot in the process of being rescued.

Could there be any redemption for a man with so many sins in his life?

Eli shook his head. "I'll head to Nick and Lisa's opening." If there were any justice, Torrino wouldn't last the trip back through the tunnels.

Good thing that wasn't Eli's call.

THE HEADSET ELI wore beeped with a signal. "Eli here."

"An ambulance found its way around the road closures,

and they'll meet you at Nick's." Her voice calmed him and gave him the courage to see the task through.

"Roger that. Water's still rising, Julia."

She paused. Probably conferring with the Clyde and Clay. When he left, the pit had almost filled, and the floor where they had put Torrino after they got him out was starting to hold water.

"Are you there?"

"I'm here."

"I'm watching the tracker. You're almost to Nick's. Any idea if paramedics will have trouble getting to him?"

"I don't know. The pit is full."

"Eli, Clay here. I know you can't get him out the way you came in. The tunnel between Clyde and Nick's house is at a lower elevation than the one to the café. It's a little farther, but …"

"I'm not sure he's going to make it if we wait any longer." Eli paused in conversation and increased his speed of movement. "I'm more worried about Clyde getting trapped down there."

"Got it."

There was a garbled conversation going on, but he couldn't make it out, and then Clay's voice was loud and clear as if talking on the phone.

"Eli?" Julia again.

"Yeah?"

"We're sending Nick and the EMTs to meet you, ETA about five minutes, then you guide them to the spot. Coms are still in operation, so if anything changes in the condition of the tunnels, let us know ASAP. Got it?"

And there was Special Agent Julia Rossi, her voice ringing out strong and true.

"Got it."

Sending Nick ahead was a good idea. He'd explored his end of the tunnels extensively. Eli's sodden clothes were weighing him down. Clyde's had to be twice as heavy. Did he have to haul Torrino higher when Eli left?

The five minutes passed slowly. Eli finally detected the sounds of footsteps and equipment coming toward him.

Thank you, God.

Nick had on a headlamp and carried a lantern.

"Good to see you, man." Eli turned in place. "Follow me."

He touched the COM device in his ear. "We're headed toward Clyde now."

"Got it on the monitor." Julia's voice again.

Her voice was soft. He liked to think it was just for him. Everything around him in the cave, tunnel, or whatever you wanted to call it, was hard and unyielding. Julia might be a tough agent, but he'd seen her soft side. He was more than ready for this to be over. Did she feel the same?

Eli filled in the paramedics and Nick on Torrino's condition when he'd last seen him. He was quiet as they waded through more and deeper water closer to the pit.

"Eli, Clyde is on the move."

Not good.

"Clyde?"

He couldn't hear an answer, if there was one, for the sound of them walking in the water. He held his hand up for them to stop.

He tapped his earpiece. "Julia, patch me through to Clyde's earpiece."

After a few clicks in his ear, the sound became clearer.

"Clyde?"

"Yeah." He was out of breath. "Had to drag him a little farther than we thought. Couldn't get a coherent message out. You guys almost here?"

"Julia? Are we almost there?"

"You should run into him any minute now."

Praise God. Clyde knelt, water rising by the moment, next to the criminal they'd been charged to find, ending, once and for all, the offshoot and remainder of the Pennington organization.

The paramedics went into full-on lifesaving mode. Was saving Torrino's life still possible?

"He's got a pulse, but it's thready. BP is dropping." Doug, the first EMT on the scene, barked orders at his partner. "We need to get him out of here right now."

Clyde clapped Eli on the shoulder. "We need to get *all* of us out of here. The water is rising fast."

TRAVELING the back roads through Amish country took twice as long as usual. The ambulance eventually made it to Marion and the hospital, where they had an Air Evac helicopter on standby.

A solemn group assembled in the tiny waiting room beyond the registration desk of Crittenden Community Hospital. Rebecca and Tripp had arrived soon after the ambulance. Eli went home to change. Then he'd return.

Conflicted about so many things, Julia sat quietly, listening to the conversation around her. In her job, it was sometimes a relief when a criminal died, but if said criminal died taking important information to the grave, it was a mixed bag of emotions.

Dr. Greer, the same ER doctor who treated Julia the day before, surveyed the group, her eyes finally landing on Clay. "Sheriff, could I have a word, please?"

Clay considered Clyde, who hadn't moved a muscle except

Reframing Trust

for his eyebrows. "I think we need to involve Agent Burke since the patient is in federal custody."

She nodded curtly. "Gentlemen?" She led them out and shut the door, cutting off any chance of overhearing.

Julia watched the doctor talking to both men, Clay nodding and Clyde pulling out his phone and making a call. When the doctor turned to go back into the ER, Clyde walked out the sliding doors and headed outside. Clay stood there for a second in the hall, his eyes closed, head bowed.

Praying?

His mouth didn't move, but he had an intense expression on his face. When he opened his eyes, he walked through the door where Torrino was being treated.

Had he died?

A weight settled on Julia's chest, and she knew her eyes were reddening as she made her tear ducts cooperate. Why would she waste tears on this man? The world would be a better place without him. Wouldn't it?

The door opened, and Eli walked in, surveyed the room, and made his goal the empty seat beside her. As he settled into the seat, he spoke quietly. "Any word?"

"Not sure. The doctor took Clyde and Clay into the hall. Clyde went outside with his phone, and Clay went back into the ER."

"I saw Clyde outside the door. He didn't get far. Rain's still coming down pretty hard."

Julia nodded. "It's been pretty dry this summer. I'm sure the farmers are glad to see it." Was it normal to discuss the weather in the face of a man dying not fifty yards away?

Her eyes lifted to his, and she wanted to crawl into his arms and hide her face against him before the tears came. The tender expression on his face was enough to start the waterworks. Until he grazed her cheek with his fingers

Then, she was a goner.

Fitting into his embrace in front of a room full of people and with a hard plastic armrest between them wasn't easy, but somehow, they made it happen.

When the door opened again, it was Clay. "Clyde's in with Torrino. He's asked for both of you, Rebecca. You and Tripp."

"Who did? Clyde?"

"No, Torrino. Said he had something to say."

Becca cringed. "I don't think—"

Tripp took her hand and squeezed it. "Come on, Rebecca. We both need to face our fears."

She stilled. "Dad, was he the one ..." When he nodded, her eyes filled with tears. Taking a deep breath, she faced her dad, nodding. Straightening, she rose. "Then let's get this over with. This might be the last chance to face the man who killed Mom."

Chapter 39

A line of scripture kept ringing in Eli's head. *The LORD is near the brokenhearted; He saves those crushed in spirit.*

The resolve on Rebecca's face touched him. What must it take to face the man who changed her life in such a horrible way and then continued? Was her spirit crushed at some point? He hadn't known her for a year yet. Nevertheless, he saw her as a force to be reckoned with.

He focused on the woman next to him. Julia, also, was such a woman. While she may not have endured the loss of her mother or the life Rebecca had been forced to live, she'd had her heart broken, as well. She'd been crushed in spirit.

But God.

Rich in mercy.

Redeemer.

Light of the World.

Provider.

Faithful.

Peaceful.

Love.

There were so many more ways to describe God. Probably an infinite number. God was close in a way Eli had never experienced before.

Ben, Clay's chief deputy, came in and sat down. "Any word?"

Julia shook her head. "He's still alive. Barely."

After about fifteen minutes, Clay came in with Clyde, Rebecca, and Tripp.

"It's over."

The sharp intake of breath from Julia stabbed him in the heart. Was this enough closure for her?

Clyde sat down, leaning forward, elbows on his knees. "He gave us the information we needed. Besides Lance, he gave us a couple of other people to find. When word gets out Torrino is dead, it shouldn't be hard to flush them out." Clyde smiled grimly. "We're keeping that information from Lance until we talk to him again. So far, I've stayed out of sight. We'll see if he remembers me later."

"He won't know what hit him, will he?" Julia spoke for the first time in a while.

"Thought you might be interested in his interrogation."

Julia's brows rose. "Does this mean ..."

"Your suspension has been lifted." Clyde looked down, then back at her, narrowing his eyes. "I think we need you on this case if you're up to it?"

If Eli had his druthers, he would keep Julia as far away from Lance as possible. He never wanted to see her hurt the way she described her relationship with him.

"Julia—"

She laid her hand on his and stopped him. "It's okay, Eli. I think it would be good for me to face him again." Her eyes were tender. "This time, it will be on my terms, not his."

What could he say? He had no authority over her. He had no say in anything she did or didn't do.

He had to trust her to God. If push came to shove, would he be willing to let her go?

A KENTUCKY STATE POLICE TROOPER transported Lance Billings to a holding cell in Paducah, closer to the FBI Field Office. In solitary confinement, FBI personnel were his only contacts with the outside world. It was the only way to keep Lance from finding out about Torrino's death. For all Lance knew, Torrino was alive and well.

They'd kept him waiting just long enough, his knees bouncing and his finger strumming on the table in front of him.

After watching him through the glass for a few moments, letting his comfort level drop as he waited, Julia entered the interrogation room alone. It was gratifying to see Lance's handcuffs locked to a round bolt in the middle of a table and his feet shackled together. A surge of power swept through her. This man, who had deceived her into thinking she had no control over her own life, had no say about the direction *his* life was headed. At least not now.

Now, she had first crack at him.

She stared down at the folder in her hand, then turned to him. If nothing else, she wanted to maintain her cool in his presence. "I understand there are a couple of guys left over from the Pennington years?"

Lance didn't know about Torrino's death. For all he knew, Torrino was weak and had spilled the information.

Clyde watched on the other side of a two-way mirror, biding his time.

"Are you the best they've got?" Lance sneered at her, his bravado not quite meeting his eyes. "They sent you in here alone?" He scoffed.

"Oh, I'm not alone." She shook her head in pity. "Lance, Lance, Lance. What have you got yourself into? How long have you been working for Torrino? Or did you work for Pennington first?"

"I'll talk when I have a lawyer."

"That's an option." She paused, opening the folder again, appearing to be studying the paper inside, which, it turned out, contained a list of things to pick up at Walmart before returning to the Renos' house.

"Or, you can get ahead of Torrino, along with a few other people, and make yourself a deal." She closed the folder and leaned back, arms folded across her chest. "Your choice."

"How do I know he talked?" The sneer was still there, but his jaw tightened. Was he faltering?

"Lance, you've been in lockup for a week. Do you think we didn't have enough time to break Torrino as well as check and double-check his story? We've had a productive week. Already caught one of the guys he mentioned, and he's ready to talk." She shook her head. "Bless your heart."

She picked up the passive-aggressive phrase after spending several weeks in the South.

The glare he shot her way made her laugh. "I forgot, you and I aren't used to Southern colloquialisms, are we? I've been down here for a while, so I picked up that one. It's a useful expression. There are *so* many ways to interpret it, depending on the situation. Guess what it means this time?"

He huffed. "Okay, I'll humor you. What does it mean?"

Julia's smile broadened, and she looked down her nose at him. "In your case? In your case, it most definitely means, 'You've made some foolish choices.'"

That made him angry, so he shot back with an oath and then jabbed. "Really? What happened to your partner? Oh yeah, he's in federal lockup. So, who's the fool?"

"Oh, Frank Stafford?" She smiled at him broadly. "I no longer have a partner. And yes, he's in Federal Prison in Marion, Illinois. I understand he's been getting death threats, being so close to Pennington's headquarters." She took a deep breath and stared at him, adrenaline flowing through her veins. "Huh. Wonder if that'll happen to you?" She waved a hand. "Anyway, they tried giving me a few new partners." She shrugged. "They didn't approve of the way I did business these days."

She hoped her smile was cold enough to give him pause.

"What about Carrie?"

"What about her?" Now, he was sullen.

She turned a page over in the file folder. "How long have you known her?"

"I'm sure you have the answer to that in your folder."

Julia nodded. "Oh, I do. I wanted to get it on the record. Says here you met in college through mutual acquaintances." She avoided his gaze for a moment, silent, then considered him, watching his every move, it seemed. "After a little research, we learned that Carrie Miller's mother is Gabe Torrino's sister." Shaking her head, she said, "Huh. The blonde hair had me fooled. Is it natural?" She couldn't resist the jab.

He bowed his head and swore under his breath before facing her again. "It's natural, and she's not involved."

"So, you do love her."

Lance nodded.

"The whole time we dated and were engaged, you loved her and were using me for information?"

He said nothing, then nodded, lips in a firm, angry line.

"You may as well verify it. For the recorder."

"Yes." He breathed out in a snort. "Satisfied? I just had to get on your good side." An eyebrow raised, and the slimy expression came back. "It wasn't hard."

ELI WANTED to go through the mirror and strangle Lance Billings. How had Eli been so wrong?

When Julia spoke again, he was impressed with her calm. Her professionalism.

"When did you start working for Torino? College?"

Lance nodded. "I borrowed some money to pay off a poker debt."

"Setting things in motion with Pennington's organization when you couldn't pay it off?"

He didn't answer. When Lance lifted his eyes, Eli could tell he'd been bested. All this happened after Eli left the university. Would things have been different if he'd been there for his friend?

"Verbally, for the record, please."

Eli didn't know when he'd been so proud of anyone. She kept her cool when he would have flattened him.

Lance stared at her sullenly, then spoke into the microphone. "Yes."

Kicking himself, Eli talked himself down. Lance would have pulled Eli into the mix if he'd been there. With his ties to Clementville, he might have been caught in the middle between his family and his friend, possibly with disastrous results.

There was a scuffle in the hallway leading to both the interrogation observation rooms.

When Julia's head shot up, her face was impassive, stirring pride in Eli as he observed.

Julia closed her folder and rose. "That must be the other guy we picked up. Let's get you back in the holding cell so I can interrogate this scumbag. Oh, I mean this *other* scumbag. Or do you prefer dirtbag?"

The door opened, and an officer who measured at least six feet, five inches entered with the key to the lock on the table.

Eli breathed a sigh of relief. It wasn't over completely, but soon.

JULIA TREMBLED INSIDE, but she refused to let Lance Billings have the last word. "Thanks, Paul. I'll be next door if you need me."

The officer nodded abruptly and shoved Lance in front of him. In the room next door, a rumpled Clyde Burke, complete with an orange inmate jumpsuit, sat at a table similar to the one to which Lance was chained moments before. Projecting a broken persona, he held his head in his hands.

When Lance stopped abruptly at the sight of Clyde, the officer prodded him forward. He stalled. "Wait a minute. I've seen him before. He worked for Pennington. Like, high up, then he dropped off the map."

Clyde looked up at Lance, and he paled.

Julia pretended to light up. "Well, he does speak." She smiled calmly. "We'll see what Mr. Burke has to say, and then we'll decide if the evidence you just shared gives you a shot at the deal too."

Lance turned frightened eyes back to Julia, then looked back and forth between her and Clyde before Officer Paul took him by the arm and was buzzed through the door and out of her sight.

When the door locked behind him, Julia closed her eyes

and sagged for a few seconds outside the room where Clyde waited.

After a few seconds, she stood, squared her shoulders, and entered the second interrogation room, where Clyde sat patiently.

"Remind me not to face you on the wrong side of the interrogation room." He grinned. "You can take these off of me, now, please."

She arched a brow, thoughtful. "Hmm. Only if you give me the information we're looking for. After all, you were the last person to see Torrino alive."

"And I'm also the last person who can offer you—" Clyde stopped when Julia drew her finger across her throat to cut him off.

Clyde narrowed his eyes and glanced toward the mirror. "Ah. A conversation for another time."

Did Eli hear that?

Chapter 40

Moving day for the Burke family saw all hands on deck. Eli was spending a Saturday at the house where he'd spent the last few months working. This time, he carried in boxes, not lumber.

Two boxes deep, he peeked around them to see Rebecca in front of him. "Where to?"

She stopped, biting her lip. "Oh ... That was supposed to ... Sorry, I got sidetracked. These go upstairs to the small bedroom in front."

It was warm, but was it warm enough for Rebecca's face to be so red? He continued upstairs, proud of the job they did on the house. The attention to detail in the finishes gave it the atmosphere of a house with history. A history beginning today.

"Whoa there, cowboy."

Julia. Eli had hoped he would run into her today. Three weeks ago, she returned to Louisville. Texting back and forth and talking on the phone didn't take the place of being physically in the same room. Finishing up paperwork on the Torrino case hadn't happened quickly enough for his taste.

Meeting at the top of the stairs wasn't optimal. The soft humor in her voice when she called him "cowboy" didn't help. He would prefer a room far away from everyone else, on the other side of a closed door.

"Where are these headed?" She read the label and frowned. "Did you see this?"

"Lady, I don't read the boxes. I just carry 'em."

"Cute. Look."

The label, plain as day, said "Nursery."

Julia's eyes bulged as her hands went to her mouth. She scanned the area for anyone who might overhear, then mouthed a silent squeal and gentle jump up and down, mouthing, "They're pregnant!"

He'd seen many moods of Julia Rossi, but this one? This one made him laugh. Deep down, what he wanted, step-by-step—and, yes, he visualized each step—was to throw these boxes on the floor, pick her up in his arms, carry her down the steps, put her in the truck, take her to the courthouse, marry her, and then ...

"Eli?"

His mind had swerved far away from where he was, and from the expression on her face, she was concerned about where he'd gone.

"Hmm?"

"I think I lost you there for a minute." Her visage cleared, and she covered her mouth again, whispering, "They're going to have a baby."

Granted, he was a man. Babies weren't on his radar. He hadn't lived around his cousins who had babies until now. Trace and Hannah hadn't gone down that road yet ... he didn't think, anyway. When would they have had time? Julia's reaction seemed a little over the top, in his opinion.

"I know what 'pregnant' means." He laughed at her

reddening face. "Do women always react this way when another woman is expecting?"

Her rosy complexion relaxed, and her smile grew. "When it's a friend, yes. It's a blessing. And now, when things have finally settled down for Clyde and Becca, it's the perfect gift."

"All I know is this box is supposed to go in that small front bedroom." He pointed to the closed door. "Is that it?"

"Probably." She turned to the door. "I'll bet she didn't intend to let the cat out of the bag today."

A gentle thud on the other side of the door stopped them, and Eli's eyes met Julia's with a frown. "Do they have a pet?"

"I didn't think so." She turned the knob and quietly pushed the door open to catch two surprised individuals.

"Sam?" Eli was stunned.

There, in front of them, hair mussed, both of them red-faced, was his little sister in the arms of the neighboring farmer, Jay Carrino. The box on the floor next to them explained the *thud*.

"Oh! We didn't mean to ..." Julia's eyes widened.

Sam's rosy face turned even rosier, if possible, when she turned to the young man holding her in his arms. "No worries." She whispered to Jay. "Should we tell them?" Jay nodded. Sam glanced from Julia to Eli and then to Jay, her expression softening when she got to him.

"We're getting married." Samantha reached up and kissed Jay on the lips.

"When—?"

Sam sent a withering glance his way. "While you were off catching bad guys and rescuing Julia." She chuckled. "We've been dating all summer. It's been nice staying under the radar —much less interference from the big brothers."

Eli was flummoxed. "I mean, I knew Jay had been around more than not, but ..."

Julia took his arm and pulled him toward the door. "I think congratulations are in order, and a promise that we can keep a secret." She looked closely at Eli and emphasized the word *secret*. "Okay?"

"Thanks, Julia. We want to tell everybody at the picnic later, so don't breathe a word."

"I wouldn't begin to know what to breathe." Eli shook his head.

"Set the boxes there," Julia said, winking at Eli, then turned to Sam. "We'll close the door behind us."

Out in the hallway, Julia broke down, laughing. "I wish you could have seen your face."

"This day keeps getting weirder and weirder." He shook his head. "I'm afraid to open door number two for fear of what I'll find. And here I thought I was ahead of the game, knowing Jay was Sam's date for Mandy's wedding."

Julia bit at her bottom lip.

"Maybe we should check out door number two?" She spoke quietly, tilting her head, and then his mind returned to where it had gone when he blanked minutes earlier.

ENTERING WHAT WOULD, when all the Burke's belongings were in place, be a beautiful master bedroom, Julia walked over to the French doors leading to the balcony overlooking the Ohio River. She opened them to allow the sweet summertime breeze to float in. "Rebecca told me this was the best view in the house."

Eli came up behind her and put his hands on her shoulders, not saying a word. She leaned into him.

Where was the life of the party? The guy who couldn't sit still in church? The man who dated girls barely long enough to know if the relationship had any potential? Until Carrie, and then that folded before he was ready.

In the last two years, Julia had come close to death twice—no, three times. Life was short. Dad's heart attack and surgery were proof.

All around them, across the world, and in this small community, people were getting engaged, marrying, blending, and starting families. When she became engaged to Lance, she'd thought she was on the right track.

Look where that got her.

Except for her small family, she didn't trust many people. Frank Stafford had proven she had to be more discerning in her work relationships and Lance in her personal ones. Not everyone did the right thing.

Encountering Mr. and Mrs. Reno—Grandma and Grandpa—had been eye-opening. They cared infinitely for their family, growing larger, it seemed, by the minute. Their loving relationship together was second only to their individual relationships with God.

Could she trust God? He'd let a lot of things happen she couldn't understand and didn't appreciate. Coming to Clementville a second time. Meeting Eli. Connecting with the Paducah FBI Field Office. Were these all bits and pieces of God's plan for her life?

Eli squeezed her shoulders, and her mind went right back to meeting Eli and the first time he kissed her, unlike any kiss she'd ever experienced.

When he kissed the crook between her neck and her shoulder, she shivered, then smiled. He'd been quiet long enough for his taste.

"What are you thinking about?" He treated the other side of her shoulder the same, and this time, it tingled so intensely that she either had to laugh or cry.

Instead, she turned in his arms, sliding her hands up to reach around his neck, barely giving her time to welcome the kiss he was so eager to give.

After a satisfying few minutes, she rested in his arms, her head relaxing on his chest as she listened to his heartbeat. Strong. Steady. And for all the ways Eli talked about his inability to commit and his bad judgment when it came to women, this was the real Eli.

Strong. Steady.

Leaning back, she gazed into his eyes. The gold flecks in his deep blue eyes caught her, refusing to let go. To be honest with herself, Julia didn't want to let go.

"I have an interview on Monday."

The disappointment on his face made her sad. "So, you're leaving tomorrow?"

She nodded, clamping her lips together as she smoothed the furrow between his brows, making him come in for another gentle kiss.

"I'm not ready for you to go yet."

"I know."

He held her close, and she burrowed her face deeper into his shirt, taking in the very essence of Eli Reno.

As a Special Agent with the Federal Bureau of Investigation, Julia had experience in keeping her emotions and opinions in check. Her job was keeping secrets. Sometimes, those secrets were a matter of life and death.

And sometimes secrets were kept to push pause on a situation. The physical attraction between them was palpable even as they both shied away from verbally committing to the word *love*.

"What if I asked you to stay?" His words were soft and a little muffled as he nuzzled her neck once again.

Pulling back, she tilted her head. "What if I did?"

"Did what?"

"Stay." She pulled away, not quite letting go as they stood with their hands clasped between them. The wheels of Eli's mind were moving. Julia could see it in the way he considered her. His eyes narrowed as his face crinkled into a smile.

"If you did, I hope I wouldn't waste any more time."

Her lips twitched into a smile. "I'd say we've used our time together wisely." She stood on tiptoes and kissed him lightly, her smile growing as he pulled her close again.

"I love you, Julia Reno." Was it her imagination, or was his voice shaking?

And ... Oh.

She laughed, and tears filled her eyes. She pressed closer, if possible. "That's Rossi, cowboy." She sniffed and let out the breath she'd been holding.

"Trying it out. Seeing how it sounds."

Chapter 41

If her eyes were glowing as much as his, Julia would be in trouble—decidedly the best kind of trouble—before the weekend was over.

"It sounds ... nice."

She had no doubt concerning her initial response to his declaration. Was she ready to commit to it verbally? What if her experience with Lance wasn't an anomaly? What if she couldn't trust her instincts?

What if.

A part of her, well-trained as she was, doubted her viability as an agent.

But gazing up into his eyes, she saw something new. He'd been hurt, too, yet now he put himself on the line emotionally as much as she had ever put herself on the line professionally.

The realization staggered her. She trusted her training more than she trusted God, who promised to be near the brokenhearted. To save those crushed in spirit.

Studying him, she applauded his patience. Had she hurt him by hesitating? She lifted a hand and held it gently on his cheek, her lips lifting when he closed his eyes and took in a deep breath.

When she asked him once if he trusted her, he didn't hesitate. Simply asked if she trusted him.

"I love you, too, Eli."

He bent and placed his lips on hers gently, more tender than any kiss they'd shared to date. No rush, no agenda, just love, affection, and commitment.

Since the first time their lips touched, she wondered how it would feel to be sure.

Now she knew, and the sigh she released between kisses incited Eli to pull her even closer, almost lifting her off her feet. Or was she floating?

"Don't leave." Eli's voice was husky, words inserted between kisses. She sensed his frustration, and she continued smiling while he was trying to lay one on her.

"Whoa there, cowboy." His frustration ignited something inside her that she was afraid she couldn't stop. Her Quantico training had taught her to segment different aspects of her life. Put emotions into different rooms.

Right now, those metaphorical rooms broke through walls to become one big open-concept great room of love, desire, humor ... and forever.

He lifted his head. "I don't want to."

"Me, neither, and that's why you need to 'whoa.'" Her grin pulled him back in. "We can revisit this part of the conversation later."

"So, we're in a conversation?"

"Oh, yes. An important one." Chewing on her lip, she flitted her glance away from him and then back. "I didn't say where my interview was."

Eli closed his eyes. "It's DC, isn't it? I knew they'd want you there eventually. I mean, I'll move there in a heartbeat, if it's what you want ..."

She froze, her heart pounding. "You'd do that for me?"

His brows furrowed. "Of course, I would. If you get assigned to Timbuktu, I'll be there beside you."

All her life, she'd hoped to find someone out there who would love her as much as her dad loved her mom. After a while, she began to think love had passed her by. This man—this funny, dear man—who she was determined to paint with the same brush as Lance—would pick up his life and follow her anywhere.

"It's a good opportunity ..."

"I'm sure it is. You deserve it." The mix of pride and resignation on his face thrilled her in a way she hadn't expected. It empowered her in a different way. Not as a feeling of superiority but a feeling of utter gratitude to her God, who laid His plan out in front of her. Hers for the taking.

She bit her lip. "My interview is with Clyde Burke. Paducah Field Office." The combination of surprise, relief, and disbelief on his face made her laugh out loud. "He wants me to be a team leader since he's being promoted to Special Agent in Charge."

"So ... let me get this straight." Stunned, he swallowed, his Adam's apple bobbing with emotion. "You want to stay? *Here?* With me?"

She picked at a button on his shirt and deflected, peeking up at him coyly. "Well, I was hoping it would be with you. I was prepared to stay with Grandma and Grandpa until I convinced you I was worth the trouble."

Eli picked her up off her feet and swung her in a circle. When he stopped, he held her in the circle of his arms and gazed at her, shaking his head. "I'm not sure what I've done to deserve you."

"You didn't do anything. I've thought a lot about why God lets bad things happen. Even in the Bible, it's hard to understand sometimes—until you consider the big picture. We were going in opposite directions until we collided here. When I learned the only way to survive was to trust God, the pieces came together."

"We weren't ready before now." His eyes never left hers. "I'm sorry you had to go through what you did with Lance." He pulled her to him and held her there, comforting her in a way she'd never experienced. The simple act of a hug came from somewhere deep inside, in those places even she hesitated to visit, drawing her to him even more if that were possible.

One simple verse from the *Song of Songs* ran through her mind as she rested there in his arms: *I've found the one whom my heart loves.*

Acknowledgments

Dear Reader,

Every book comes with obstacles, and this one is no exception. As I wrapped up this, the last volume in the RenoVations Inc. series, there were health scares, re-starting an old career, and the amazing news that I would be a grandmother.

Finishing a series is bittersweet. On the one hand, I'm ready to write about new characters. On the other hand, this fictional community has become a part of my life. I can visualize what it would look like if it existed, and I can, in my mind, drive around and point out where these characters live, work, and solve mysteries. Everything has to end, though, and I couldn't find one more single Reno cousin who hadn't found their happily ever after.

There's no way any book could come to fruition without the patience and encouragement of my husband. Thank you for enjoying cooking and loading and unloading the dishwasher.

To my family, friends, and readers, thank you for asking me when my next book is coming out. It keeps me going.

To my publisher and editors, without Linda and Amy, you wouldn't see this finished product. Thank you.

To my "Windows Quadrilogy" sisters, Amy, Heather, and Erin, we got together to write a series and have stayed together as friends, advisors, sounding boards, and accountability partners. Without you, I'd have given up long ago.

To God, who, without the sacrifice of His Son, Jesus, and the presence of the Holy Spirit, I would not have the strength or even a reason to get through another day.

So thank YOU, dear reader, for making it this far. I hope you've enjoyed the trials, tribulations, humor, and love of the Reno family. If you make it to Crittenden County, in Kentucky, I hope you recognize a few landmarks and the ambiance I've included in these stories.

Keep reading, loving, and worshiping,
Regina Rudd Merrick
Psalm 37:4

About Regina Rudd Merrick

Regina Rudd Merrick started her journey as a lifelong lover of reading in first grade and eventually parlayed that love of literature into a degree in library science, with stints as both elementary and middle school librarians and currently as a public library director.

After finding the enjoyable world of reading and writing "fan-fiction"—original stories based on characters from familiar stories, television shows, and movies--she realized that for some reason, God had given her the ability to weave a story, whether it be in this online community or with original characters. Her first novel, *Carolina Dream*, book one of the Southern Breeze Series, was the winner of a publishing contest with Mantle Rock Publishing, LLC (now Scrivenings Press), and her writing career was born.

Now the author of seven novels and a contributor to four novella collections, Regina writes about people like all of us who sometimes struggle with their faith and trusting God. Her latest novella contribution is included in the collection, *Love in Any Season*, and her latest novels are *Window of Peace*, book two of a multi-author series entitled Stained Glass Legacy, releasing in April 2023, and *Twelve Days of Mandy Reno*, a short Christmas novel and book two of the RenoVations, Inc. series.

In 2024, she had three releases: *Carolina Connections* (January 2024), *Rebuilding Joy* (February 2024), and *Christmas ReWired* (November 2024).

Regina is wrapping up the RenoVations Inc. series with *Reframing Trust*. She has plans for a Christmas novella for 2026, and is brainstorming her next full-length novel.

Regina loves chocolate, the beach, providing keyboard and vocals in her church's praise band, historical homes, watching other people renovate on HGTV, and Hallmark movies. She and her husband of forty-plus years are empty nesters in rural western Kentucky and are the proud parents of two grown-up daughters, a son-in-law, and, most important, she's a new grandmother this year!

More from the RenoVations Inc. Series

Heart Restoration

RenoVations Inc.—Book One

For interior designer Lisa Reno things go from bad to worse when her contractor-brother falls off a ladder and breaks his leg. Now she has to deal with the past coming back to haunt her, an old house with a corpse in the creepy cellar, and her best friend trying her best to fix her up with any man that moves.

Nick Woodward is willing to do his old college roommate a favor–especially since it involves renovating his own inheritance. The last thing he wants is to get involved with anyone. When he lost his wife and unborn child so suddenly, he had made the decision to keep God and everyone else at arm's length. So far, so good.

Ah, the difference a trip to a dingy basement makes.

Get your copy here:
https://scrivenings.link/heartrestoration

12 Days of Mandy Reno

RenoVations Inc.—Book Two

Law student Amanda Reno is stuck in her tiny hometown in Kentucky to complete her studies virtually and work part-time at the Clementville Café. Her parents are stuck in Brazil, leaving Mandy to celebrate Christmas without them.

Young Sheriff Clay Lacey takes matters into his own hands, devising a plan to take Mandy's mind off her crushed expectations. She is no longer his classmate's tagalong kid sister, but a young woman he is increasingly attracted to.

How will Mandy react when she finds out Clay is the one working to make sure she has a memorable Christmas? Will she be pleased? Or will she cringe as she thanks the man who may be falling in love with her?

Get your copy here:

https://scrivenings.link/12daysofmandyreno

Rebuilding Joy

RenoVations Inc.—Book Three

Single mom Darcy Emerson Sloan has enough to do raising twins and running a restaurant. She's doing fine on her own and doesn't need the complications of a man in her life. But when her café turns into a crime scene, putting her and her children in danger, she begins to take interest in the handsome young FBI agent that comes on the scene.

Contractor Del Reno is as even-keeled as they come, but even he has his limits. And Darcy Sloan has pushed him too far. Every time he tries to help, it backfires. But now that Darcy and her kids are in trouble, he has no choice but to come to her aid and to protect her. She's just going to have to deal with it. Secret tunnels, organized crime, adorable children, and a wedding.

Just another day in Clementville.

(Previously published as Rebuilding Joy by Bellville Street Books.)

Get your copy here:
https://scrivenings.link/rebuildingjoy

Christmas Rewired

RenoVations Inc.—Book Four

When electrical engineer Trace Reno loses his job during the holidays, he decides it's time for a change. He hires on with the family contracting firm, RenoVations Inc., as assistant to the licensed electrician, Hannah Buckner.

Hannah is known for her sunny disposition, but lately, she has decided God must have forgotten her as her friends all around her find "the one," and she hasn't. When the only man in her life who shows an interest is the grouchy Trace Reno, she tries to be patient, but in her opinion, he's bossy. And even worse, he knows nothing about construction. She'd rather be single.

Love at first sight for him—pure irritation for her.

A mishap on a last-minute Christmas Eve job gives them the time together Trace craves, and Hannah makes the best of it.

Could it be possible that Trace has a gooey center beneath his crusty exterior?

Get your copy here: https://scrivenings.link/christmasrewired

A Southern Breeze Series

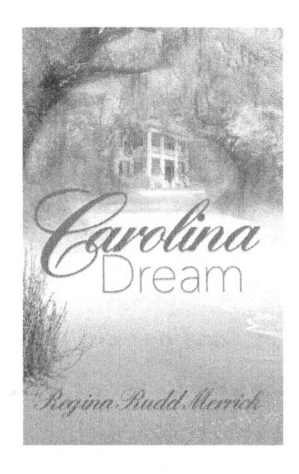

Carolina Dream

A Southern Breeze Series: Book One

Sarah Crawford wants more from life than to attend the wedding of her ex-fiancée. An unexpected inheritance in South Carolina comes at the perfect time, just as Sarah is willing to use any excuse to get out of town. When she meets potential business partner Jared Benton and discovers that a house is part of the inheritance, she is sure that God has been preparing her for this time through a recurring dream.

But will a dream about an antebellum mansion, many rooms to be explored, and a man with dark brown eyes give her the confidence to take a leap of faith, leaving friends, family, and her job behind?

https://scrivenings.link/carolinadream

Carolina Mercy

A Southern Breeze Series: Book Two

She's always gotten everything she's wanted. He thinks he has to give up everything. Her best friend's wedding is foremost on Lucy Dixon's radar. Her biggest concern is once again meeting Tom Livingston, who has ignored her since an idyllic date on the boardwalk of Myrtle Beach the previous summer. At least, it is her biggest concern until tragedy strikes. Where is her loving, merciful God, now?

When Tom Livingston meets Lucy, the attraction is instant. Soon after, his mother is diagnosed with an untreatable illness, and his personal life is pushed aside. His work with the sheriff's department, his family–they are more important. He knows about the love of God, but circumstances make him feel as if God's mercy is for everyone else, not him. Can a wedding and a hurricane–blessing and tragedy–bring them together?

https://scrivenings.link/carolinamercy

Carolina Grace

A Southern Breeze Series: Book Three

First-year Special Education teacher Charly Livingston demonstrates God's love on the outside but is resentful that God allowed back-to-back tragedies in her family.

Rance Butler is a top-notch medical intern. He's on his way to the top, and when he meets Charly, he knows things will only get better. When he discovers family secrets and a dying father he never knew, his easy, carefree life seems to disintegrate.

Even in the idyllic ocean breezes and South Carolina sunshine, contentment turns to bitterness and confusion except for God's amazing grace.

https://scrivenings.link/carolinagrace

Carolina Connections

A Southern Breeze Series: Book Four

Enjoy two novellas connected to Regina Rudd Merrick's A Southern Breeze series in one convenient volume. Both of these stories were included in multi-author collections: "Pawleys Aisle" (Coastal Promises) and "Mr. Sandman" (Candy Cane Wishes and Saltwater Dreams). Now you can complete your collection of A Southern Breeze stories with this novella duo, Carolina Connections.

Pawleys Aisle—Leaving a lucrative position in the banking world for the creative world of weddings, Chelsea Prince finds the perfect venue, Pawleys Island Chapel, next door to the perfect walled garden. Her elderly neighbor and partner-in-planning have an agreement, but when the unexpected happens, she has to deal with the cranky grandson who wants to be left alone to write the next great American novel. Since Chelsea has sworn off men, it shouldn't be a problem to ignore him and go on her way hosting weddings in the chapel. But when Marc McCallum offers up a compromise, she wonders if maybe there is one man out there who can be trusted.

Mr. Sandman—Events manager Taylor Fordham's happily-ever-after was snatched from her, and she's saying no to romance and Christmas. When she meets two new friends—the cute new chef at

Pilot Oaks and a contributor on a sci-fi fan fiction website who enjoys debate—her resolve begins to waver. Just when she thinks she can loosen her grip on thoughts of love, a crisis pulls her back. There's no way she's going to risk her heart again.

https://scrivenings.link/carolinaconnections

Other Titles by Regina Rudd Merrick

Window of Peace

Stained-glass Legacy—Book Two

Michael Connor "MC" Dunne led a charmed life. He had a plan—finish veterinary school, get married, and take over the local animal clinic. Enter the Vietnam War.

MC returns home, injured, to Park Haven, Tennessee, and soon learns there's a new vet in town, hired when the local veterinarian suffered a heart attack. So much for his plan.

Violent flashbacks and nightmares pull MC away from his faith and turn him into a hermit. His safe place is the family farm, working on the old cabin and restoring the chapel his great-uncle built in the early 1900s, with the family's heirloom stained-glass window.

Nancy Jean Baker struggles to prove herself as a competent veterinarian to the small-town skeptics of Park Haven. Fighting her own demons from a traumatic past, she's driven to succeed.

But when war veteran MC Dunne returns home, wounded and wary, Nancy discovers she's standing between him and his dream.

Can they help each other overcome their hurts and horrors? Or is their hope of happiness doomed when the past threatens to ruin their future?

Get your copy here:

https://scrivenings.link/windowofpeace

Novella Collections:

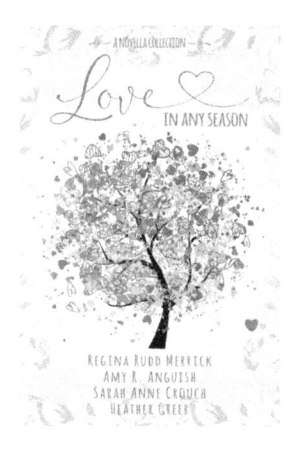

Love in Any Season

Includes "Spring has Sprung," a novella by Regina Rudd Merrick

https://scrivenings.link/loveinanyseason

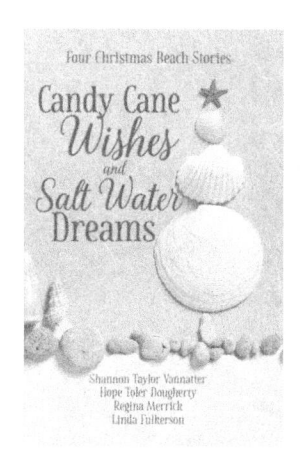

Candy Cane Wishes and Saltwater Dreams

Includes "Mr. Sandman," a novella by Regina Rudd Merrick

https://scrivenings.link/candycanewishes

Scrivenings PRESS
Quench your thirst for story.
www.ScriveningsPress.com

Stay up-to-date on your favorite books and authors with our free e-newsletters.

ScriveningsPress.com

Made in the USA
Columbia, SC
17 June 2025